R0700404163   01/2023

PALM BEACH COUNTY
LIBRARY SYSTEM
3650 Summit Boulevard
West Palm Beach, FL   33406-4198

HARPERChapters

DOWN IN THE DUMPS

A VERY TRASHY CHRISTMAS

WES HARGIS

HARPER

An Imprint of HarperCollinsPublishers

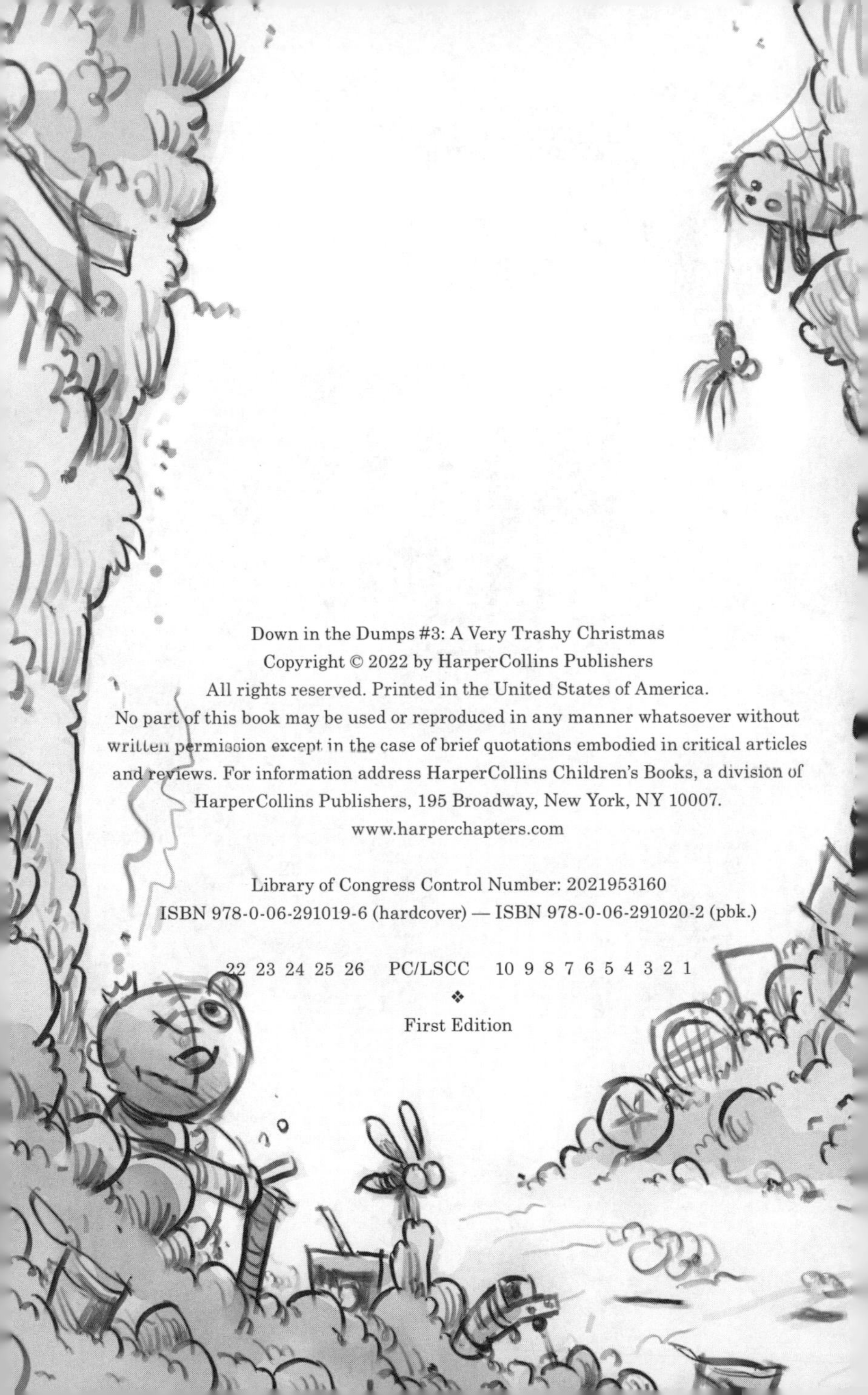

Down in the Dumps #3: A Very Trashy Christmas

 For information address HarperCollins Children's Books, a division of HarperCollins Publishers, 195 Broadway, New York, NY 10007.
www.harperchapters.com

Library of Congress Control Number: 2021953160
ISBN 978-0-06-291019-6 (hardcover) — ISBN 978-0-06-291020-2 (pbk.)

22 23 24 25 26 PC/LSCC 10 9 8 7 6 5 4 3 2 1

First Edition

CONTENTS

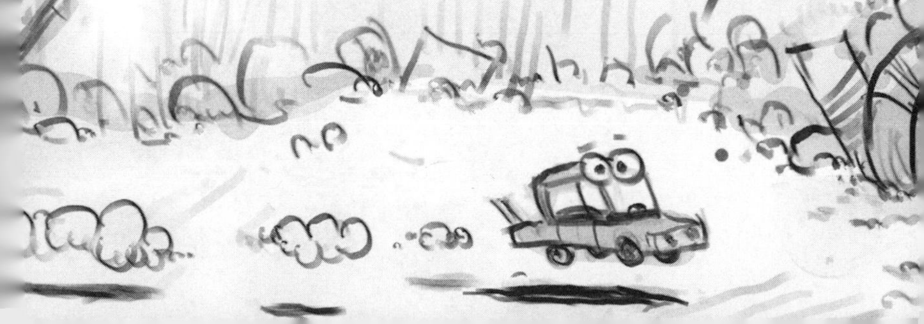

CHAPTER 1
SOMETHING FOUND

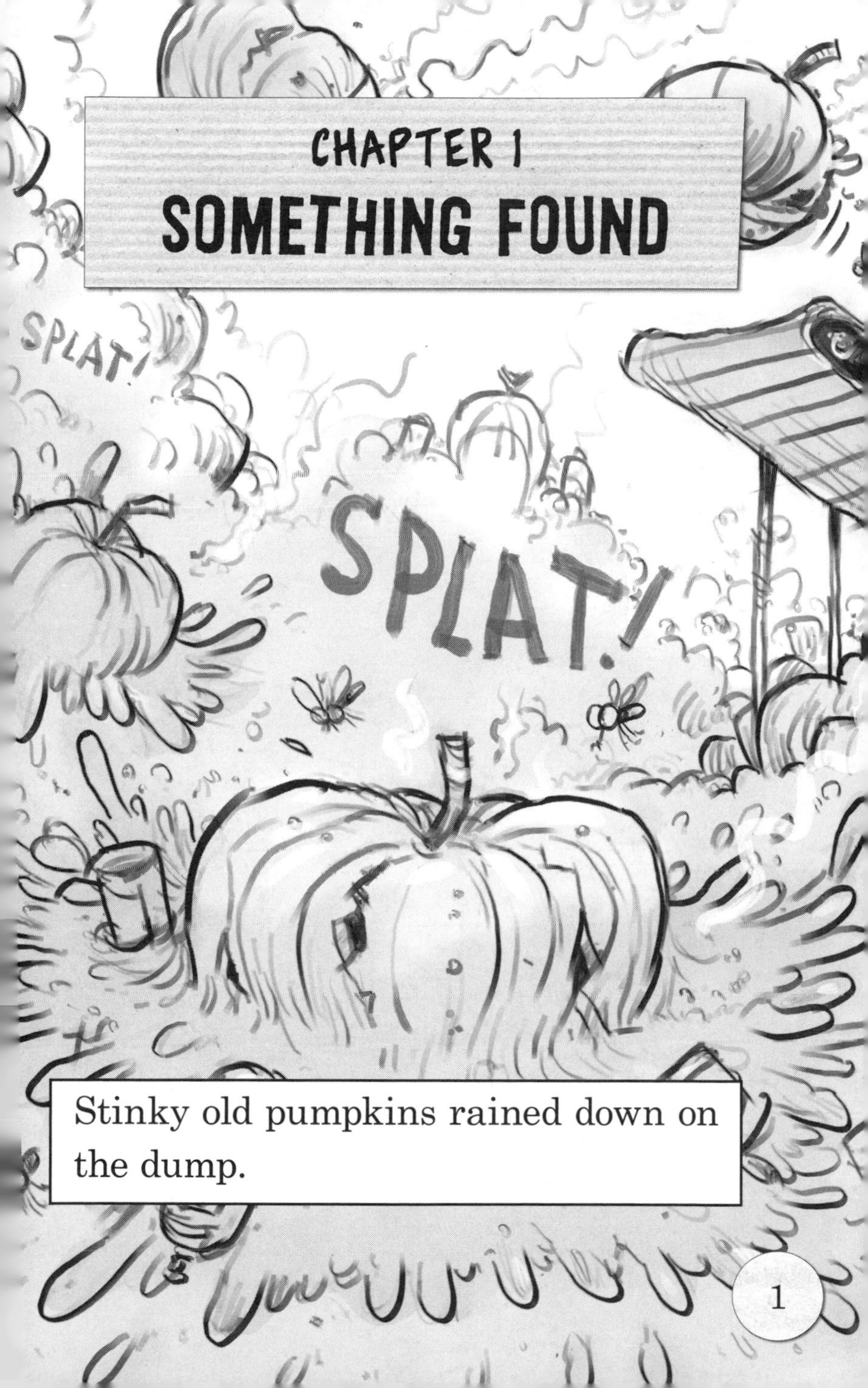
SPLAT!
SPLAT!

Stinky old pumpkins rained down on the dump.

Farmer Gunderson sent all his rotten leftover pumpkins down to the dump. Halloween was over. It was time to get ready for Christmas.

Rotten pumpkin muck was everywhere.

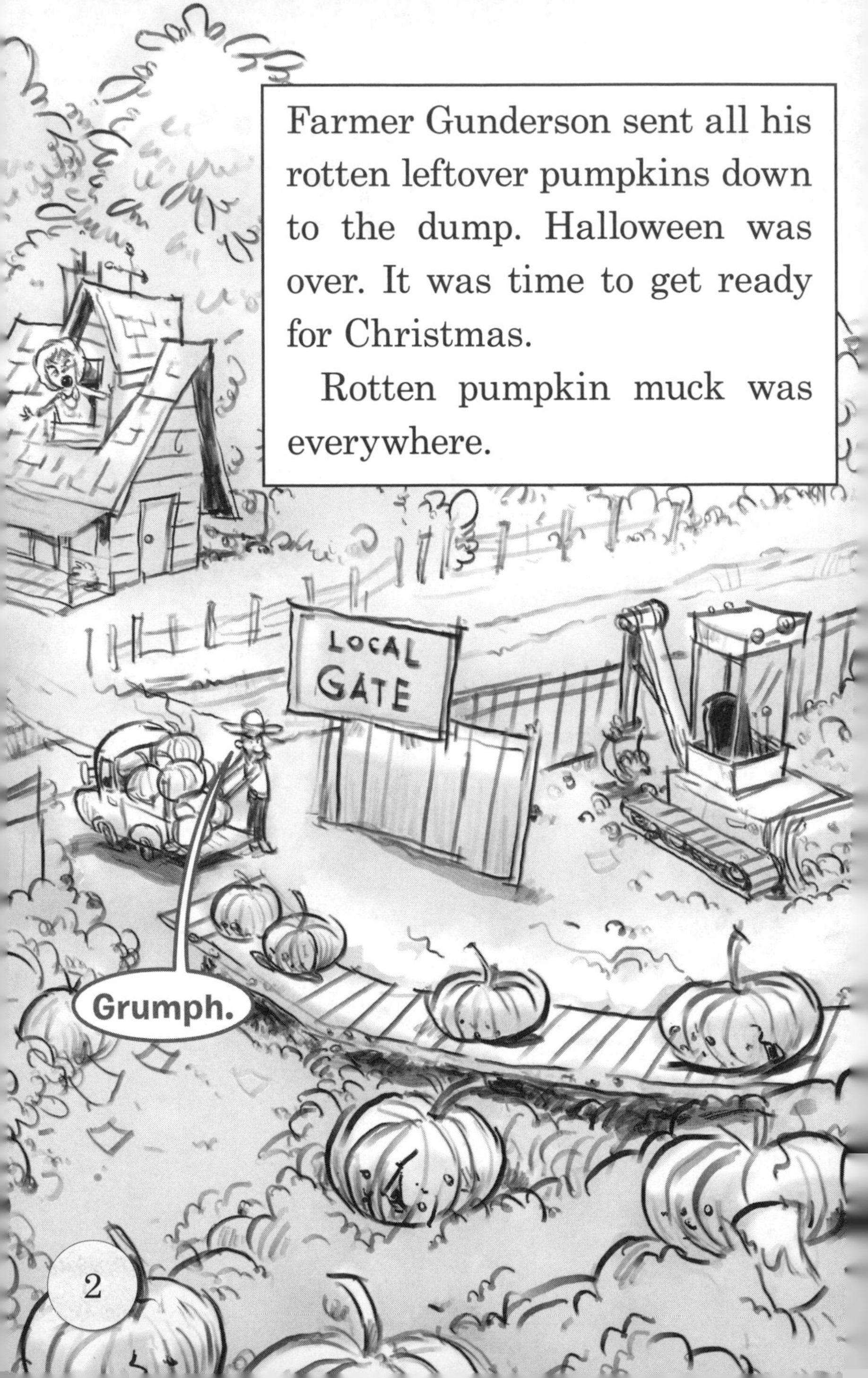
LOCAL GATE
Grumph.

Like she did every morning, Nana waited at the great pile with her BFF Moreland to greet all the new garbage.

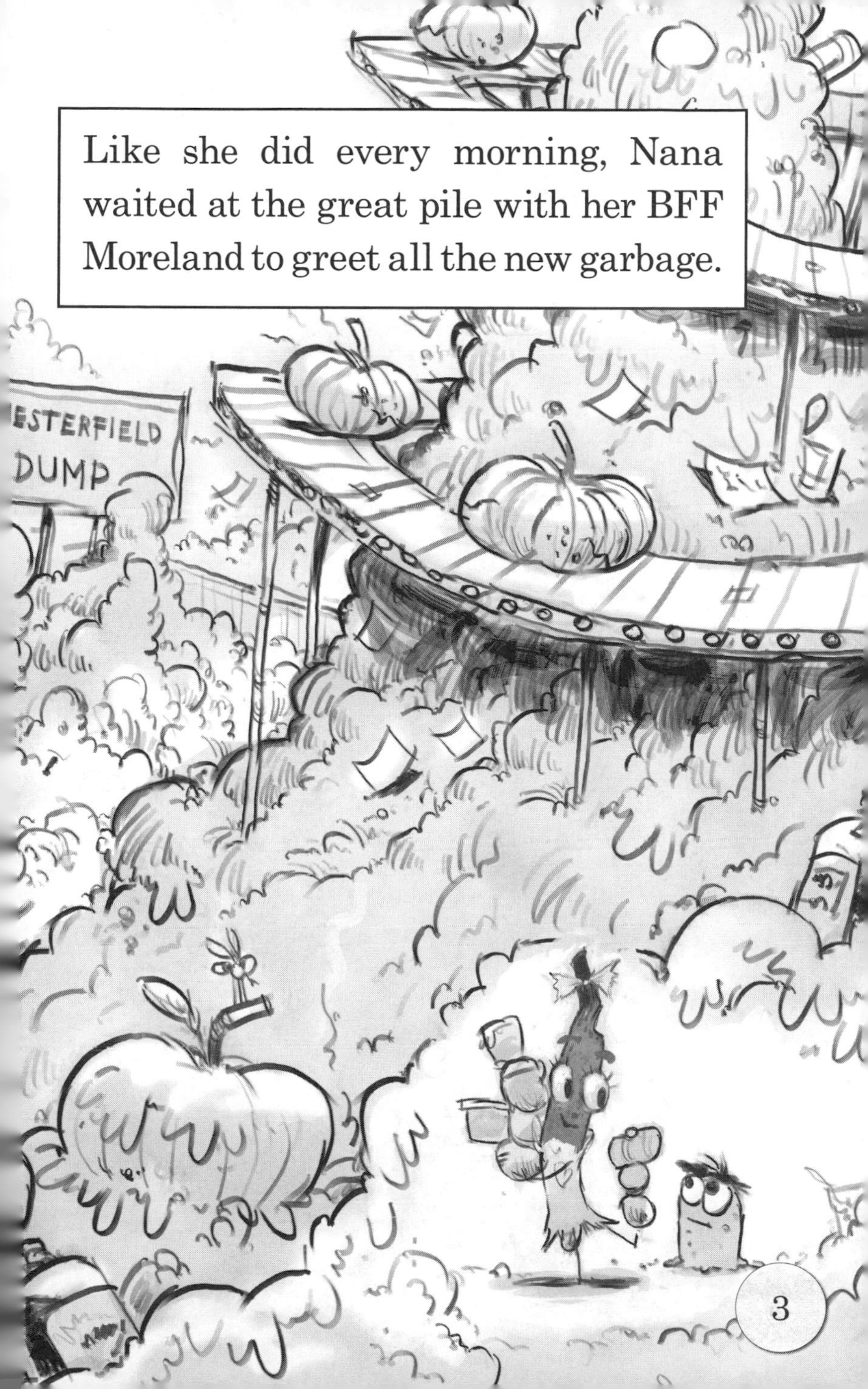
ESTERFIELD
DUMP

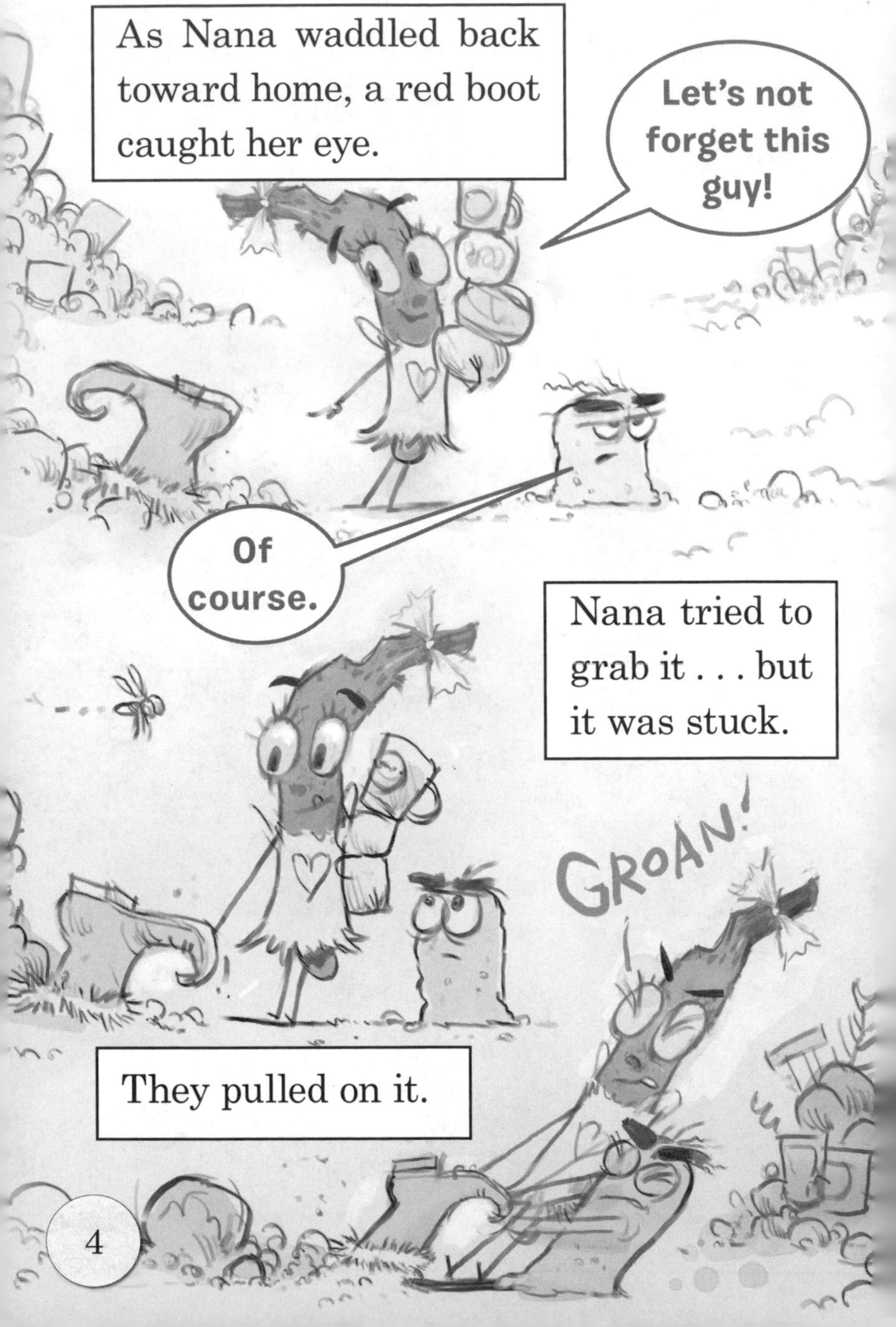

As Nana waddled back toward home, a red boot caught her eye.
Let's not forget this guy!
Of course.
Nana tried to grab it . . . but it was stuck.
GROAN!
They pulled on it.

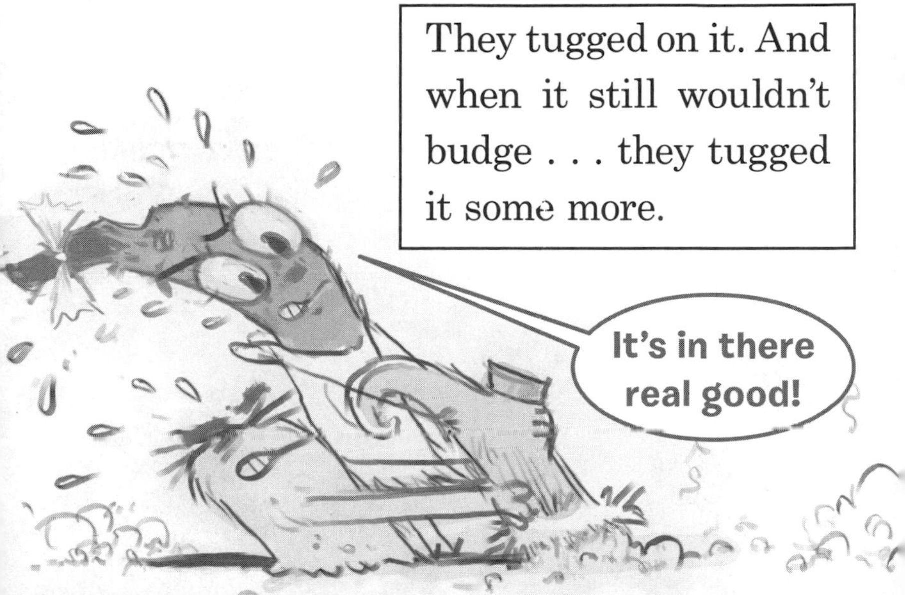
They tugged on it. And when it still wouldn't budge . . . they tugged it some more.
It's in there real good!
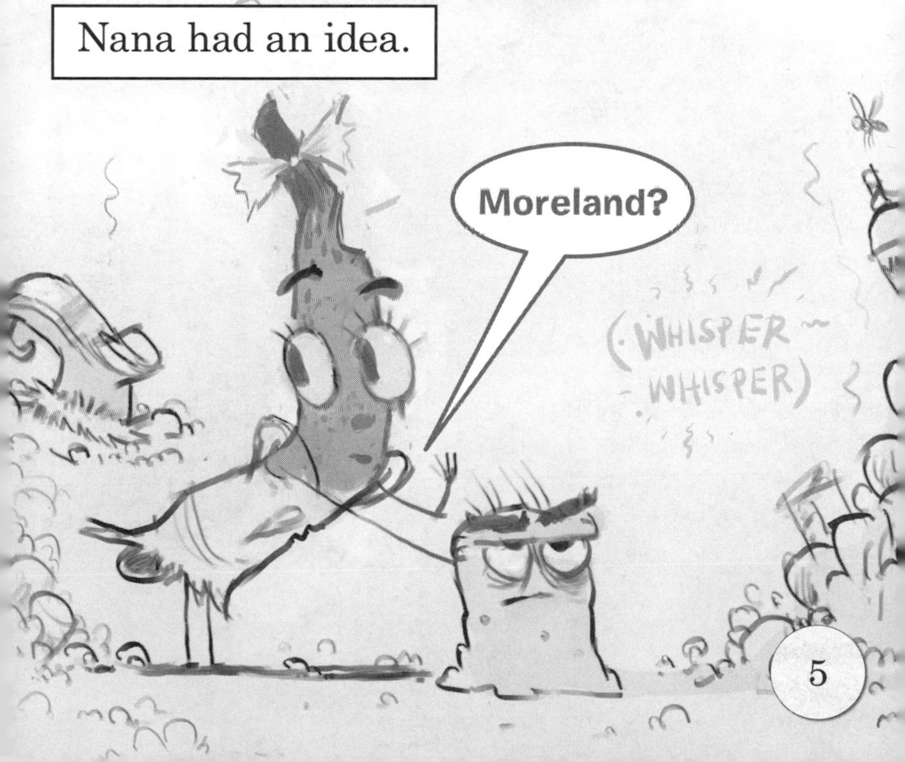
Nana had an idea.
Moreland?
(WHISPER~ WHISPER)

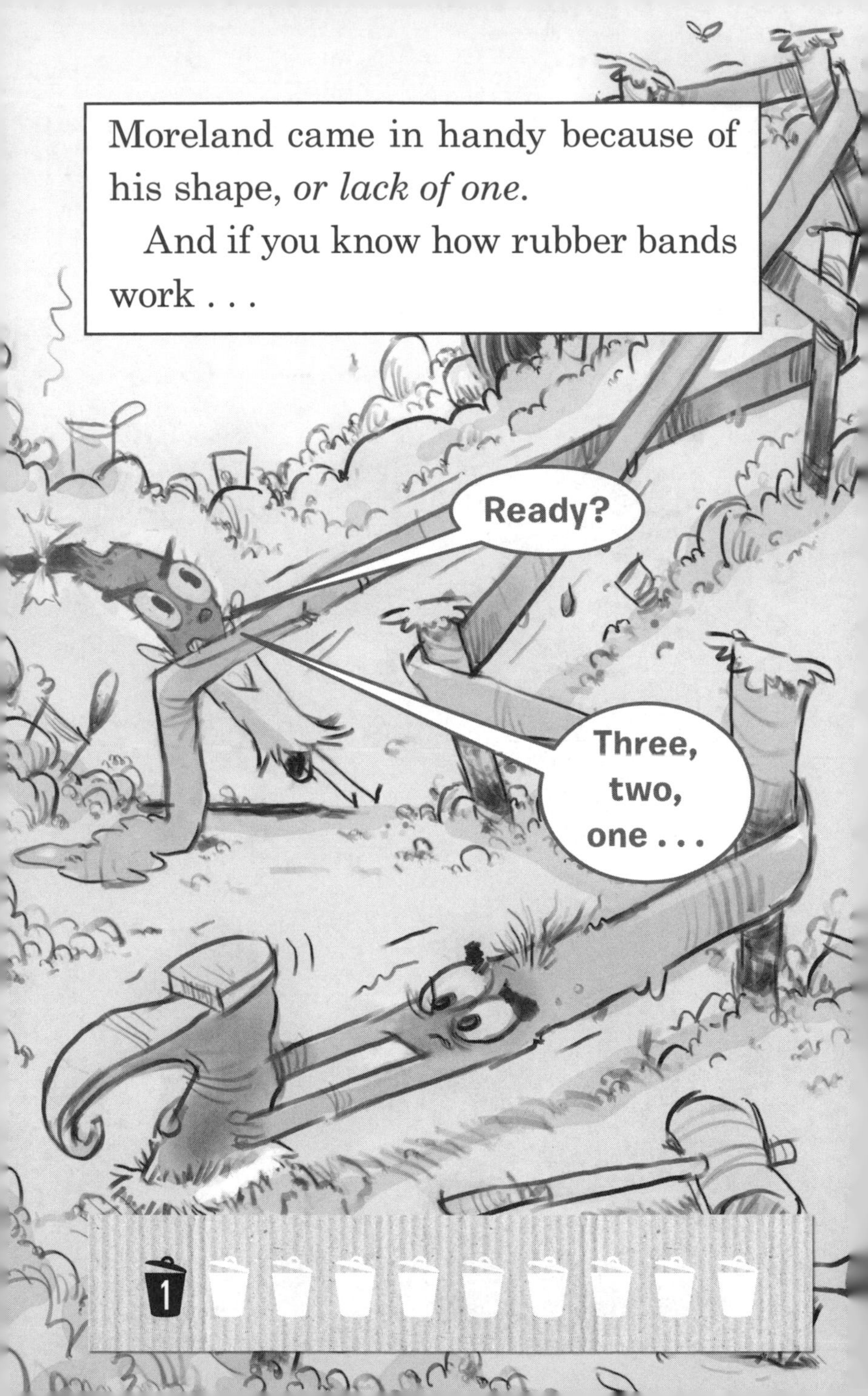
Moreland came in handy because of his shape, *or lack of one*.
And if you know how rubber bands work . . .
Ready?
Three, two, one . . .
1

CHAPTER 2
MEET STEVE!

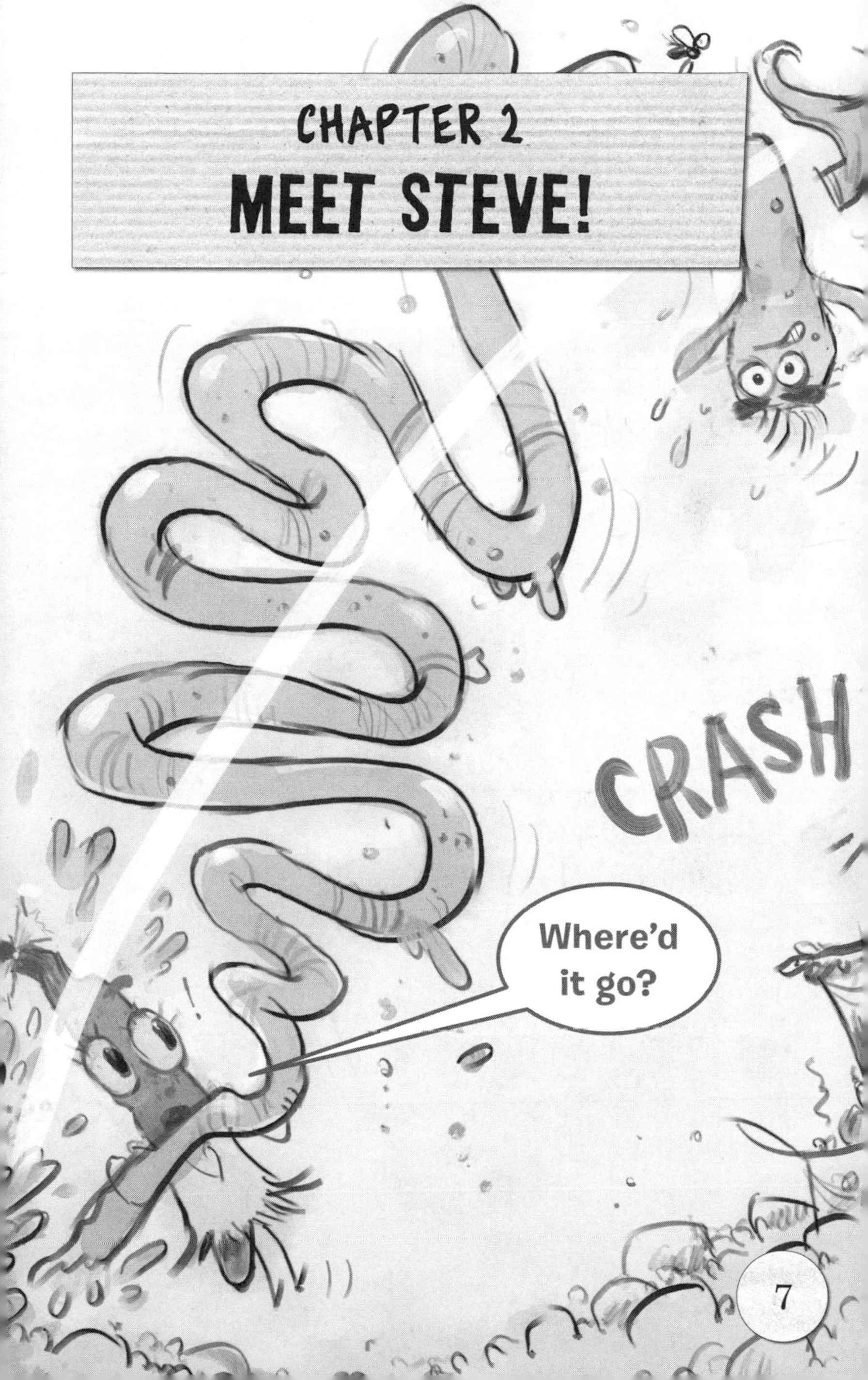
CRASH
Where'd it go?

Nana had pulled out something much bigger than a boot. It was a funny-looking doll.

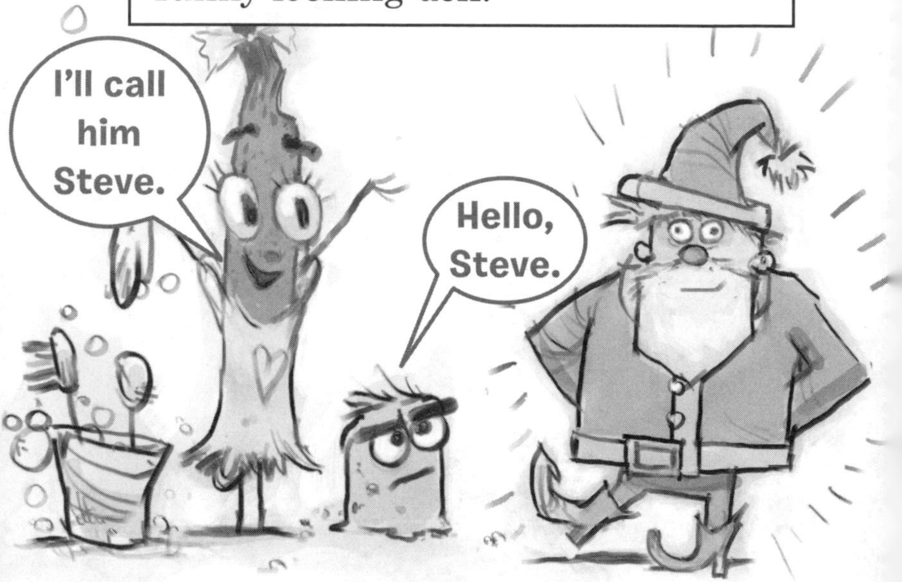
I'll call him Steve.
Hello, Steve.

They wheeled Steve back to their house and set him on top of a big mushy pumpkin.

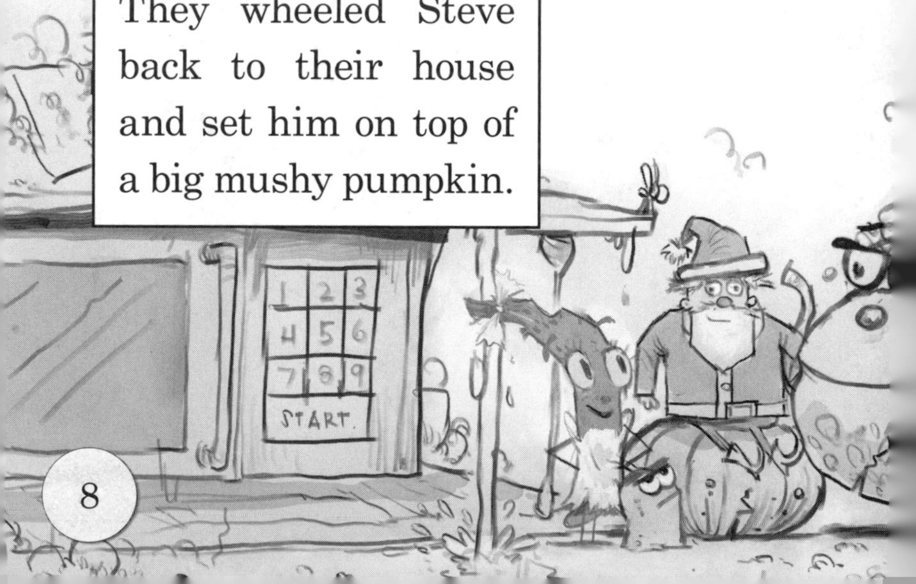
1 2 3
4 5 6
7 8 9
START

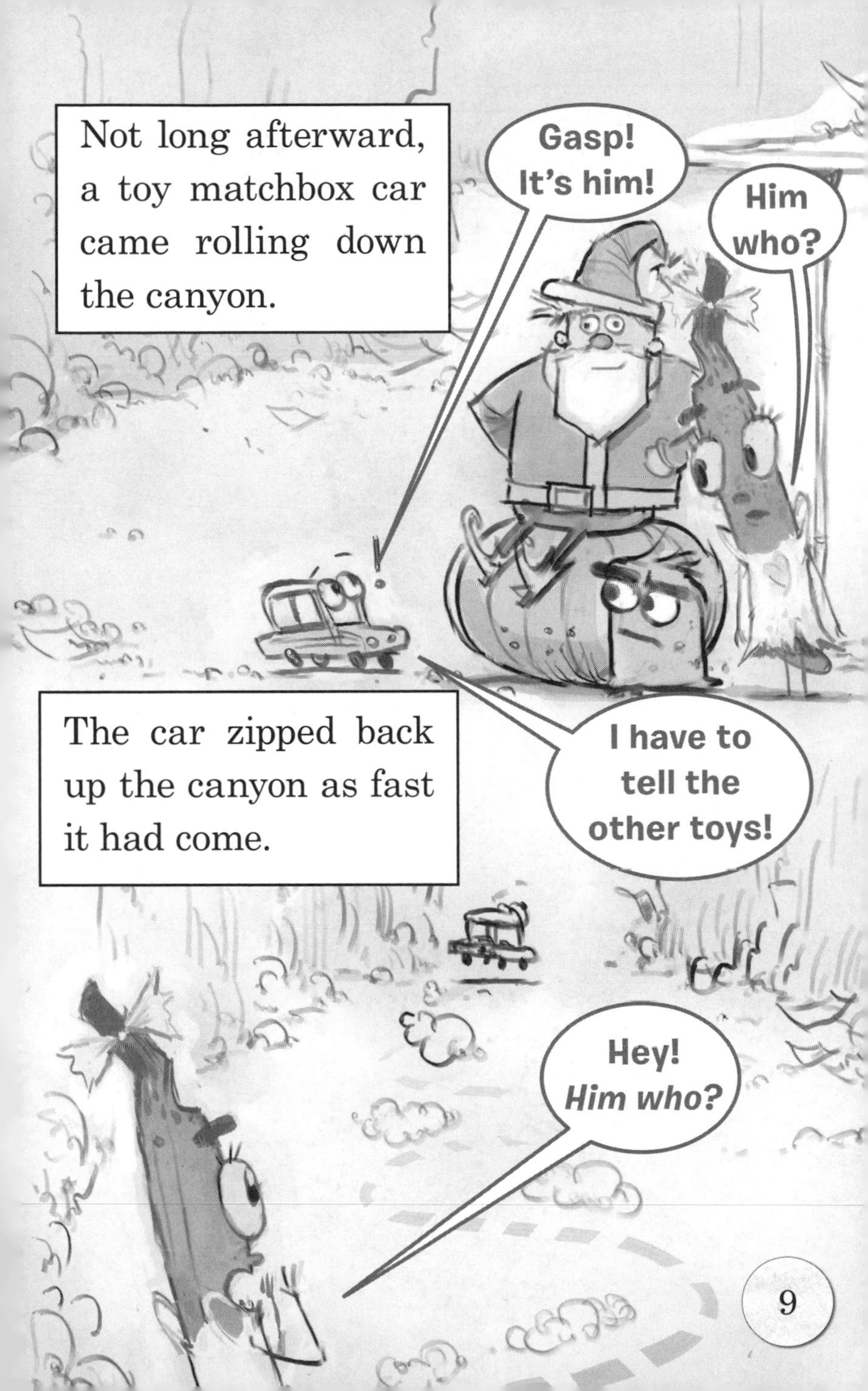
Not long afterward, a toy matchbox car came rolling down the canyon.
Gasp! It's him!
Him who?
The car zipped back up the canyon as fast it had come.
I have to tell the other toys!
Hey! *Him who?*

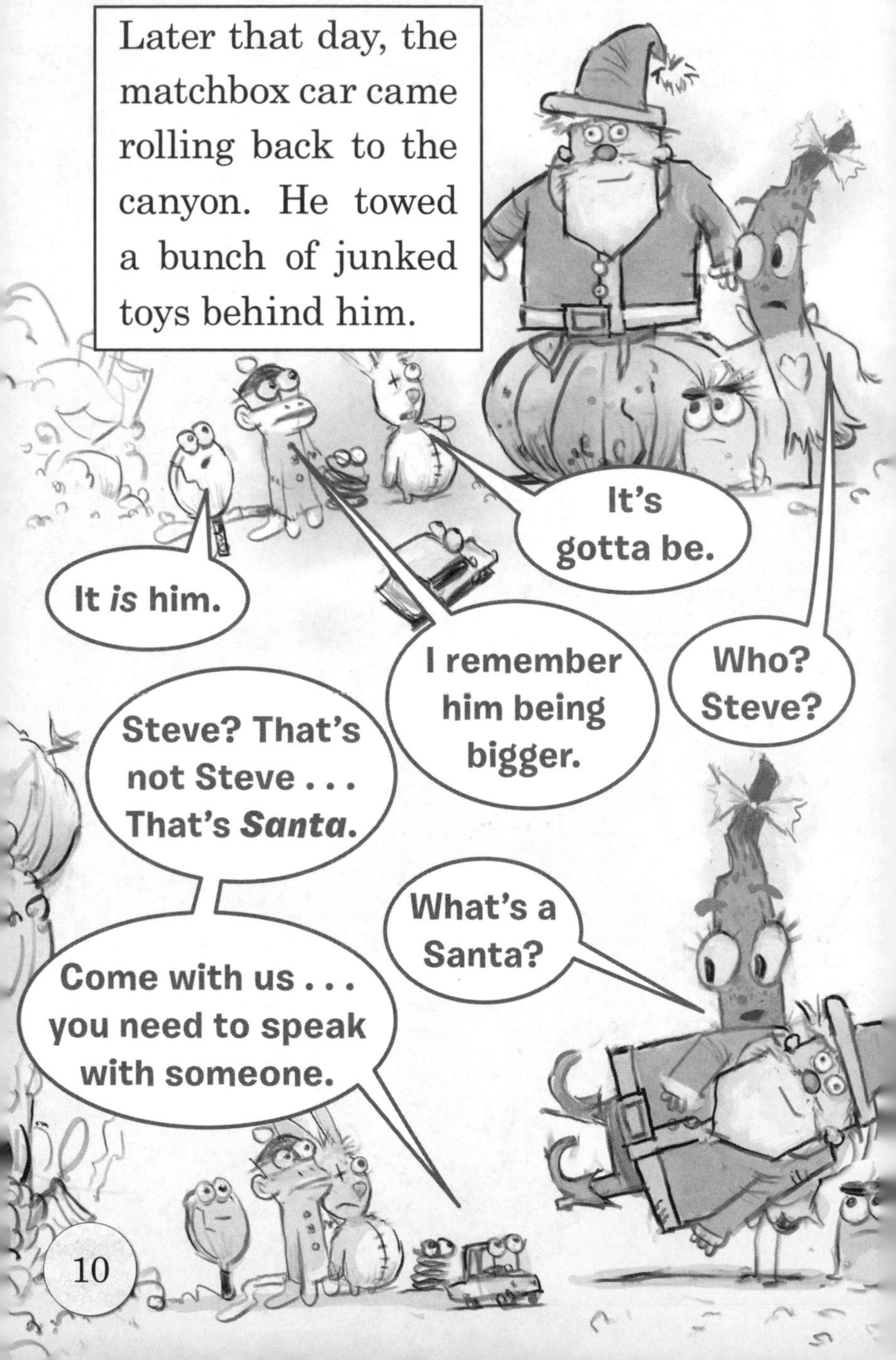
Later that day, the matchbox car came rolling back to the canyon. He towed a bunch of junked toys behind him.
It's gotta be.
It *is* him.
I remember him being bigger.
Who? Steve?
Steve? That's not Steve . . . That's *Santa*.
What's a Santa?
Come with us . . . you need to speak with someone.

Nana, Moreland, and Ms. Kettle followed the group of toys as they went down to Old Toy Canyon.

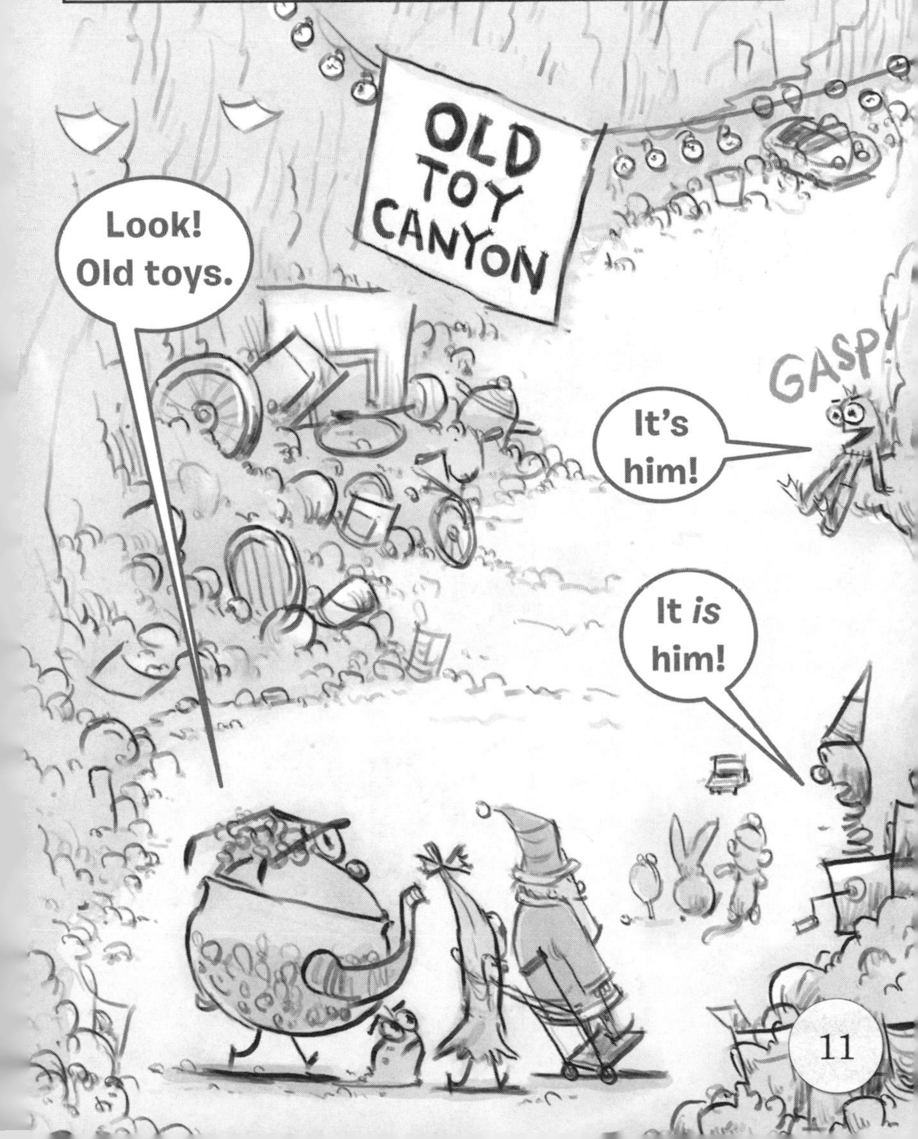
OLD TOY CANYON
Look! Old toys.
GASP!
It's him!
It *is* him!

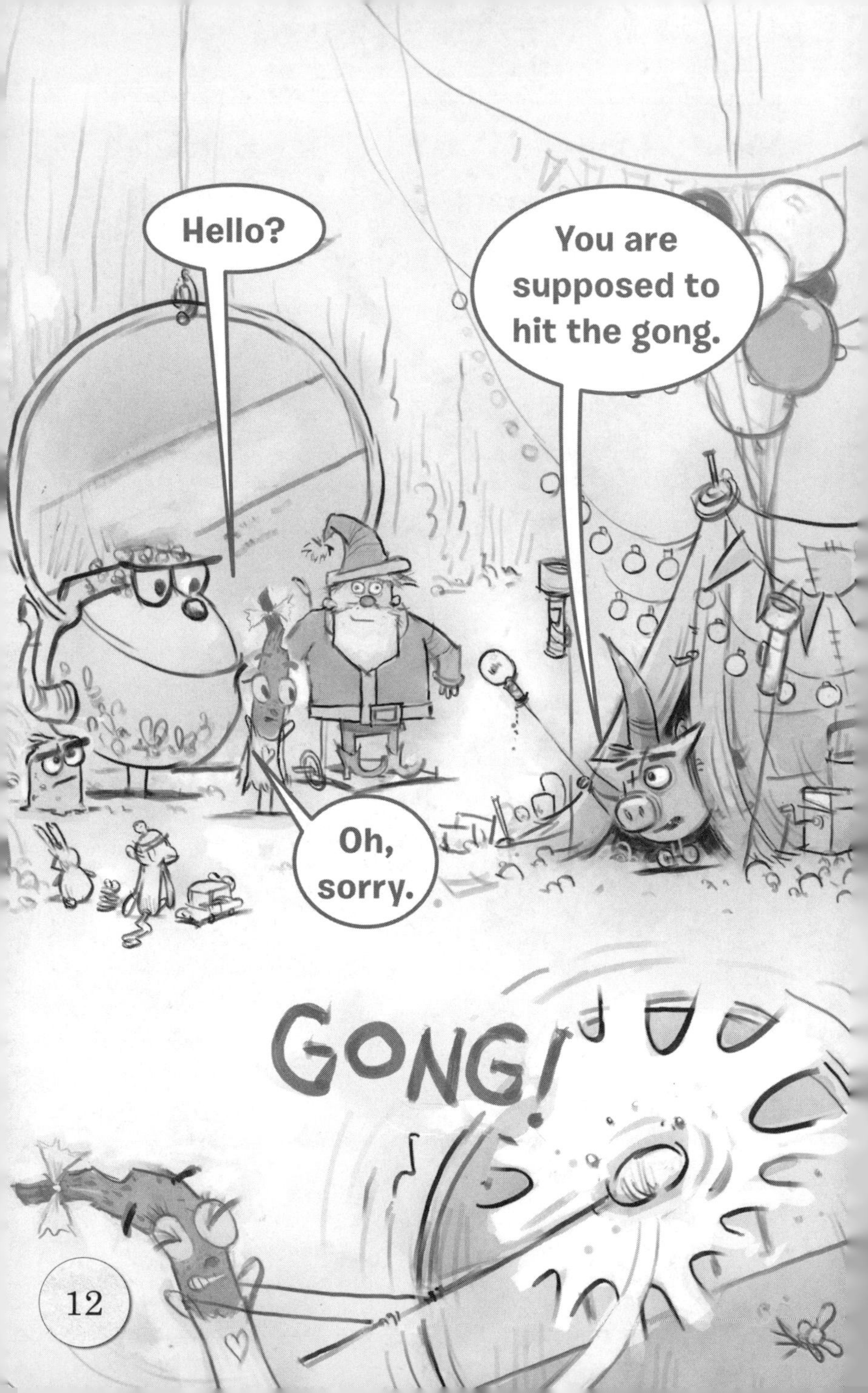
Hello?
You are supposed to hit the gong.
Oh, sorry.
GONG!

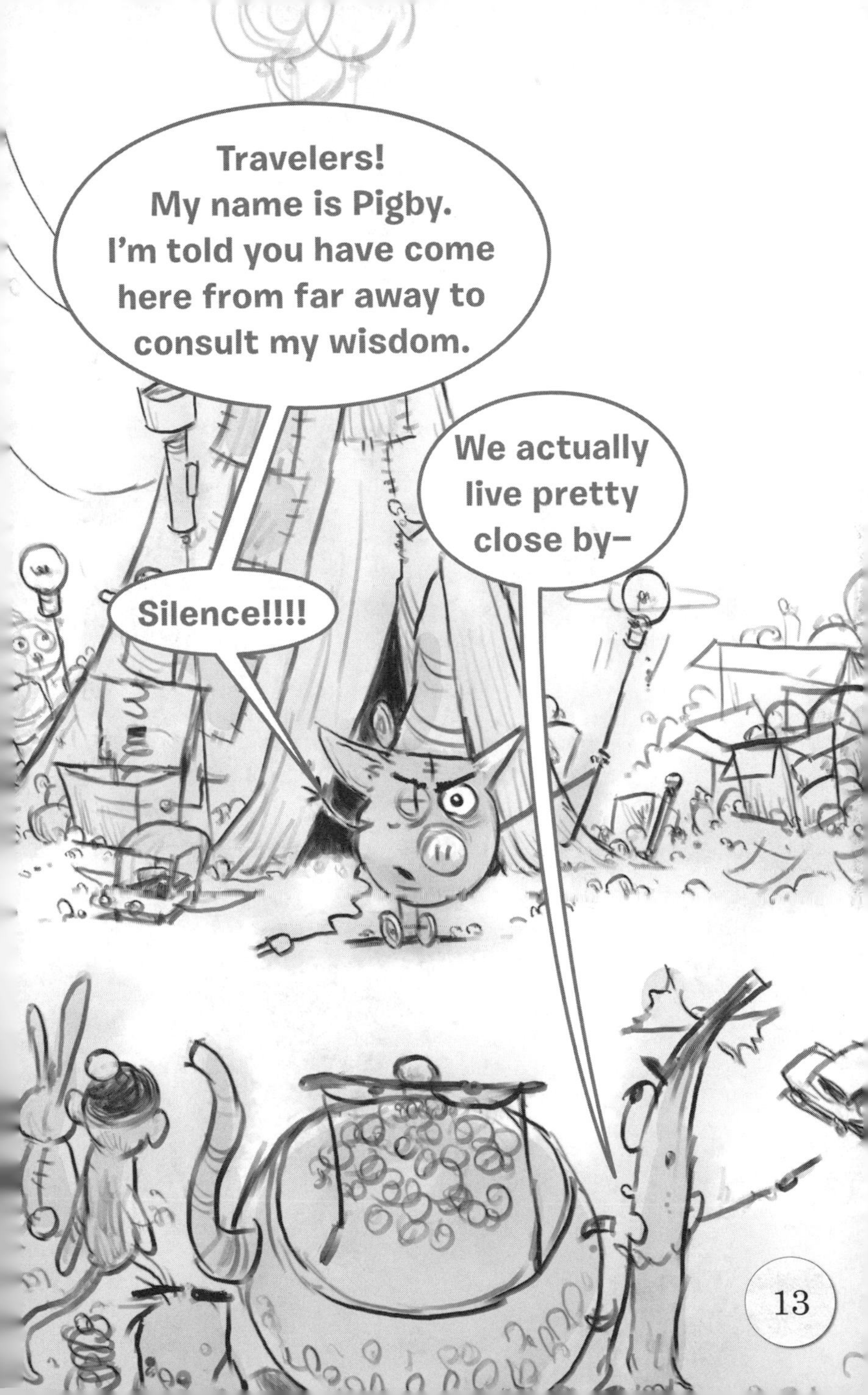
Travelers! My name is Pigby. I'm told you have come here from far away to consult my wisdom.
We actually live pretty close by–
Silence!!!!

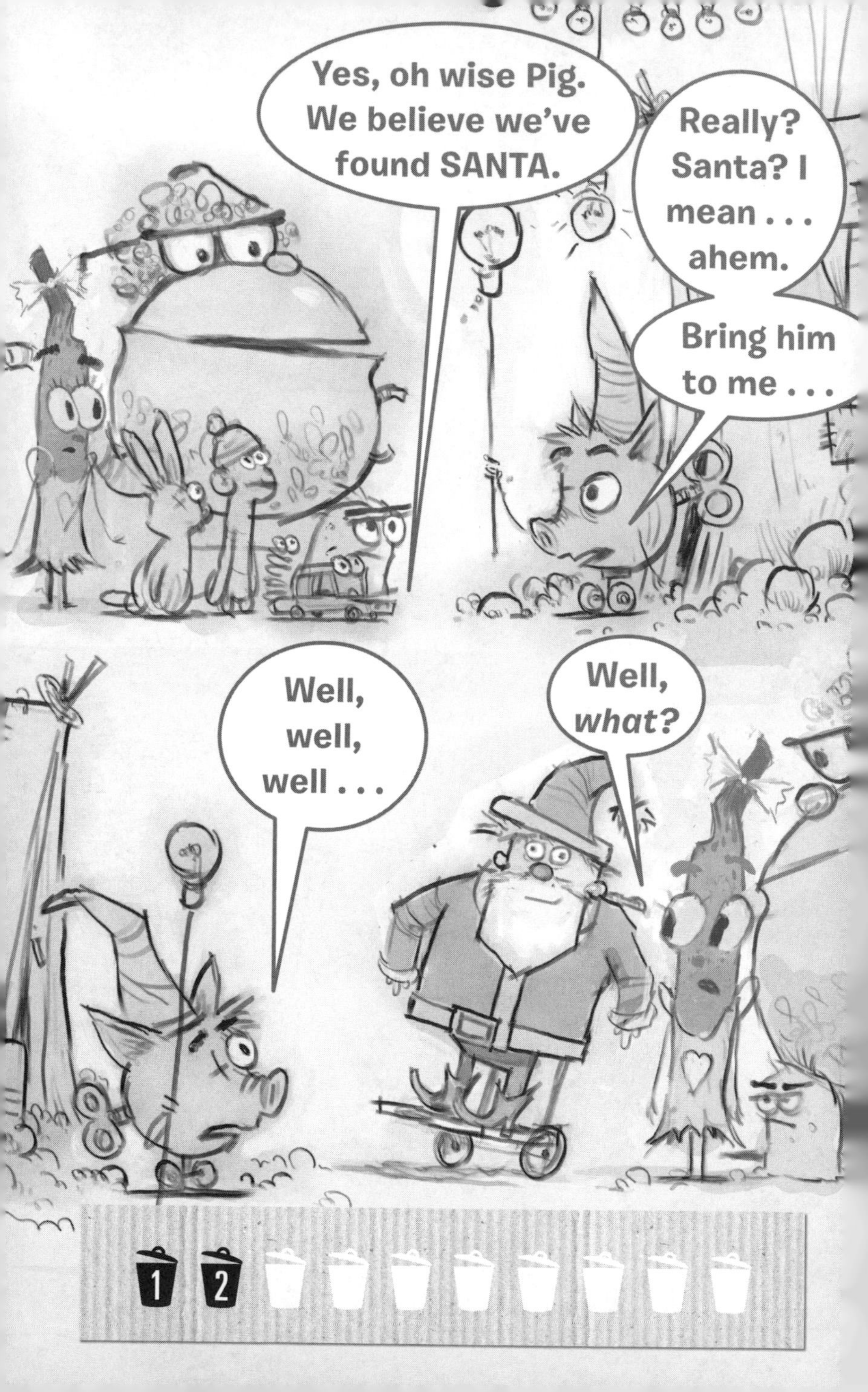
Yes, oh wise Pig. We believe we've found SANTA.
Really? Santa? I mean . . . ahem.
Bring him to me . . .
Well, well, well . . .
Well, *what?*
1
2

CHAPTER 3
THE REAL SANTA

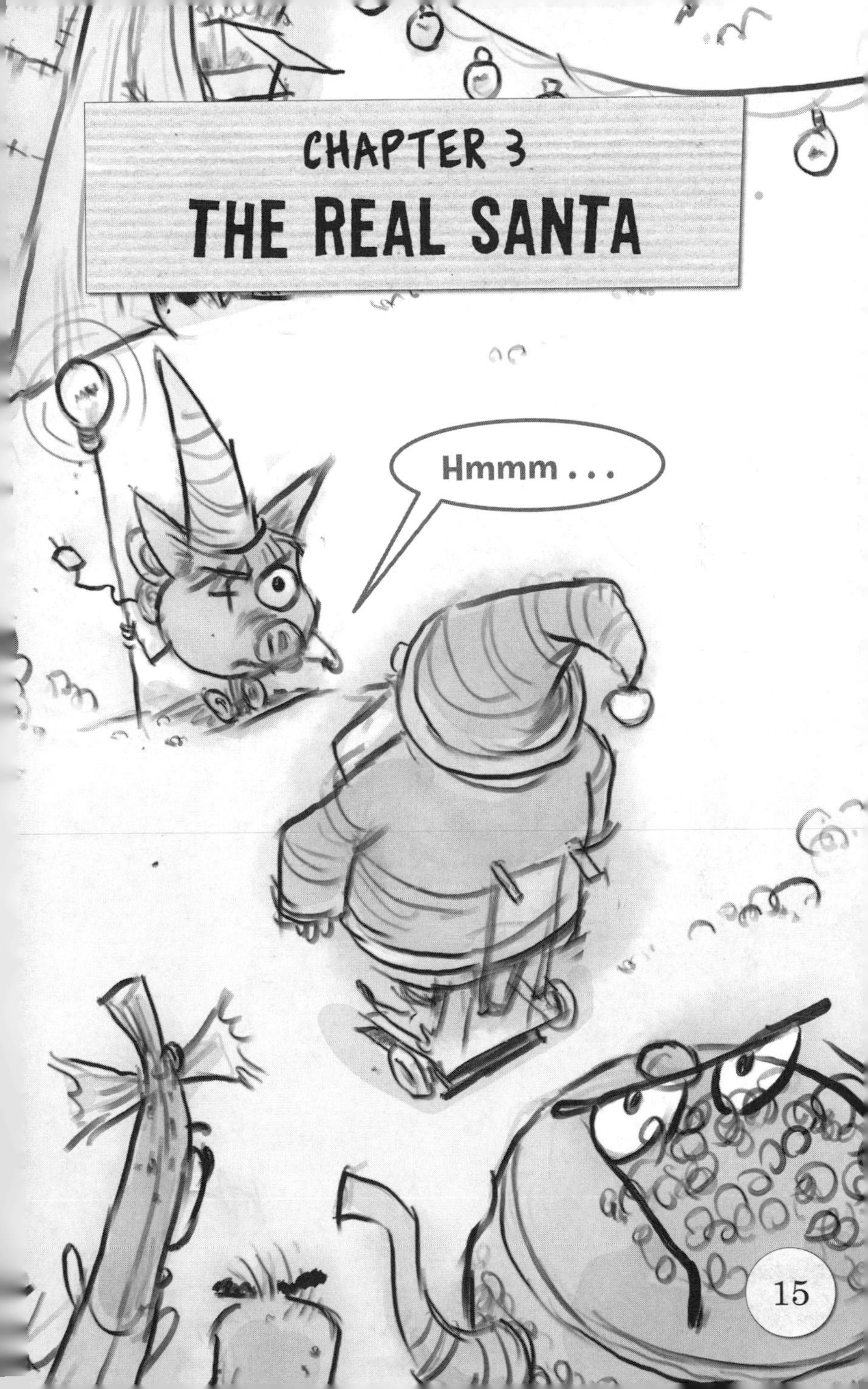
Hmmm . . .

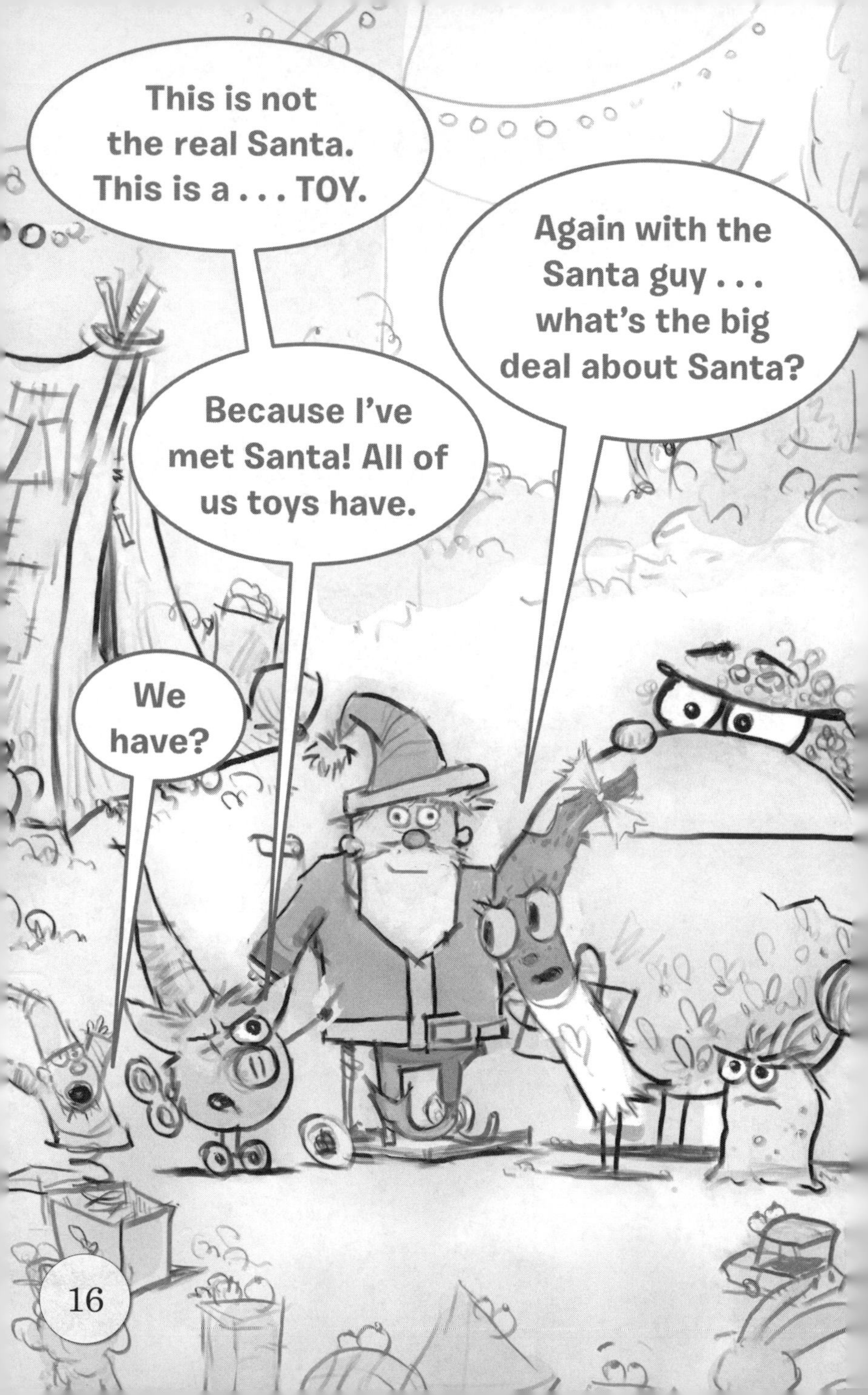
This is not the real Santa. This is a . . . TOY.
Because I've met Santa! All of us toys have.
Again with the Santa guy . . . what's the big deal about Santa?
We have?

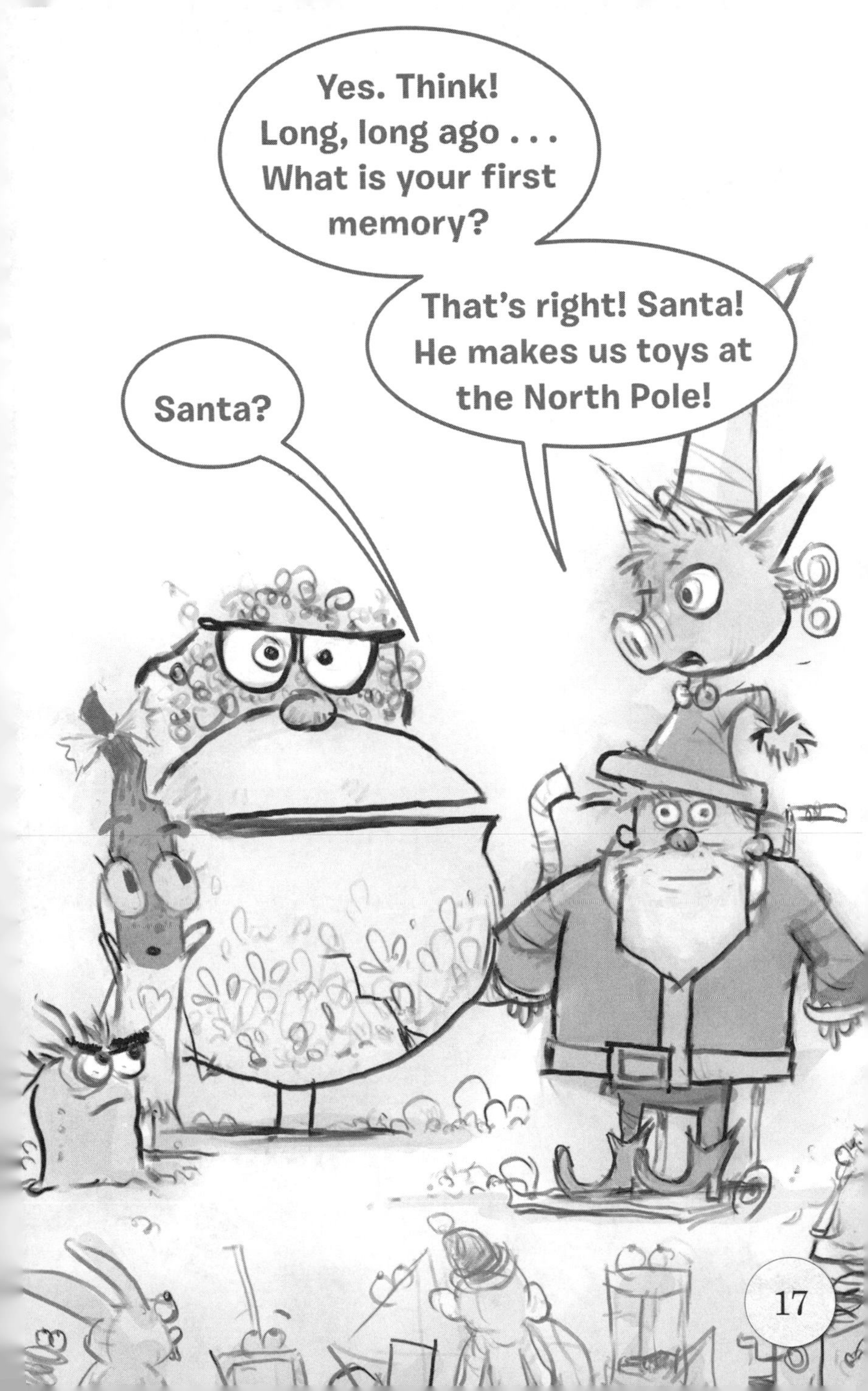
Yes. Think! Long, long ago . . . What is your first memory?
That's right! Santa! He makes us toys at the North Pole!
Santa?

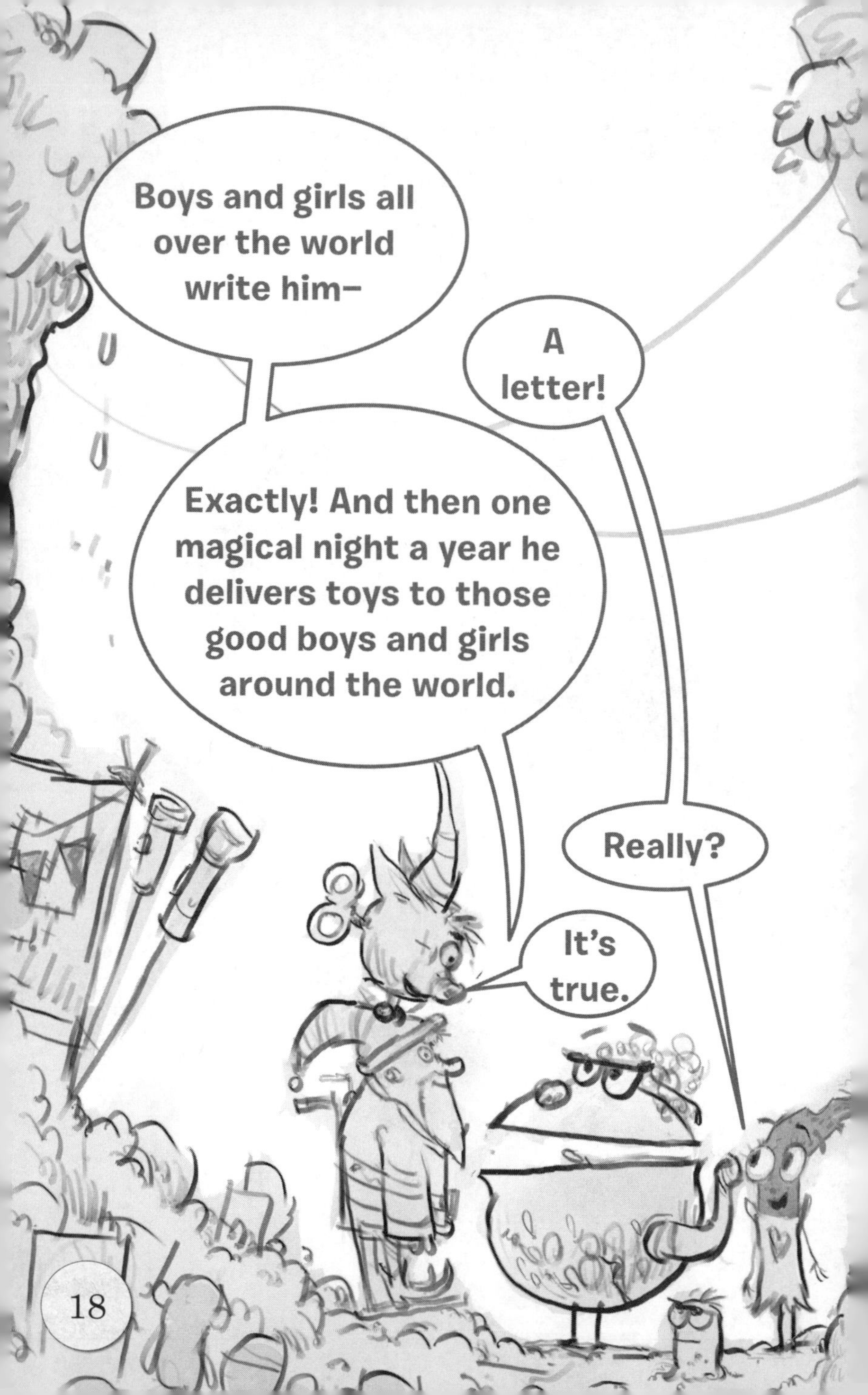

Boys and girls all over the world write him–
A letter!
Exactly! And then one magical night a year he delivers toys to those good boys and girls around the world.
Really?
It's true.

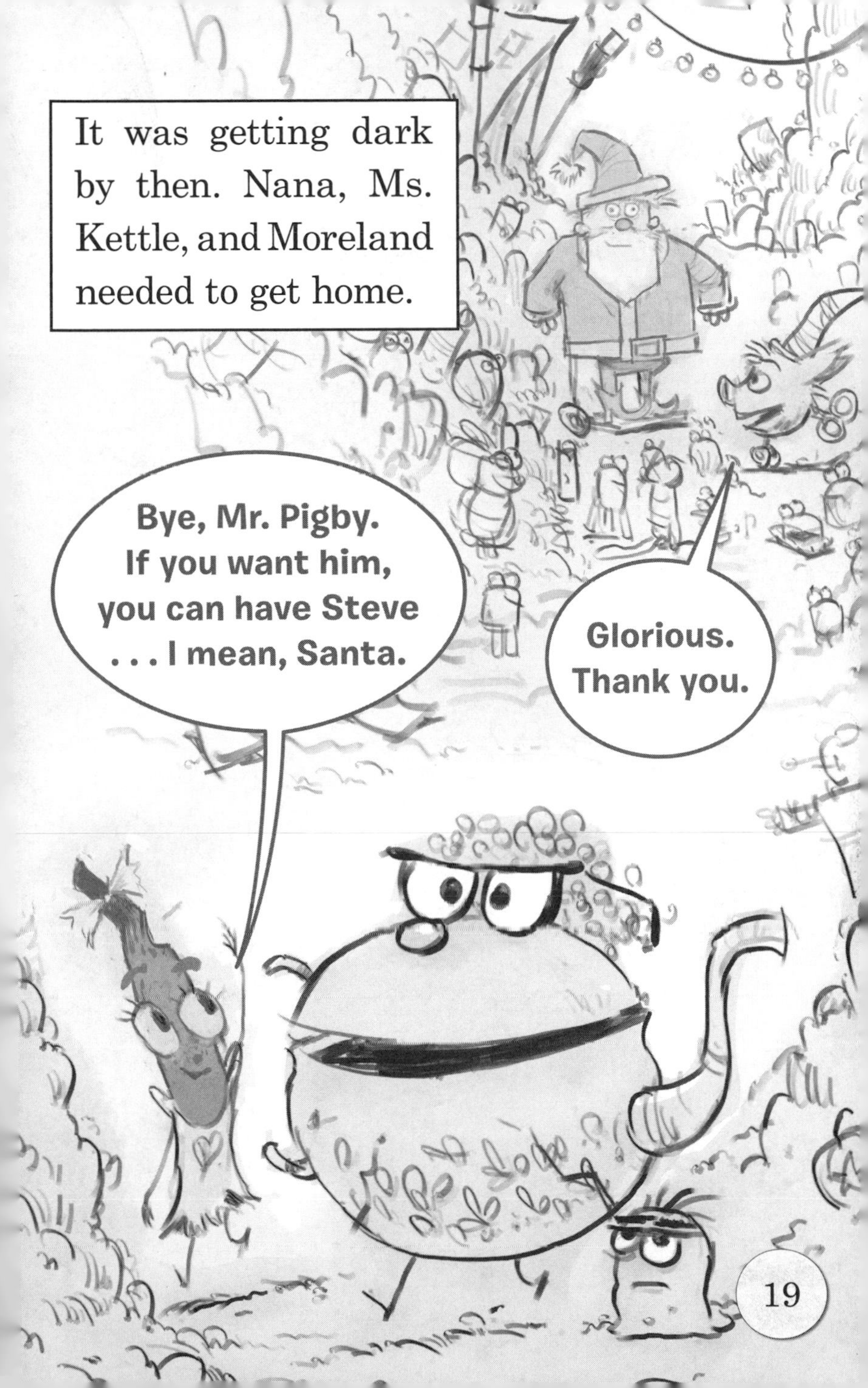
It was getting dark by then. Nana, Ms. Kettle, and Moreland needed to get home.
Bye, Mr. Pigby. If you want him, you can have Steve . . . I mean, Santa.
Glorious. Thank you.

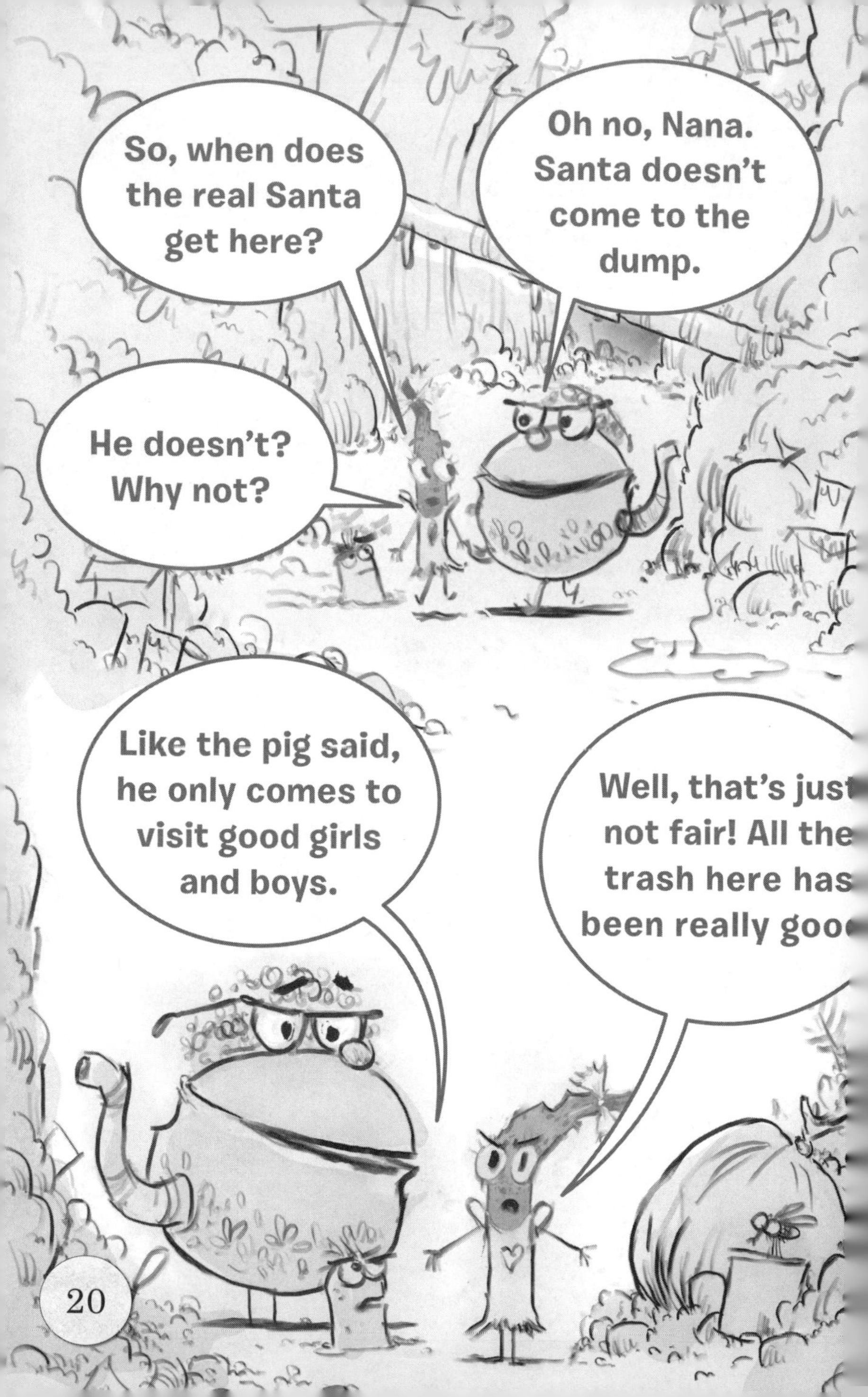
So, when does the real Santa get here?
Oh no, Nana. Santa doesn't come to the dump.
He doesn't? Why not?
Like the pig said, he only comes to visit good girls and boys.
Well, that's jus not fair! All the trash here has been really goo

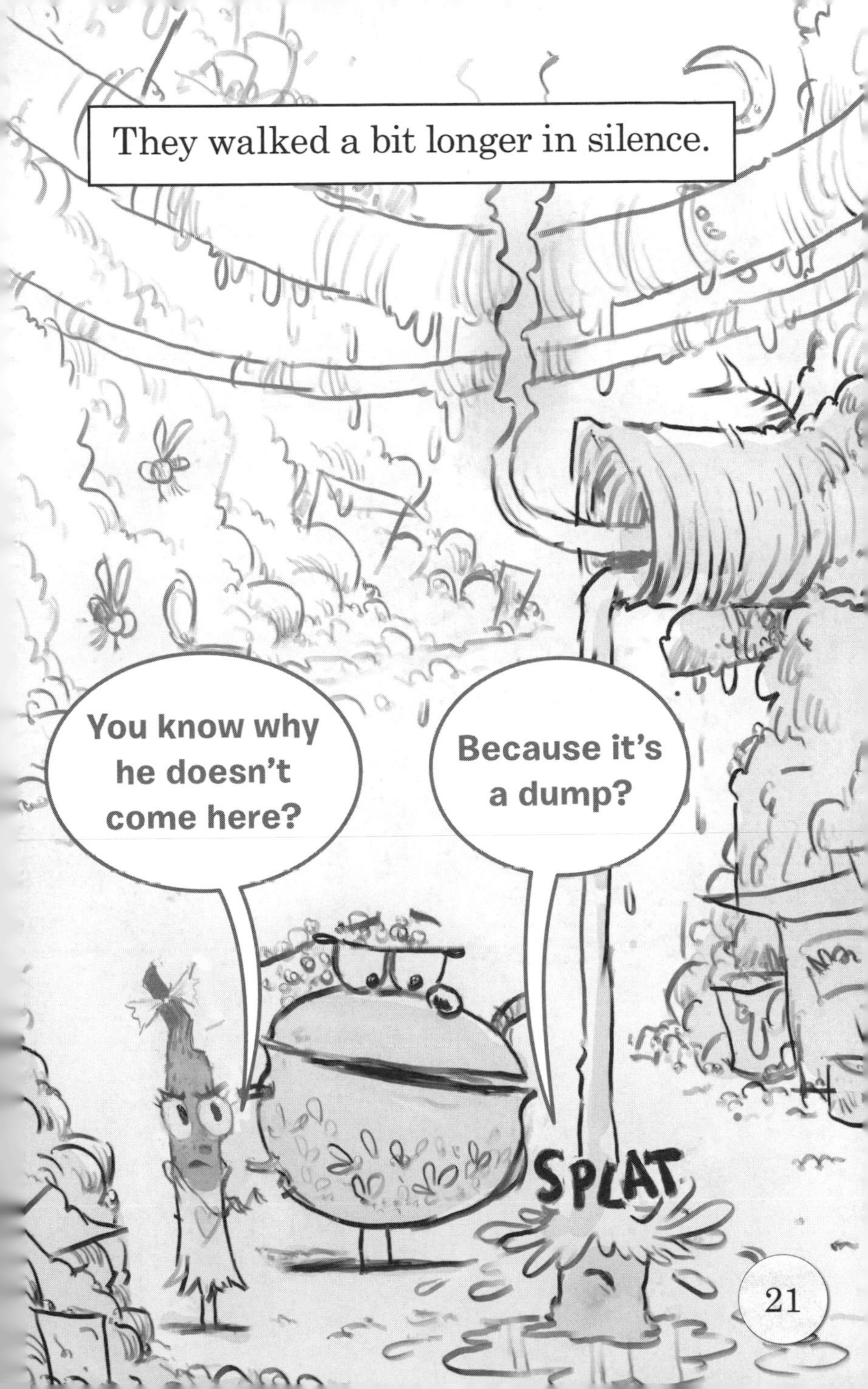
They walked a bit longer in silence.
You know why he doesn't come here?
Because it's a dump?
SPLAT

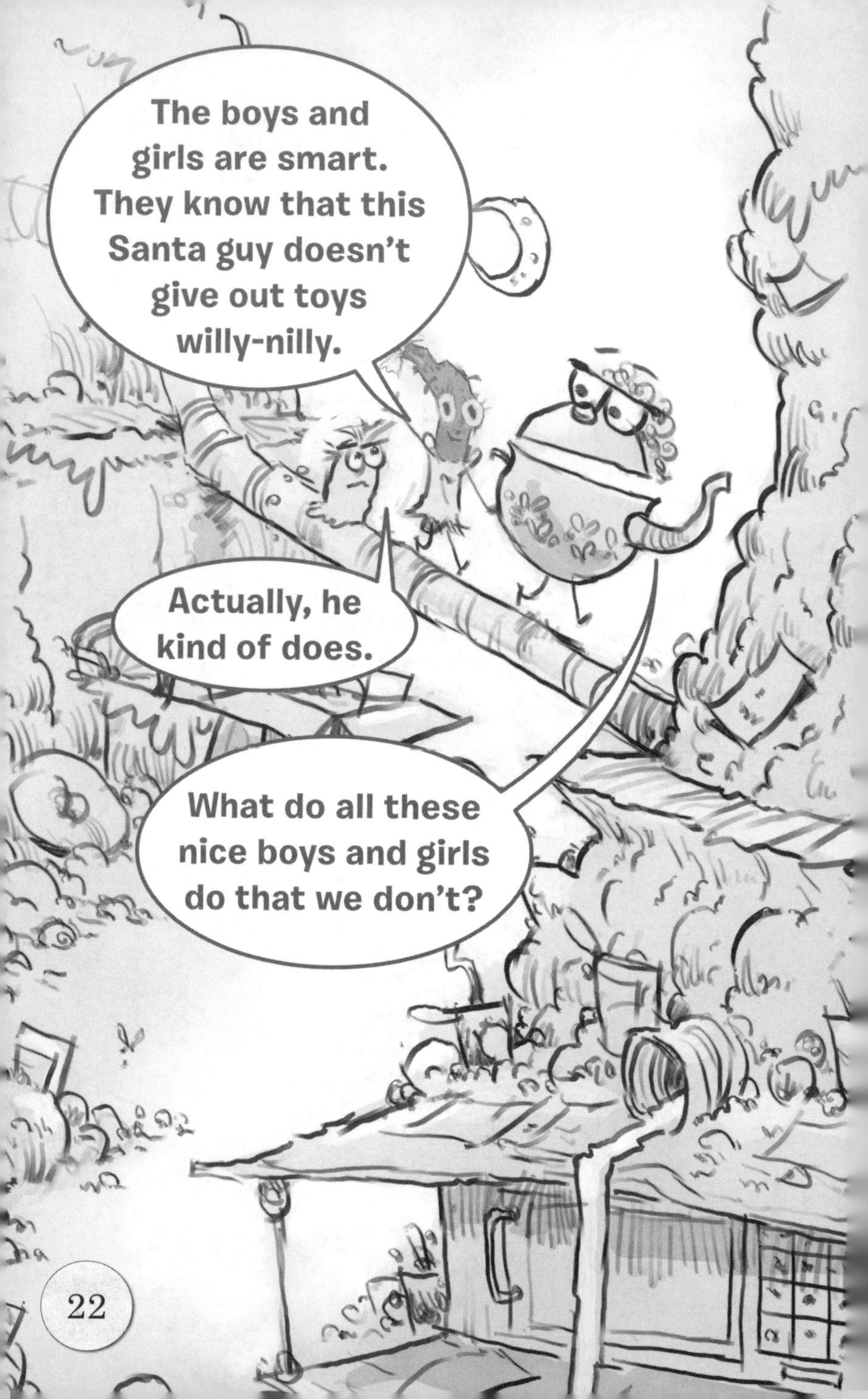
The boys and girls are smart. They know that this Santa guy doesn't give out toys willy-nilly.
Actually, he kind of does.
What do all these nice boys and girls do that we don't?

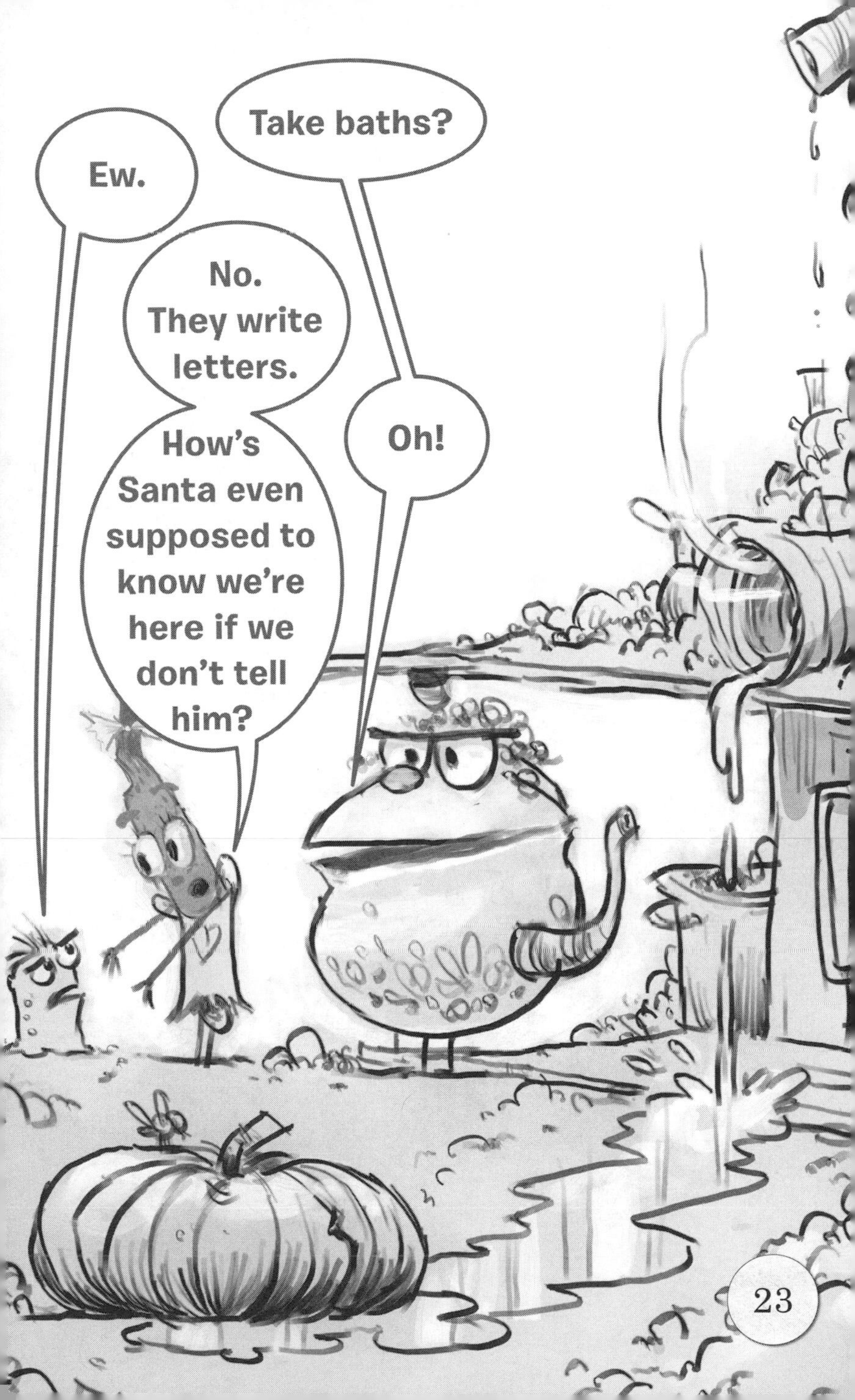
Ew.
Take baths?
No.
They write
letters.
How's
Santa even
supposed to
know we're
here if we
don't tell
him?
Oh!

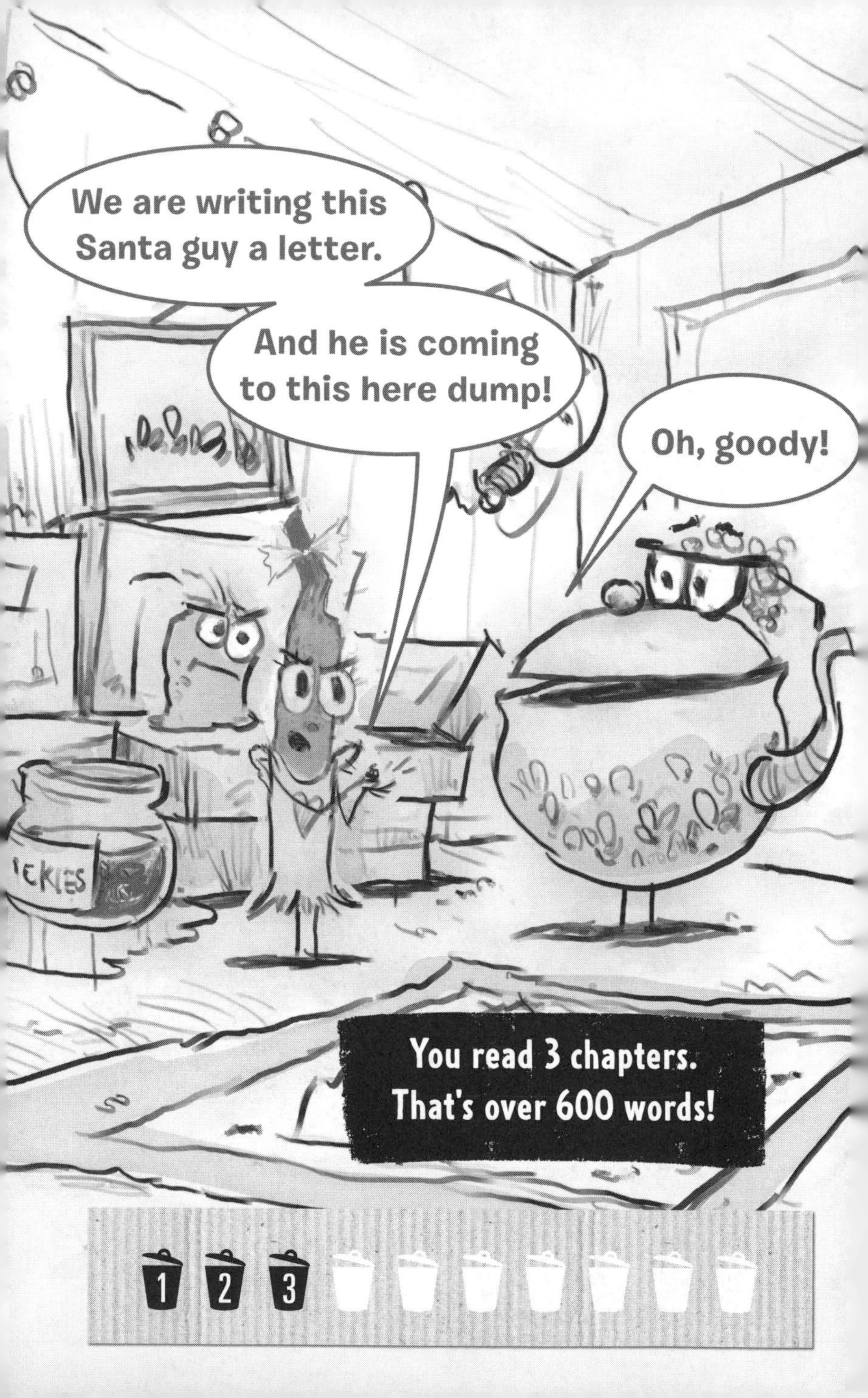
We are writing this Santa guy a letter.
And he is coming to this here dump!
Oh, goody!
ICKLES
You read 3 chapters. That's over 600 words!
1 2 3

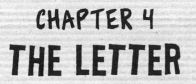

The next morning, the old microwave was buzzing with activity

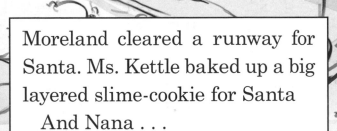

Moreland cleared a runway for Santa. Ms. Kettle baked up a big layered slime-cookie for Santa And Nana . . .

25

. . . well, she was writing the perfect letter to Santa about why they all deserved Christmas gifts.

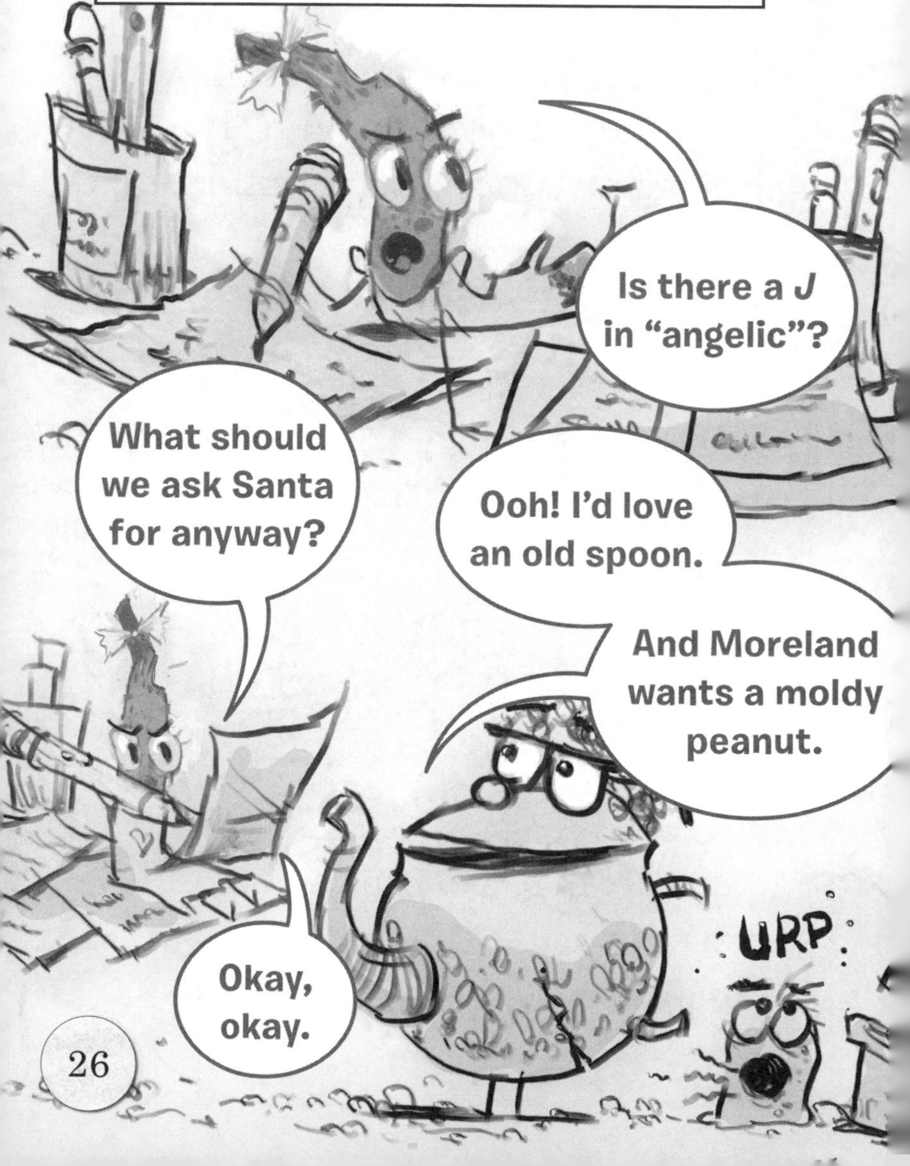
Is there a *J* in "angelic"?
What should we ask Santa for anyway?
Ooh! I'd love an old spoon.
And Moreland wants a moldy peanut.
Okay, okay.
URP

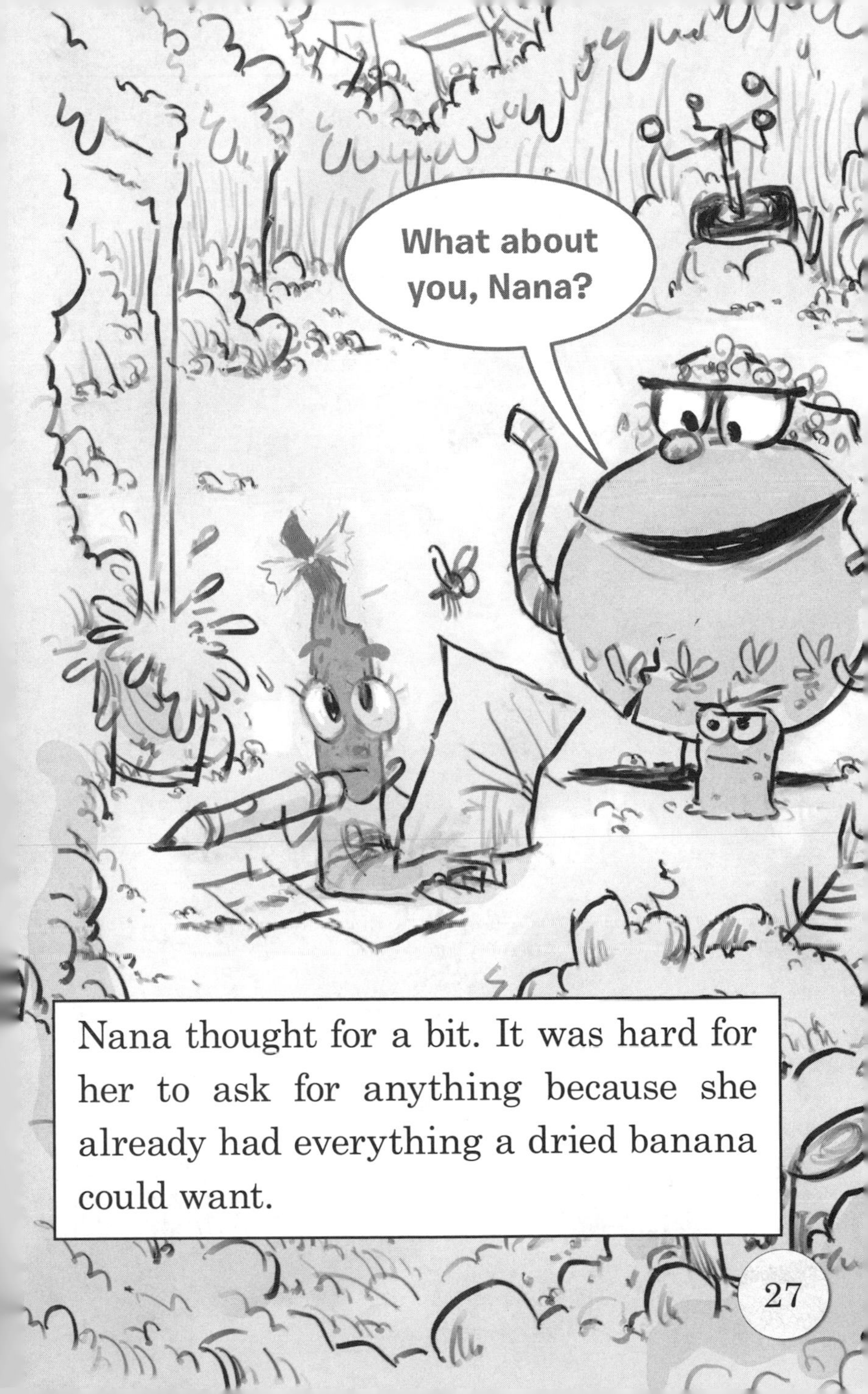
What about you, Nana?

Nana thought for a bit. It was hard for her to ask for anything because she already had everything a dried banana could want.

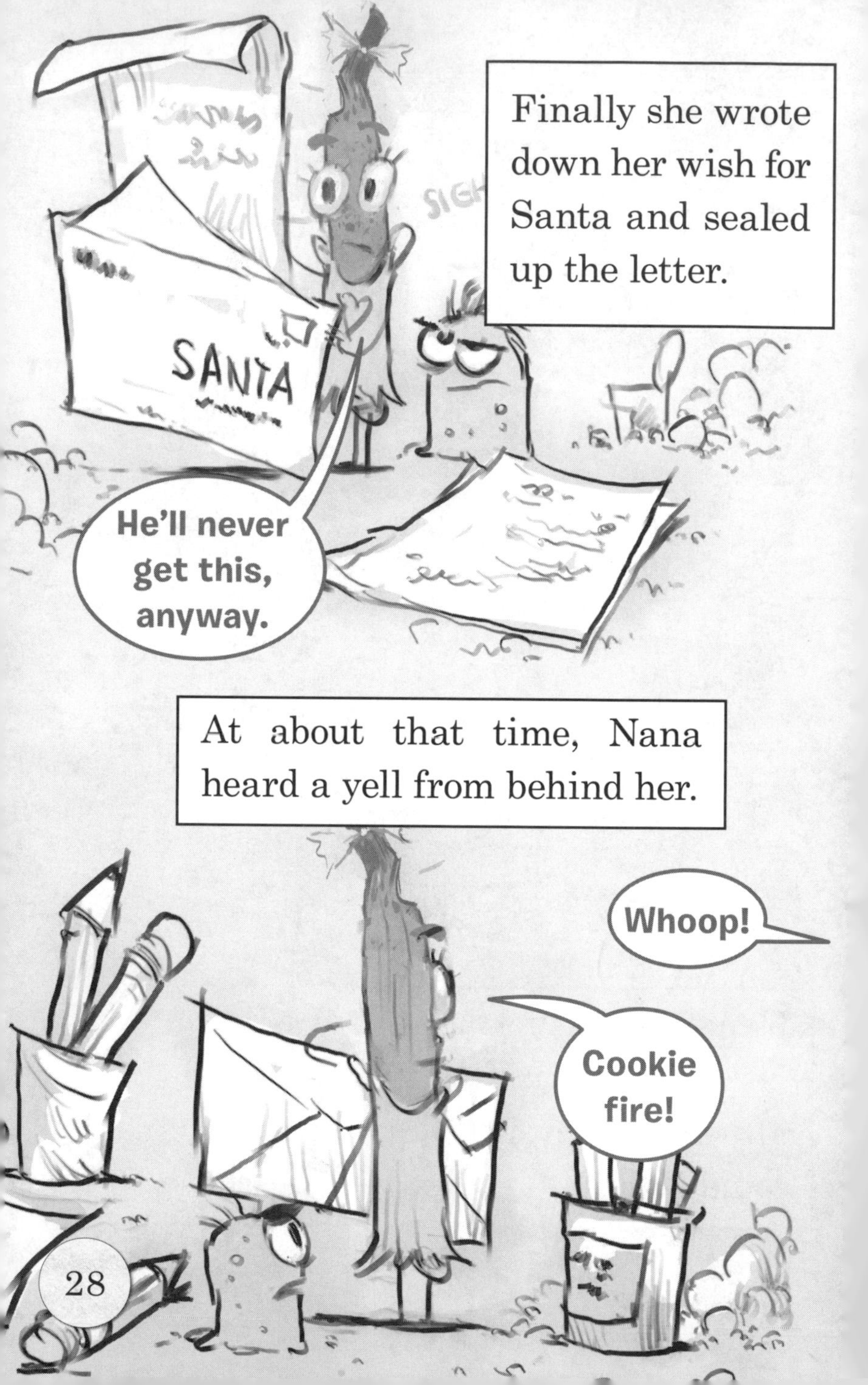
Finally she wrote down her wish for Santa and sealed up the letter.
SANTA
He'll never get this, anyway.
At about that time, Nana heard a yell from behind her.
Whoop!
Cookie fire!

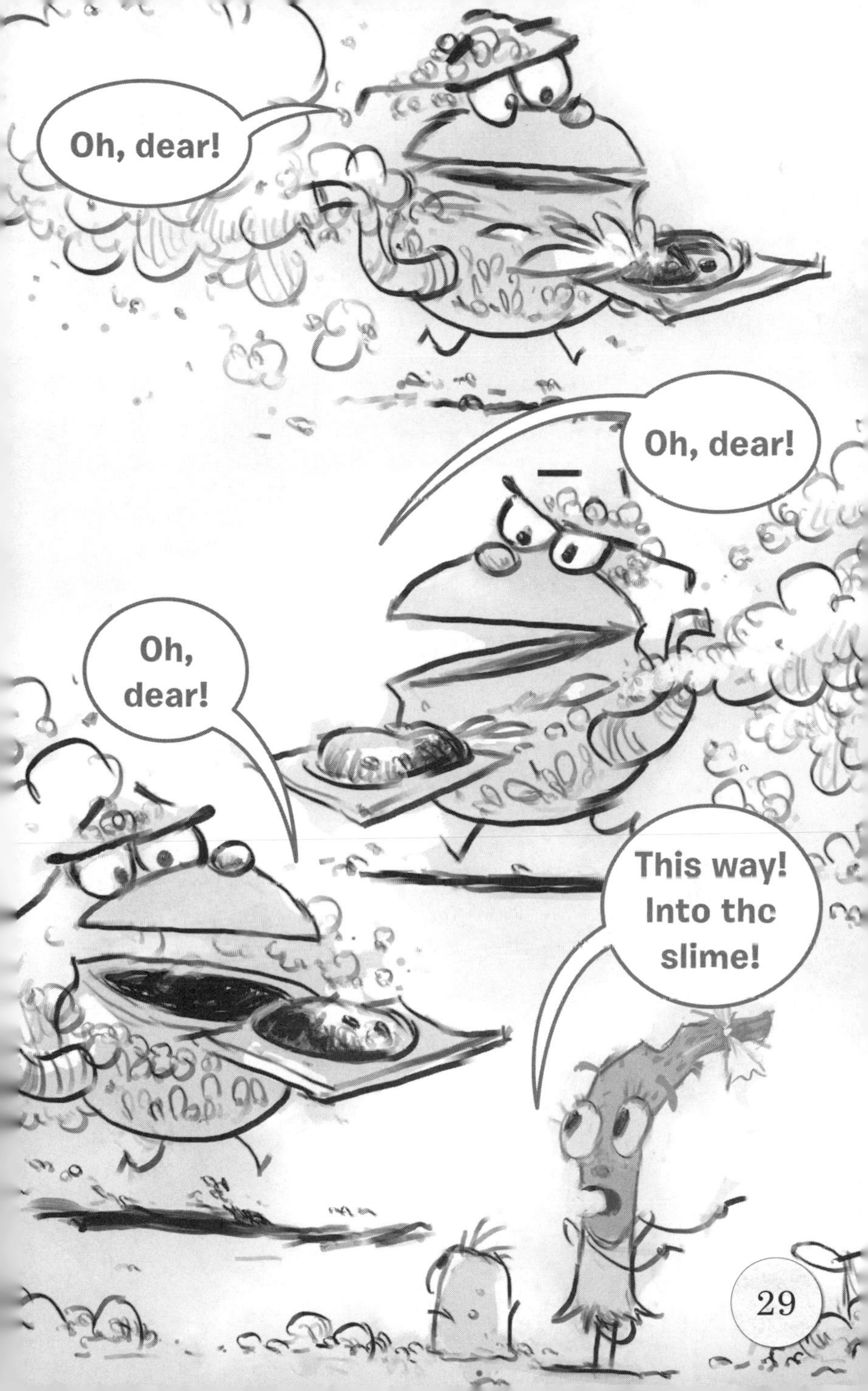
Oh, dear!
Oh, dear!
Oh, dear!
This way! Into the slime!

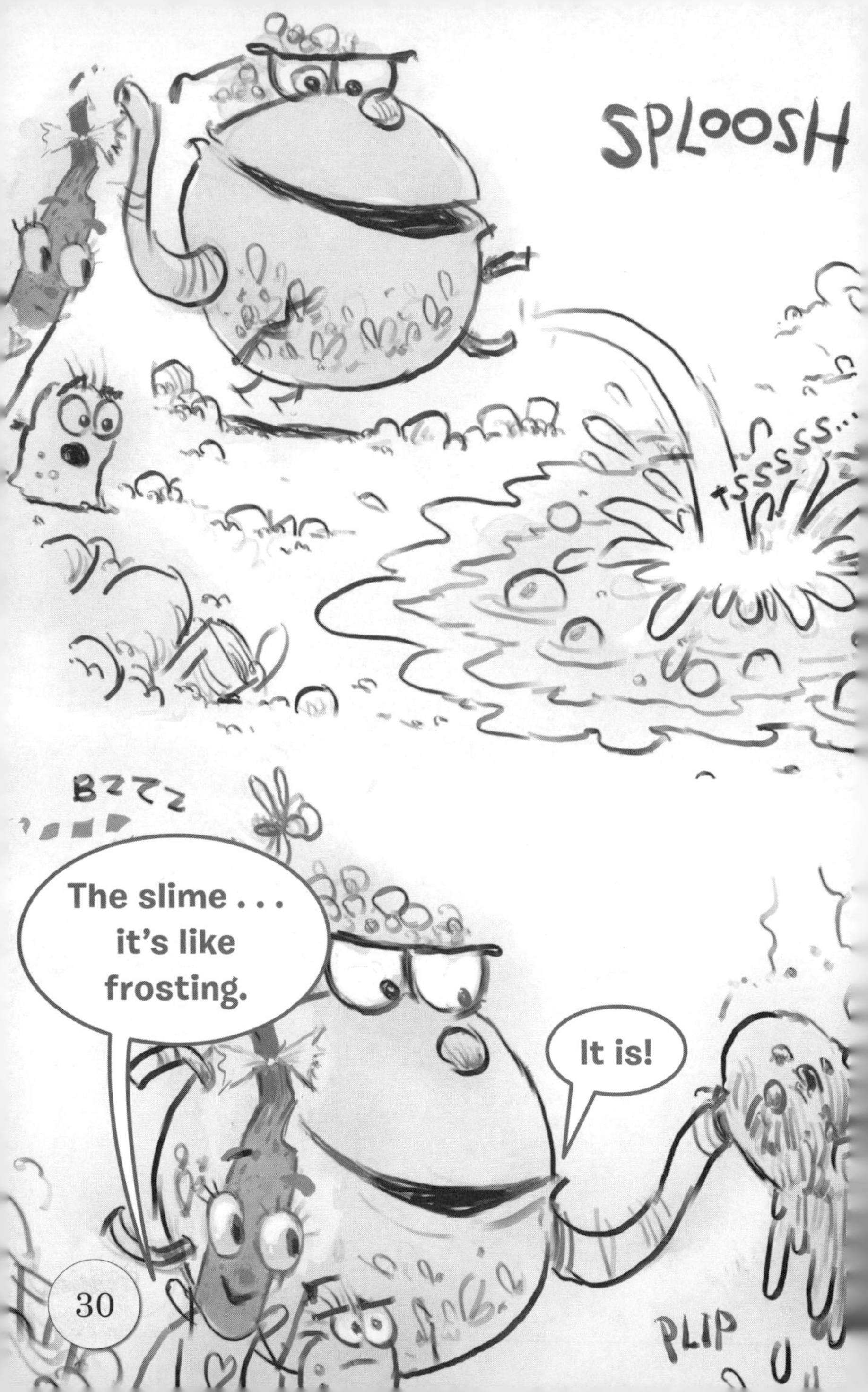
SPLOOSH
TSSSSS...
BZZZ
The slime . . . it's like frosting.
It is!
PLIP

Ms. Kettle was beaming. Her happy little accident had resulted in the perfect cookie for Santa.

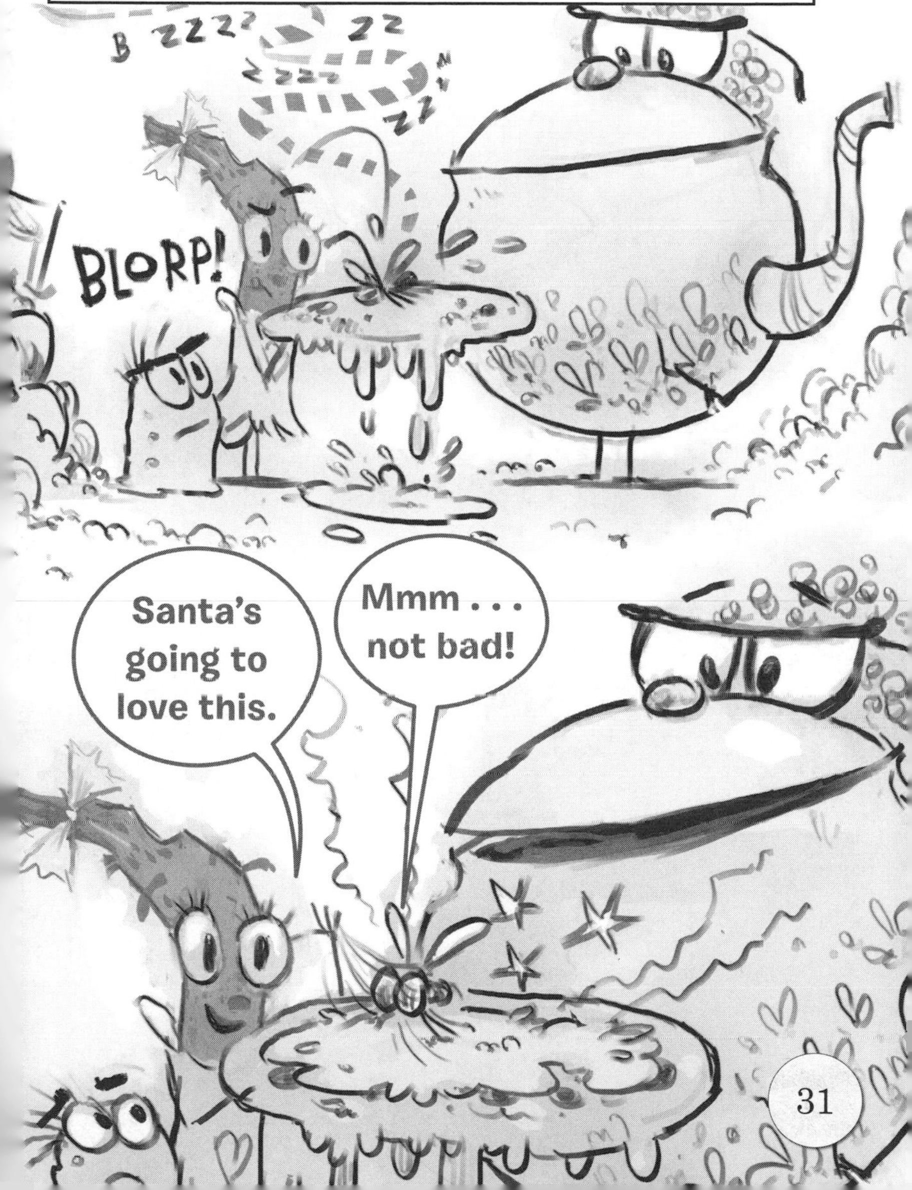
B ZZZZ
ZZ
BLORP!
Santa's going to love this.
Mmm . . . not bad!

Ms. Kettle packaged up the cookie. Nana placed the letter near it, and they stood back to admire them.

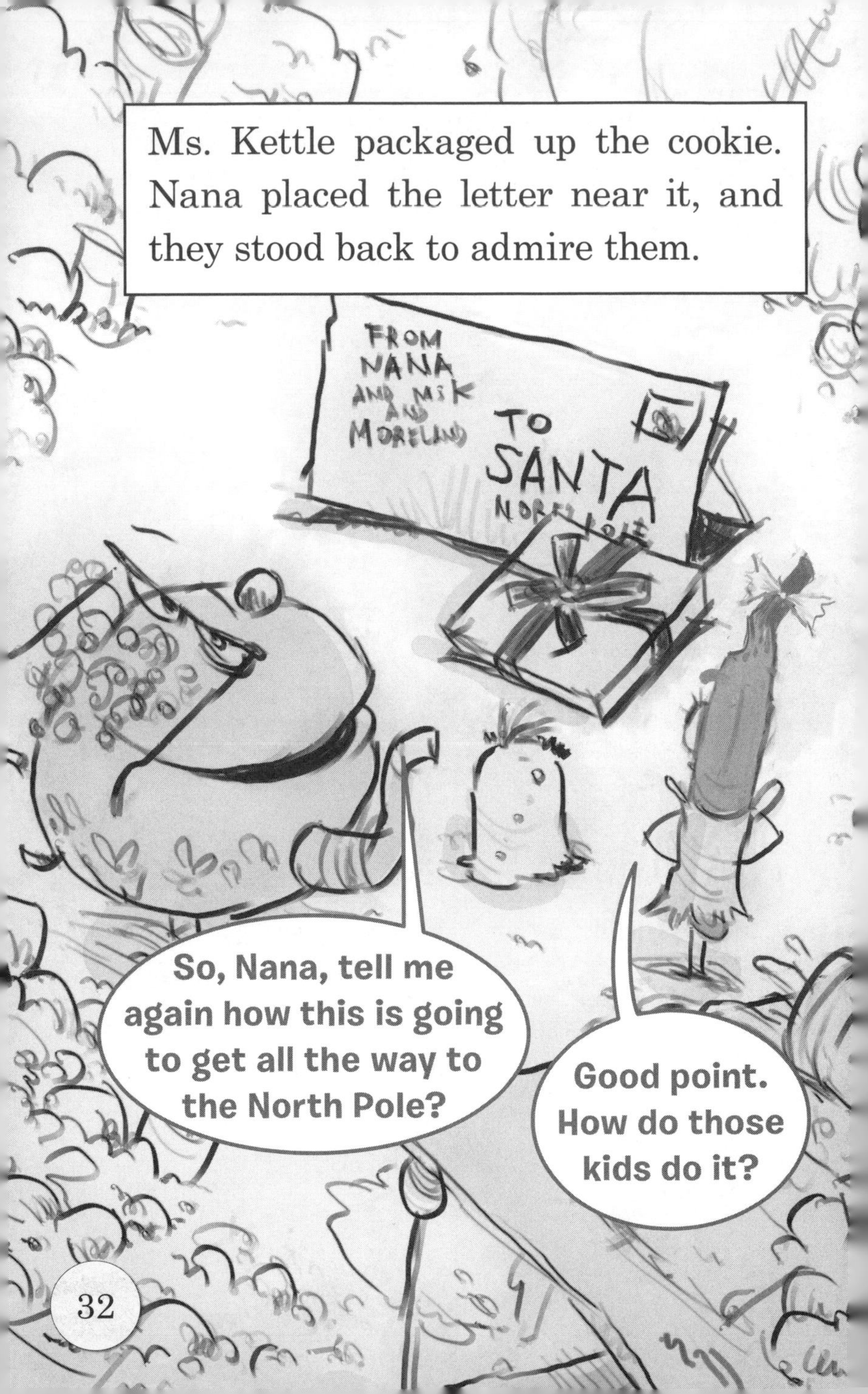
FROM NANA AND MS K AND MORELAND
TO SANTA
So, Nana, tell me again how this is going to get all the way to the North Pole?
Good point. How do those kids do it?

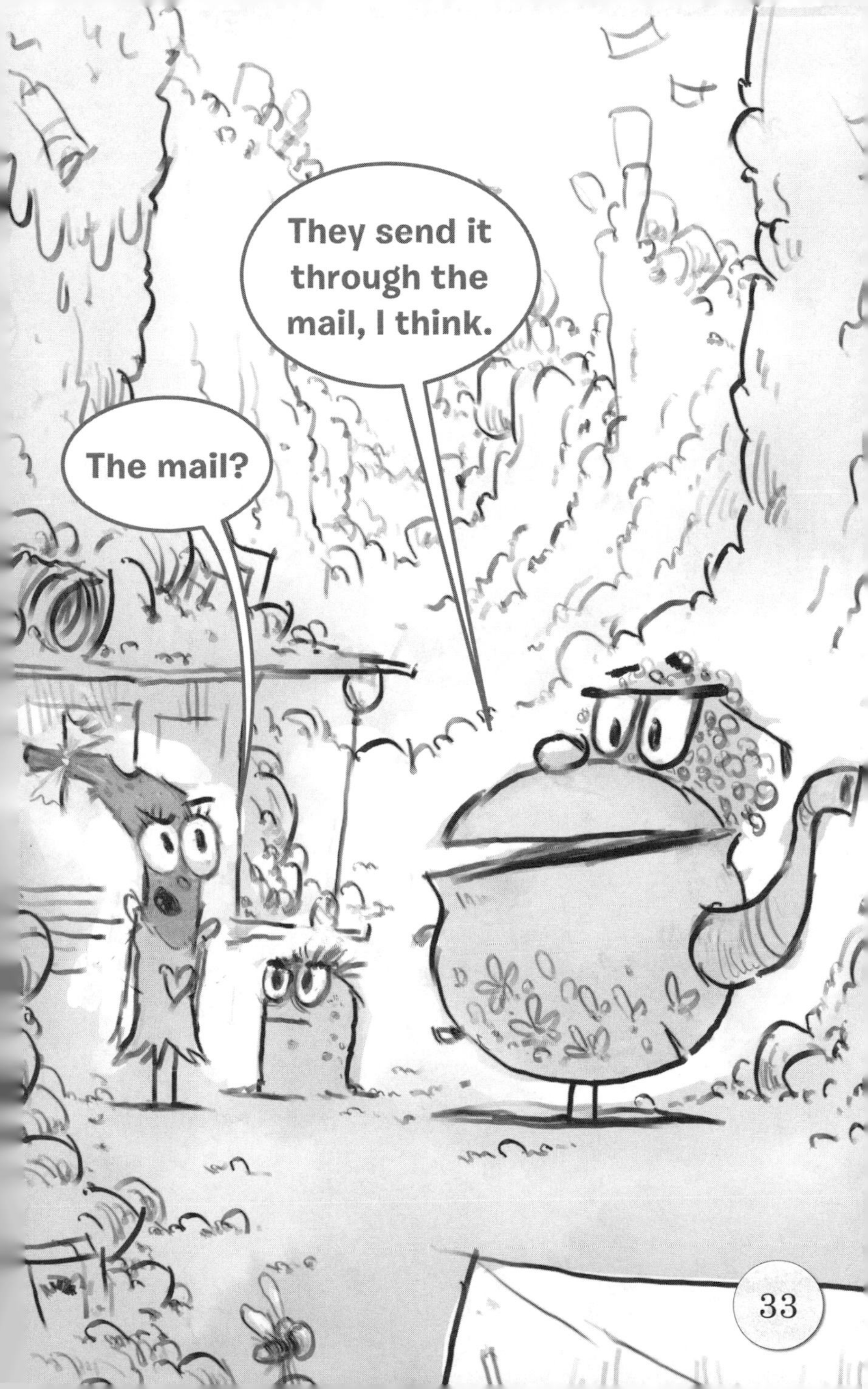
The mail?
They send it through the mail, I think.

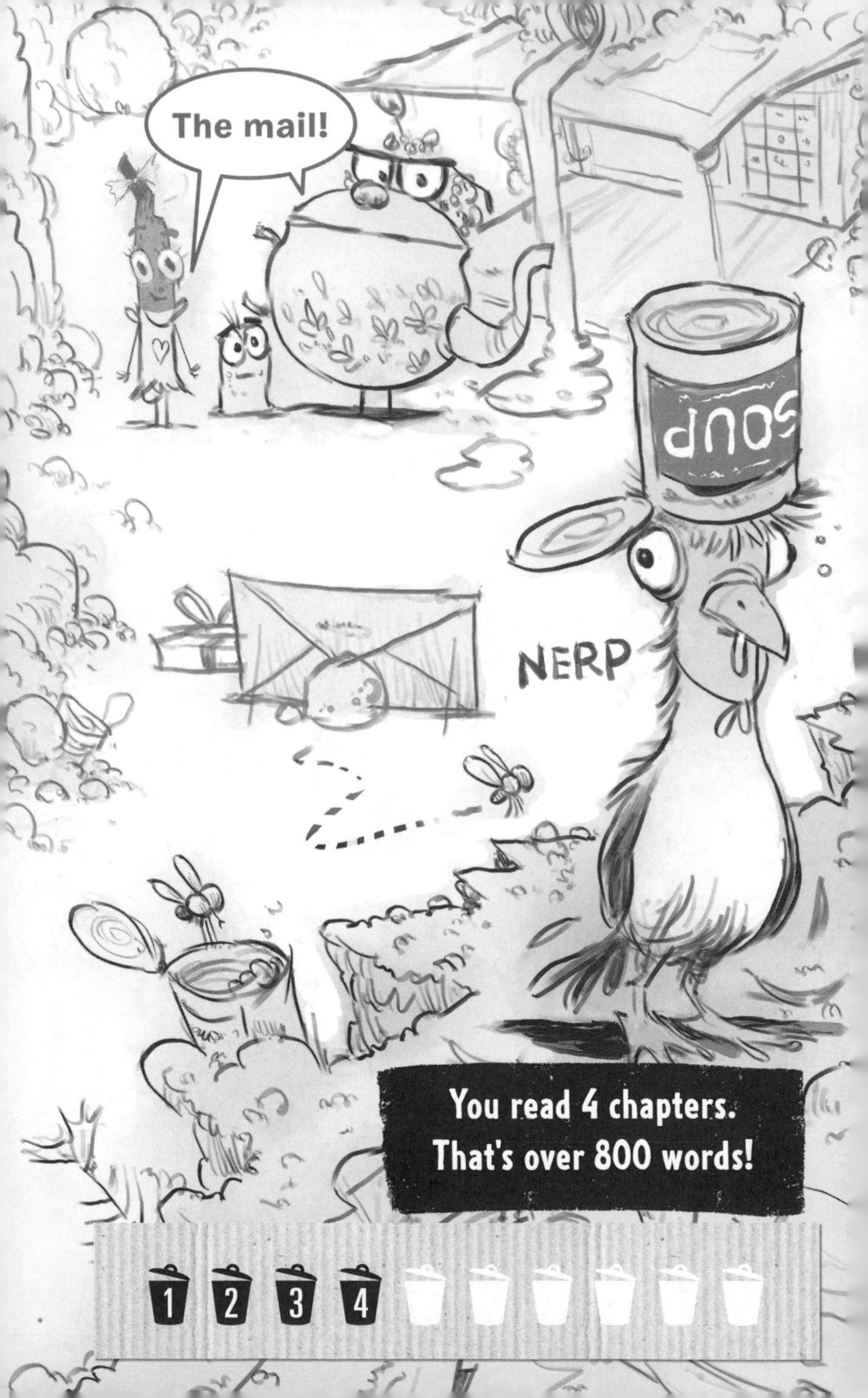
The mail!
NERP
You read 4 chapters.
That's over 800 words!
1 2 3 4

CHAPTER 5
TYSON TO THE RESCUE

Tyson was the dump's loyal seagull. Like Moreland, he ate lots of strange icky stuff that arrived at the dump.

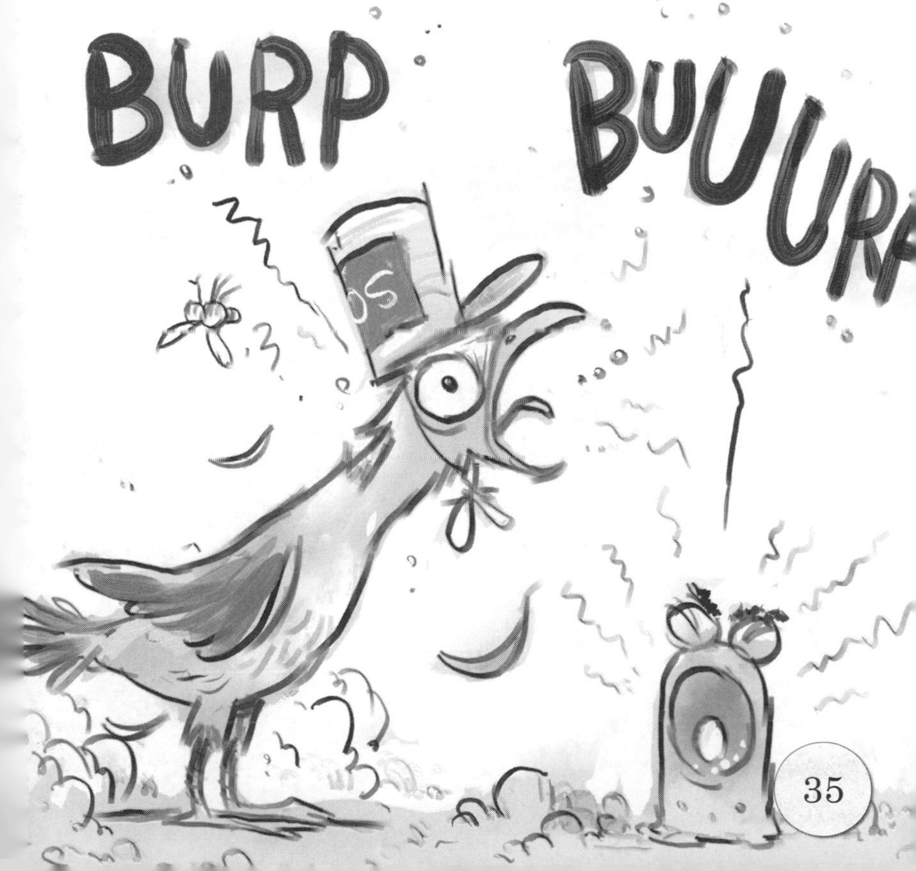
BURP
BUUURP
OS

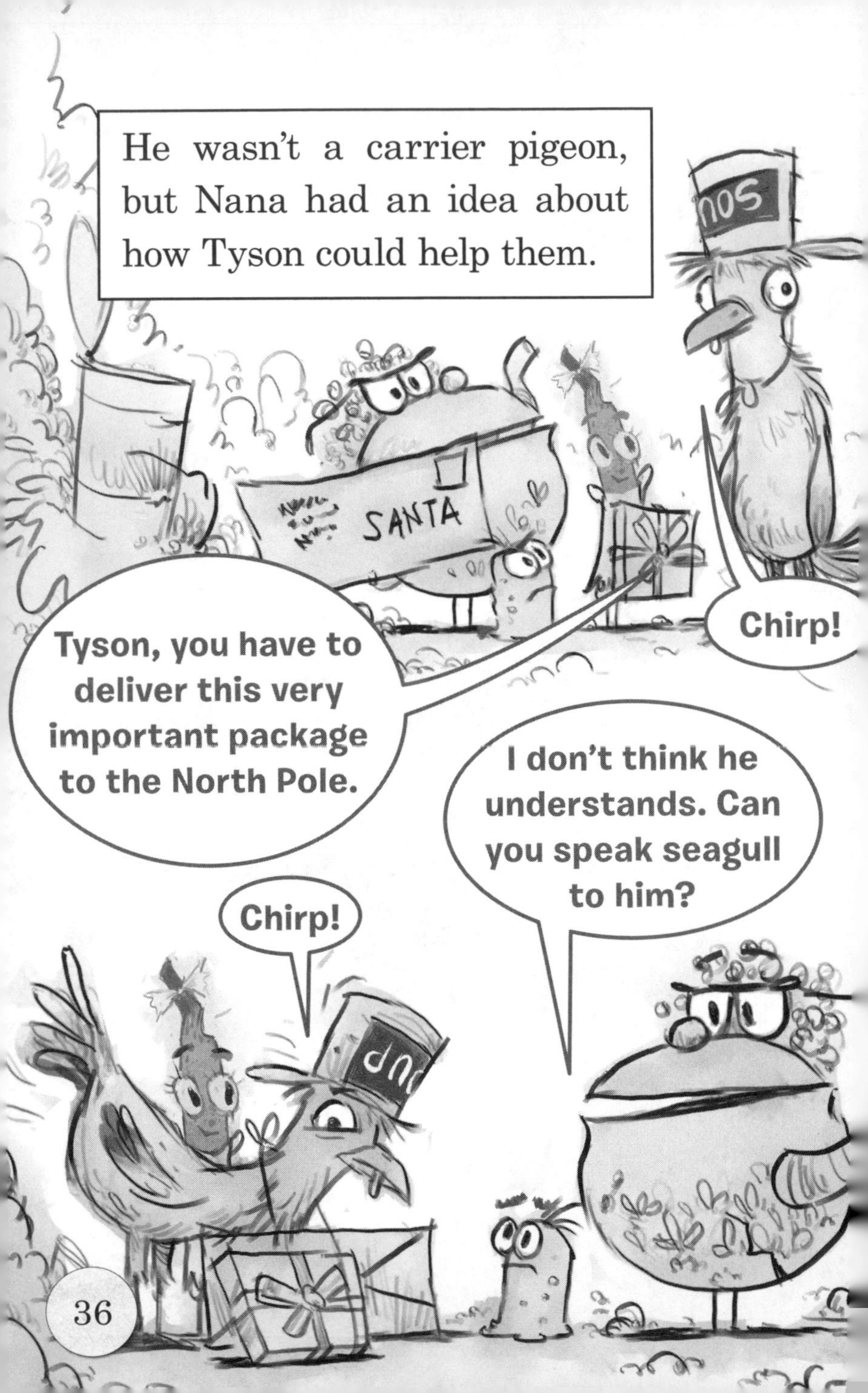
He wasn't a carrier pigeon, but Nana had an idea about how Tyson could help them.
SANTA
Tyson, you have to deliver this very important package to the North Pole.
Chirp!
I don't think he understands. Can you speak seagull to him?
Chirp!

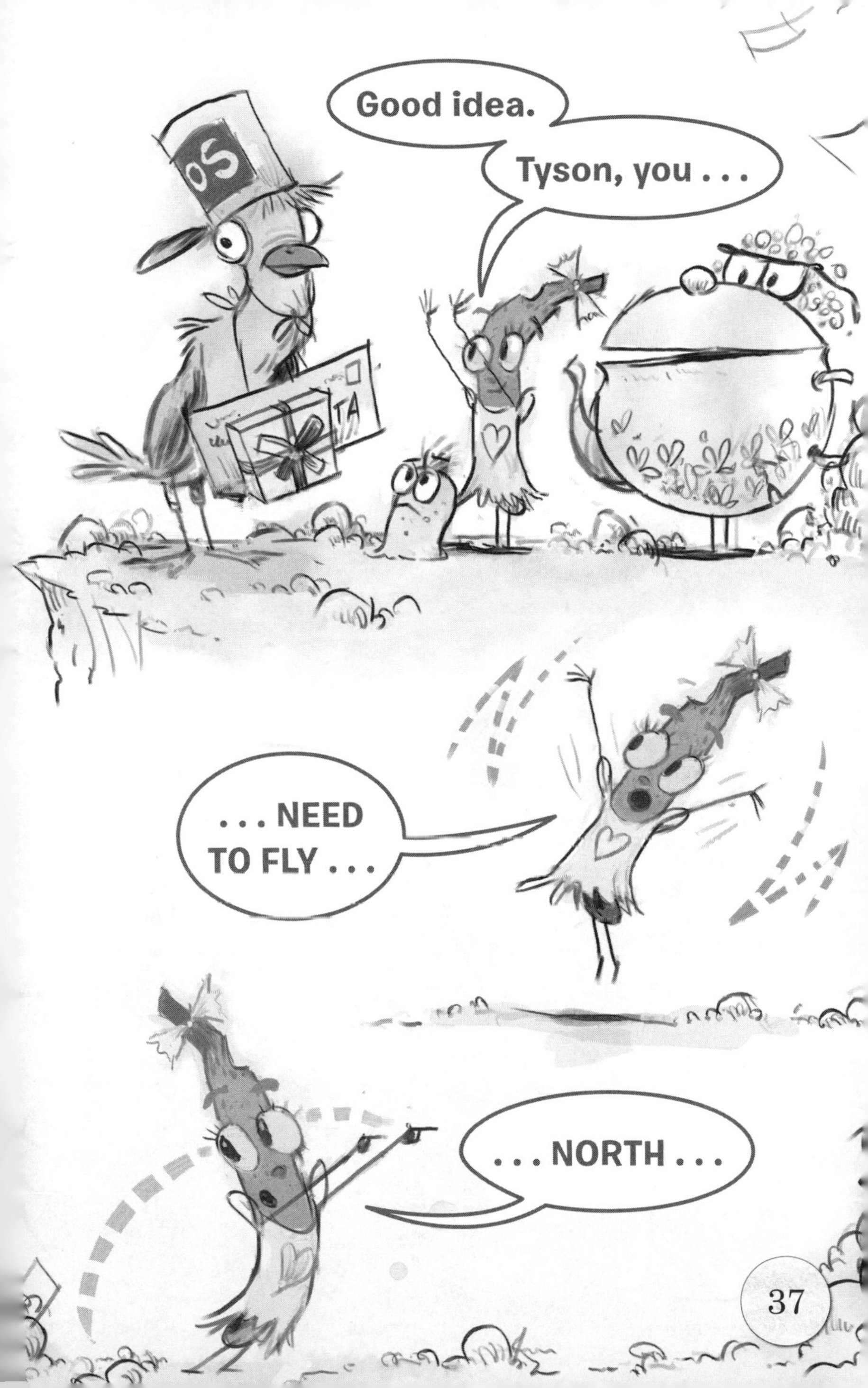
Good idea.
Tyson, you . . .
. . . NEED TO FLY . . .
. . . NORTH . . .

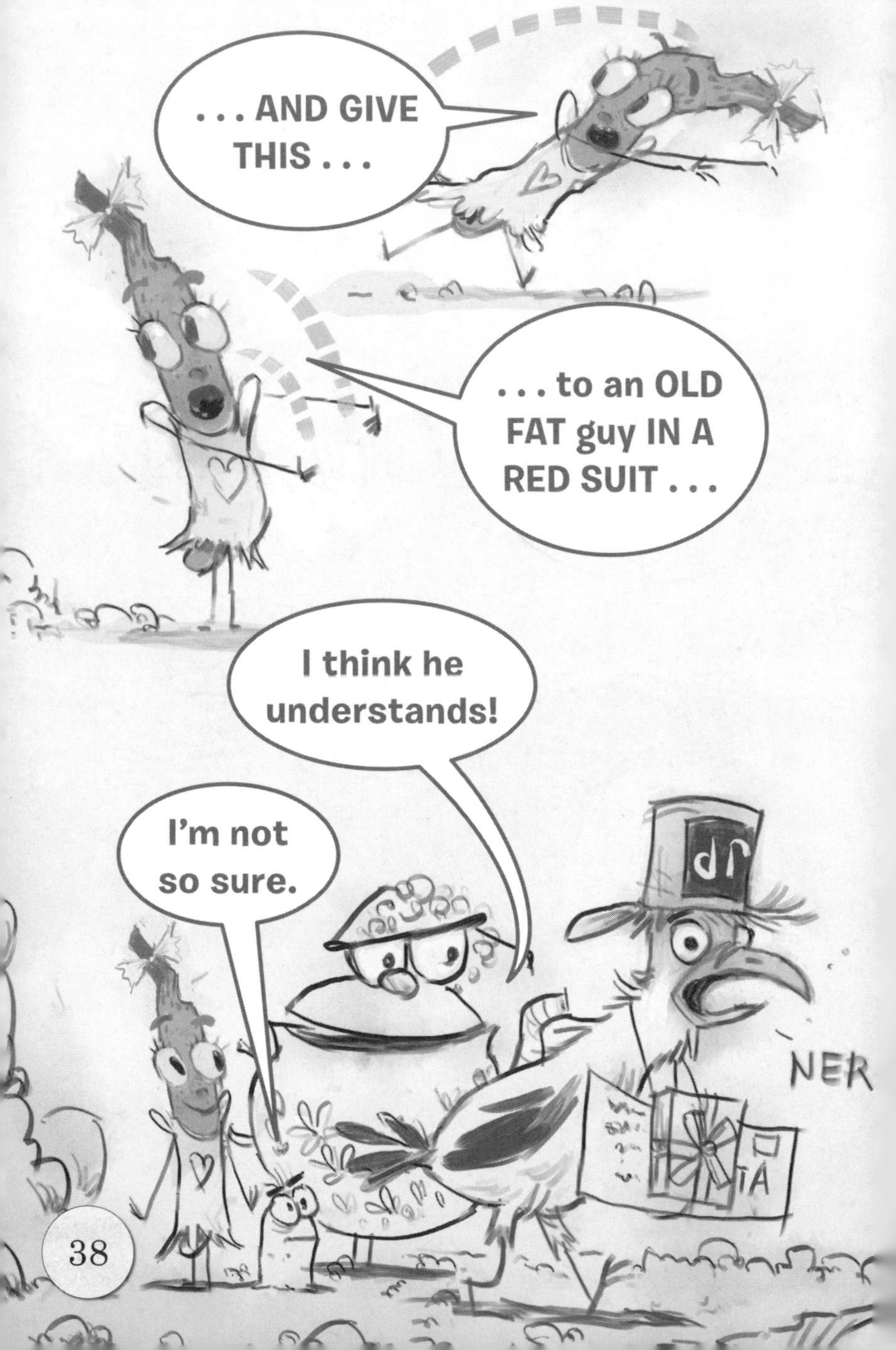

. . . AND GIVE THIS . . .
. . . to an OLD FAT guy IN A RED SUIT . . .
I think he understands!
I'm not so sure.
NER

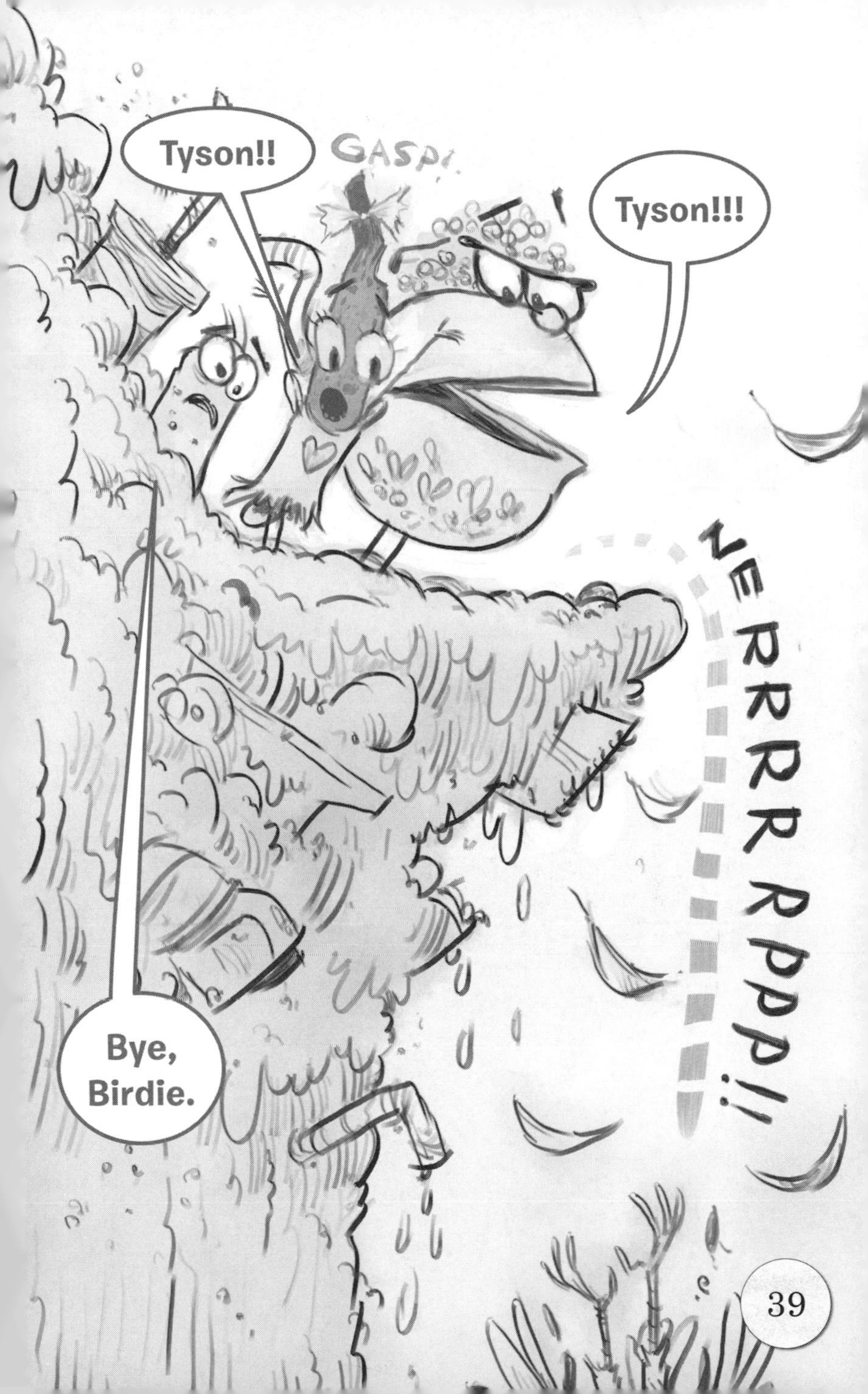
Tyson!!
GASP!
Tyson!!!
NERRRRRPPP!!
Bye, Birdie.

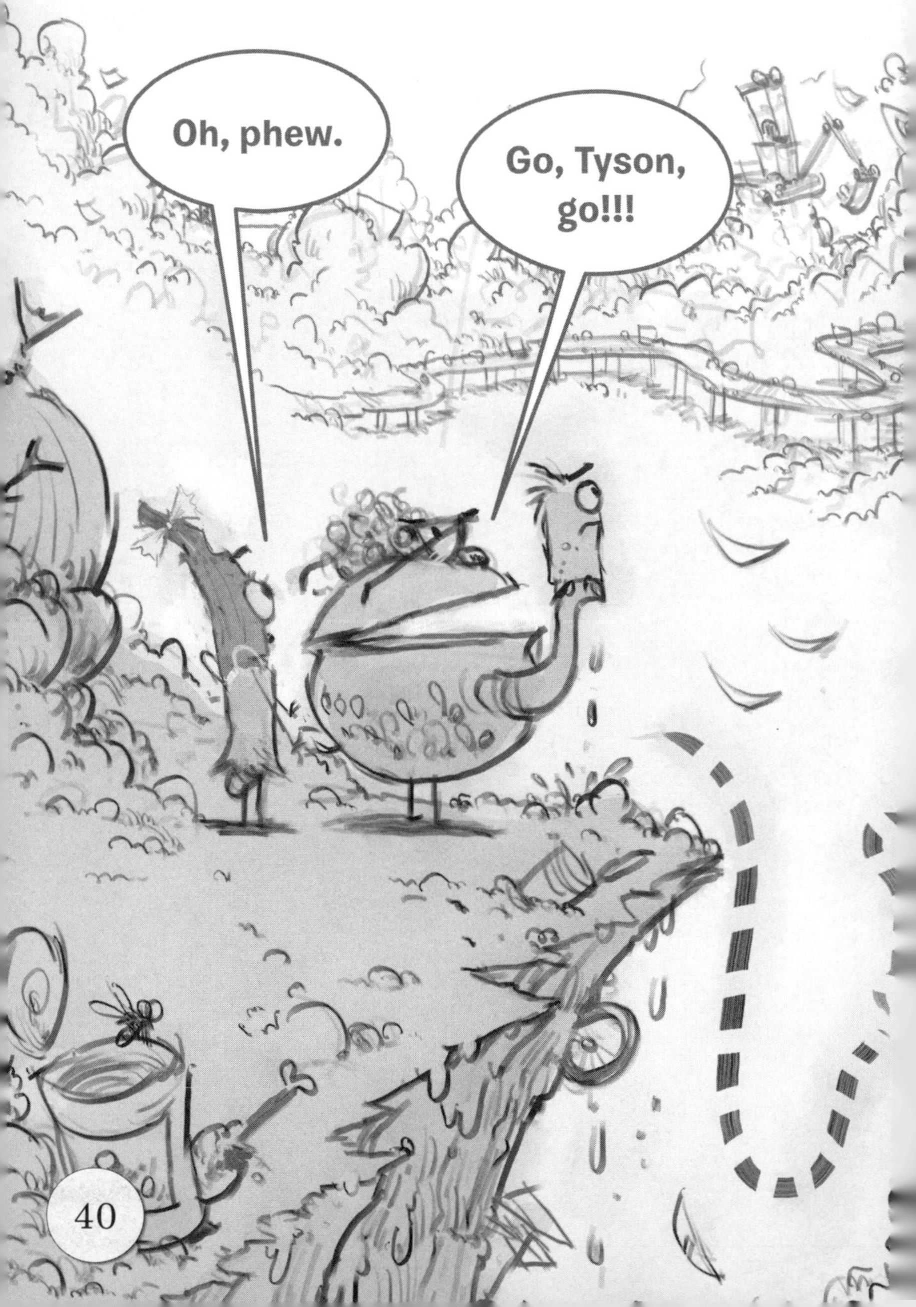
Oh, phew.
Go, Tyson, go!!!

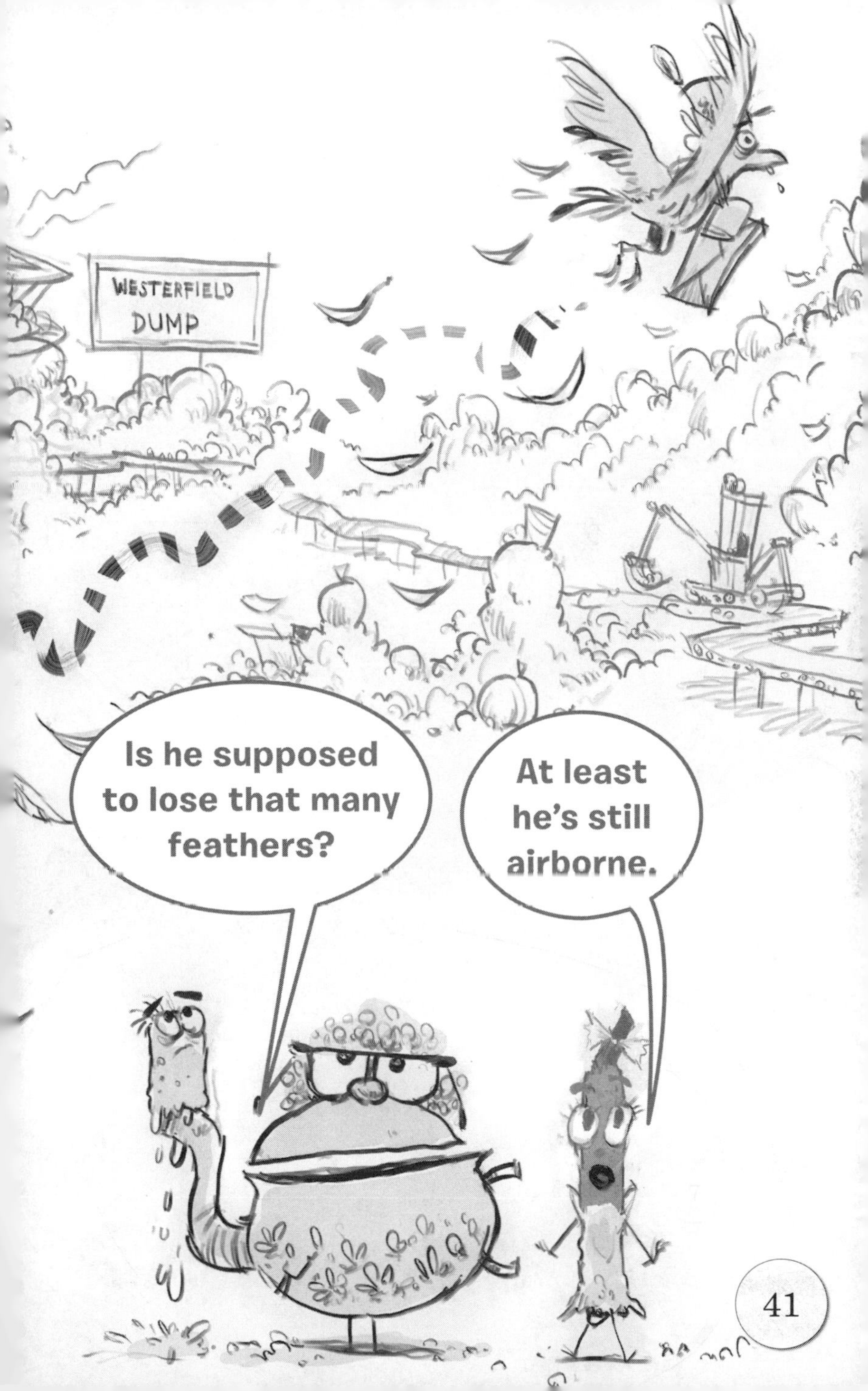
WESTERFIELD DUMP
Is he supposed to lose that many feathers?
At least he's still airborne.

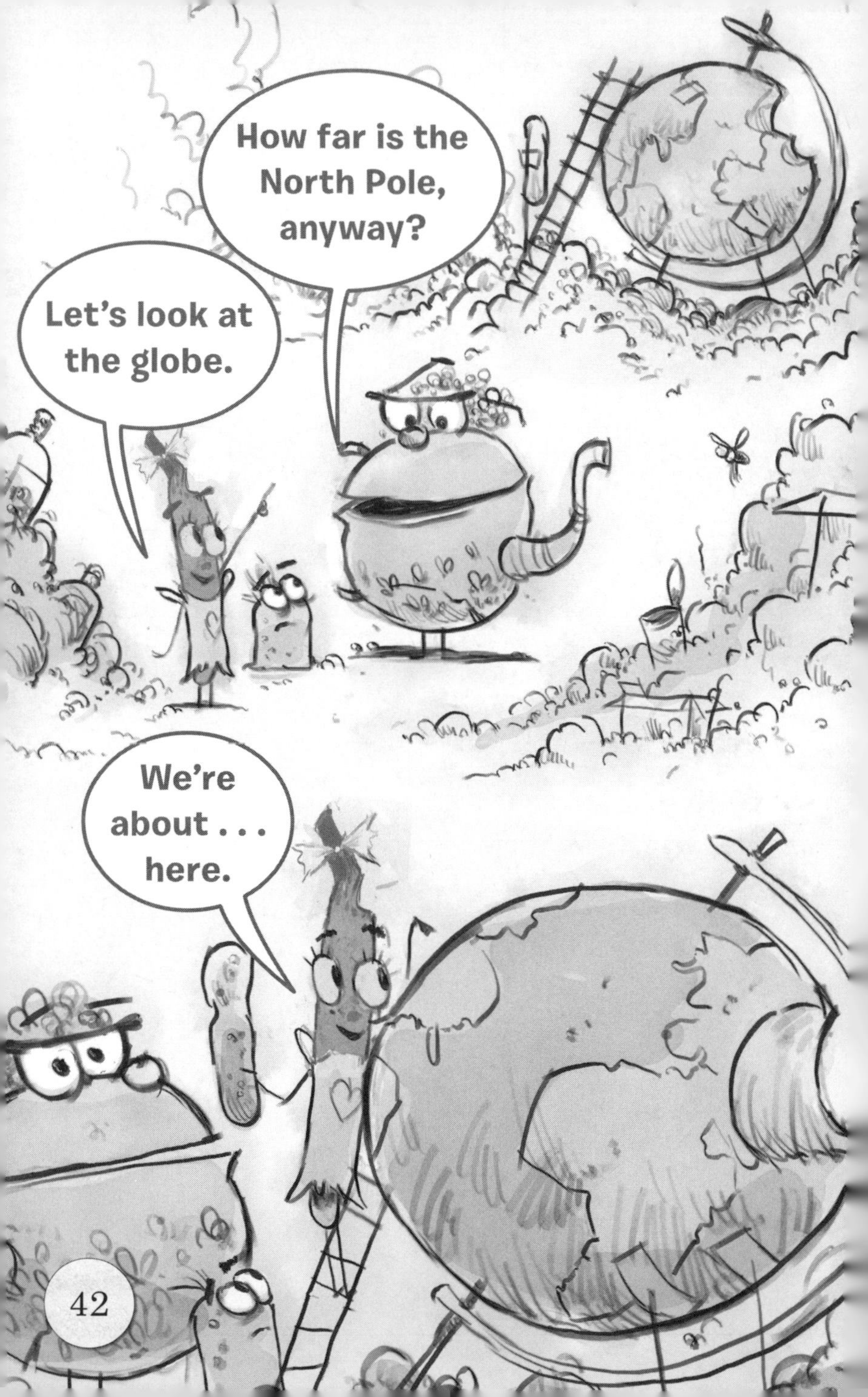
How far is the North Pole, anyway?
Let's look at the globe.
We're about . . . here.

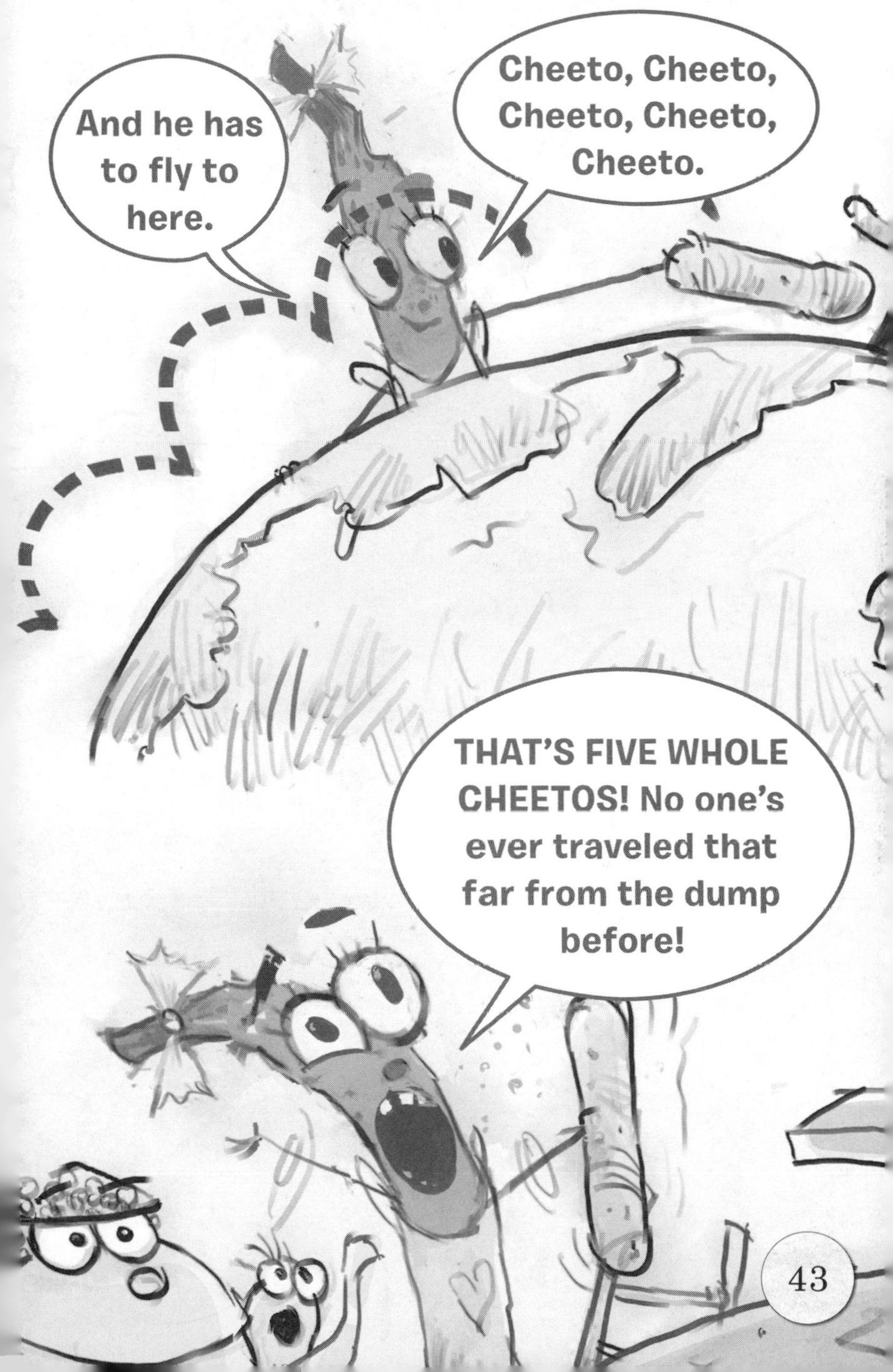
And he has to fly to here.
Cheeto, Cheeto, Cheeto, Cheeto, Cheeto.
THAT'S FIVE WHOLE CHEETOS! No one's ever traveled that far from the dump before!

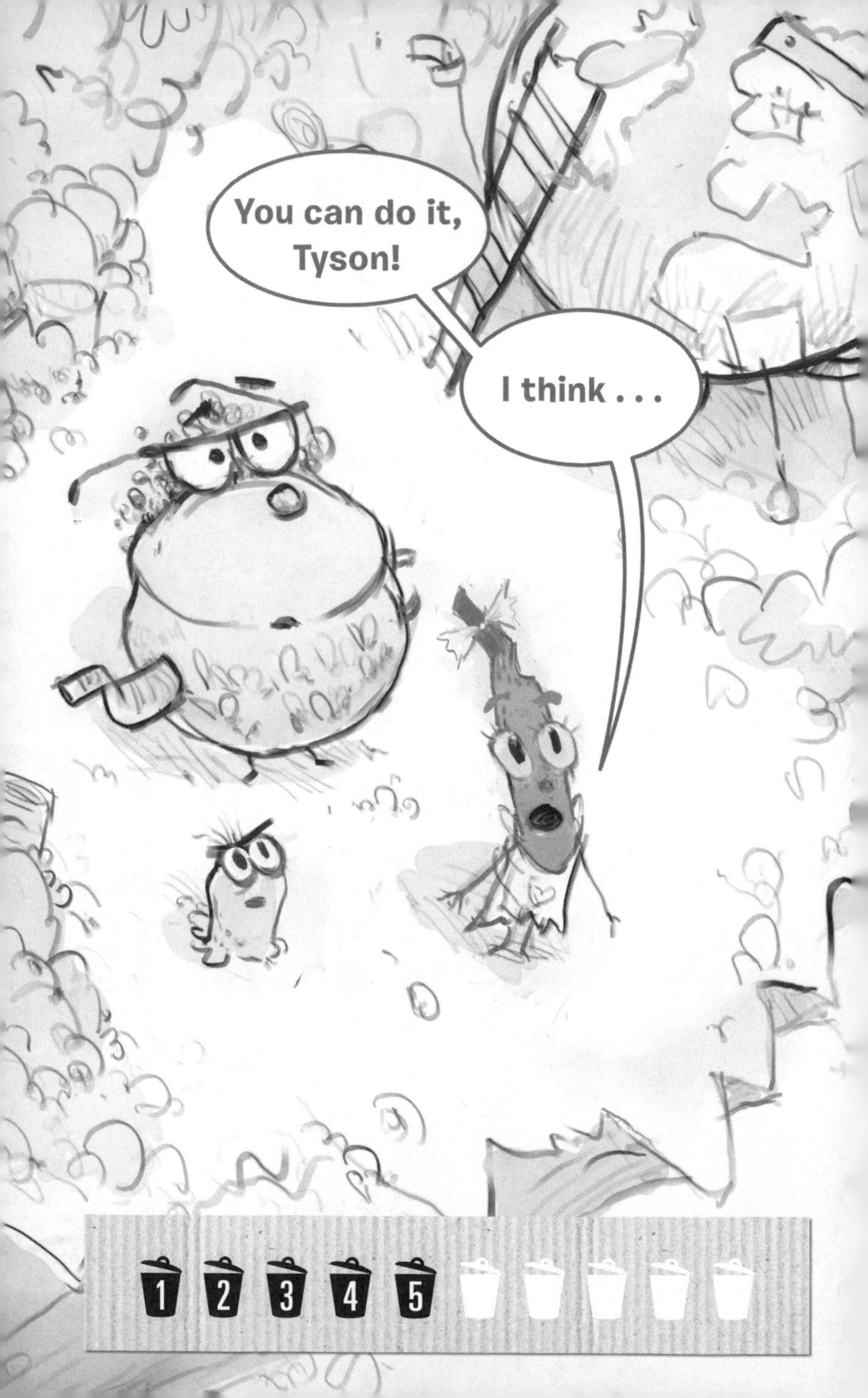
You can do it, Tyson!
I think . . .
1 2 3 4 5

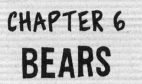

CHAPTER 6
BEARS

Days passed, and Nana set up an outpost to look for Santa and Tyson.

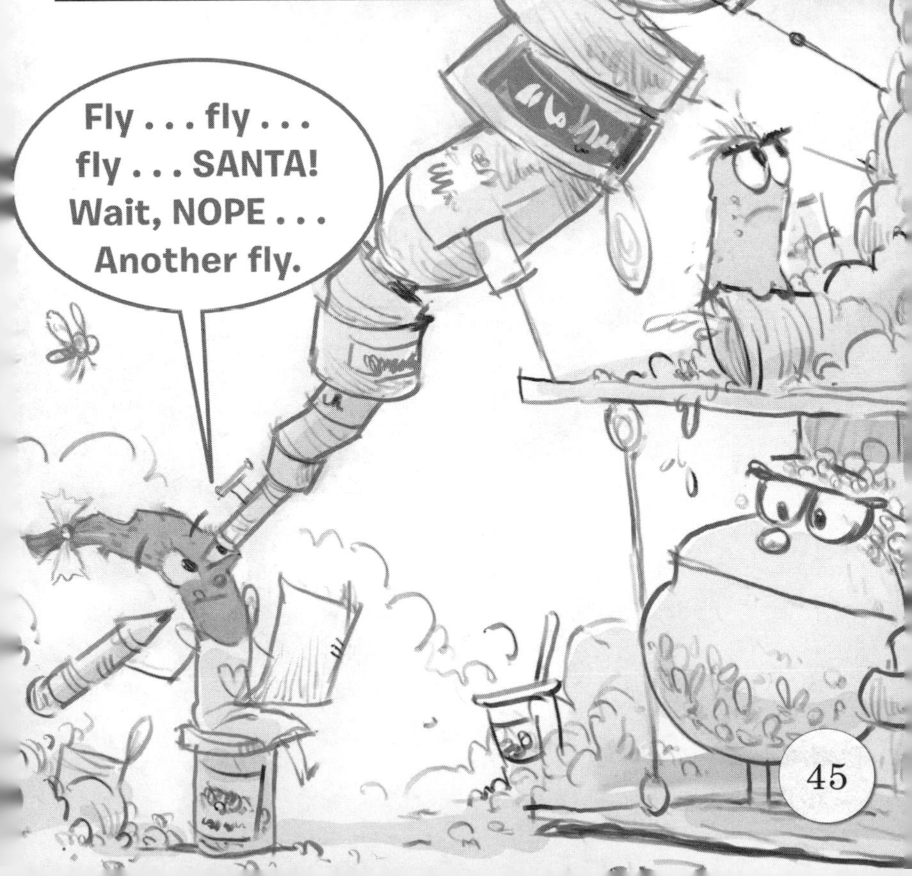
Fly . . . fly . . . fly . . . SANTA! Wait, NOPE . . . Another fly.

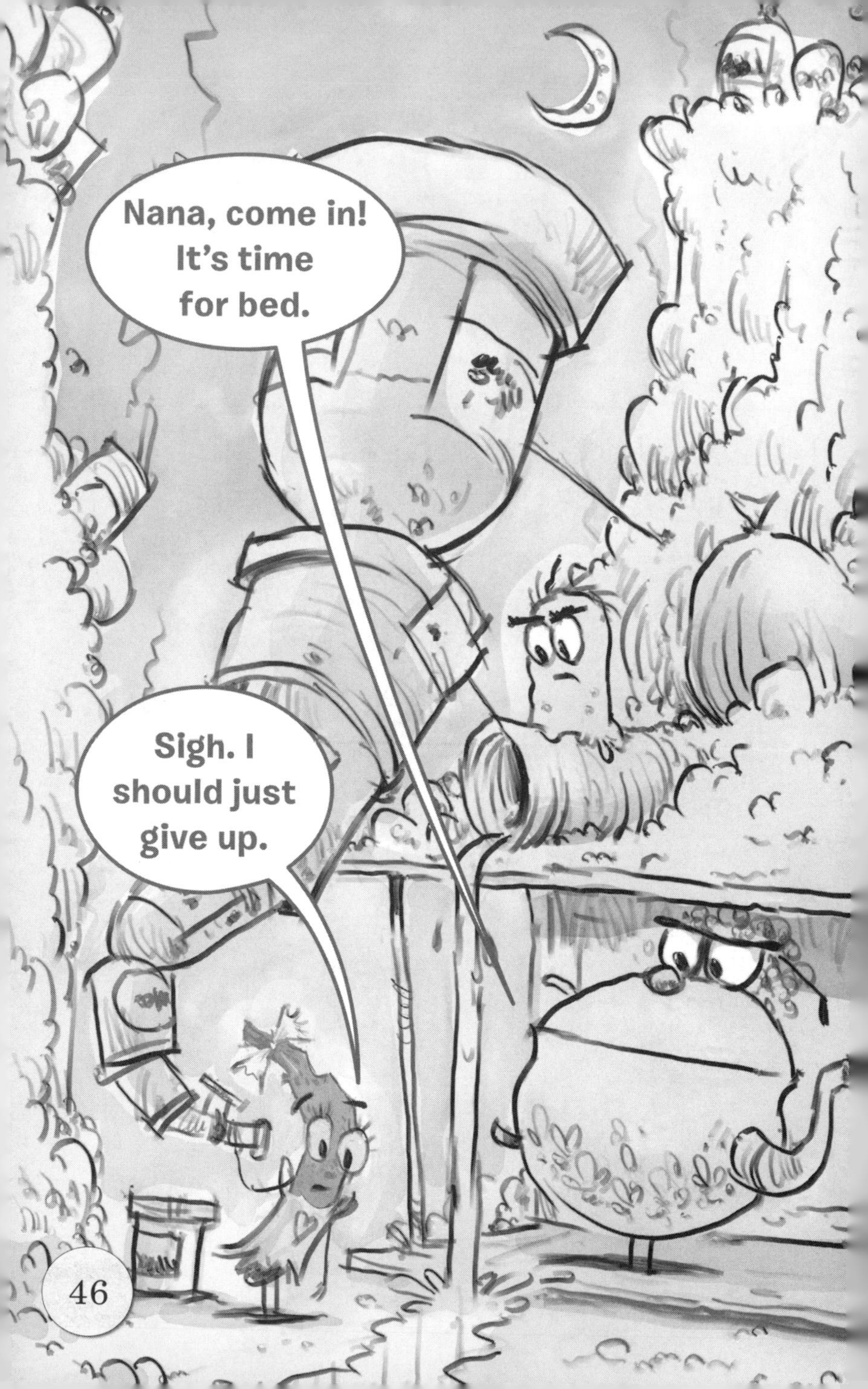
Nana, come in! It's time for bed.
Sigh. I should just give up.

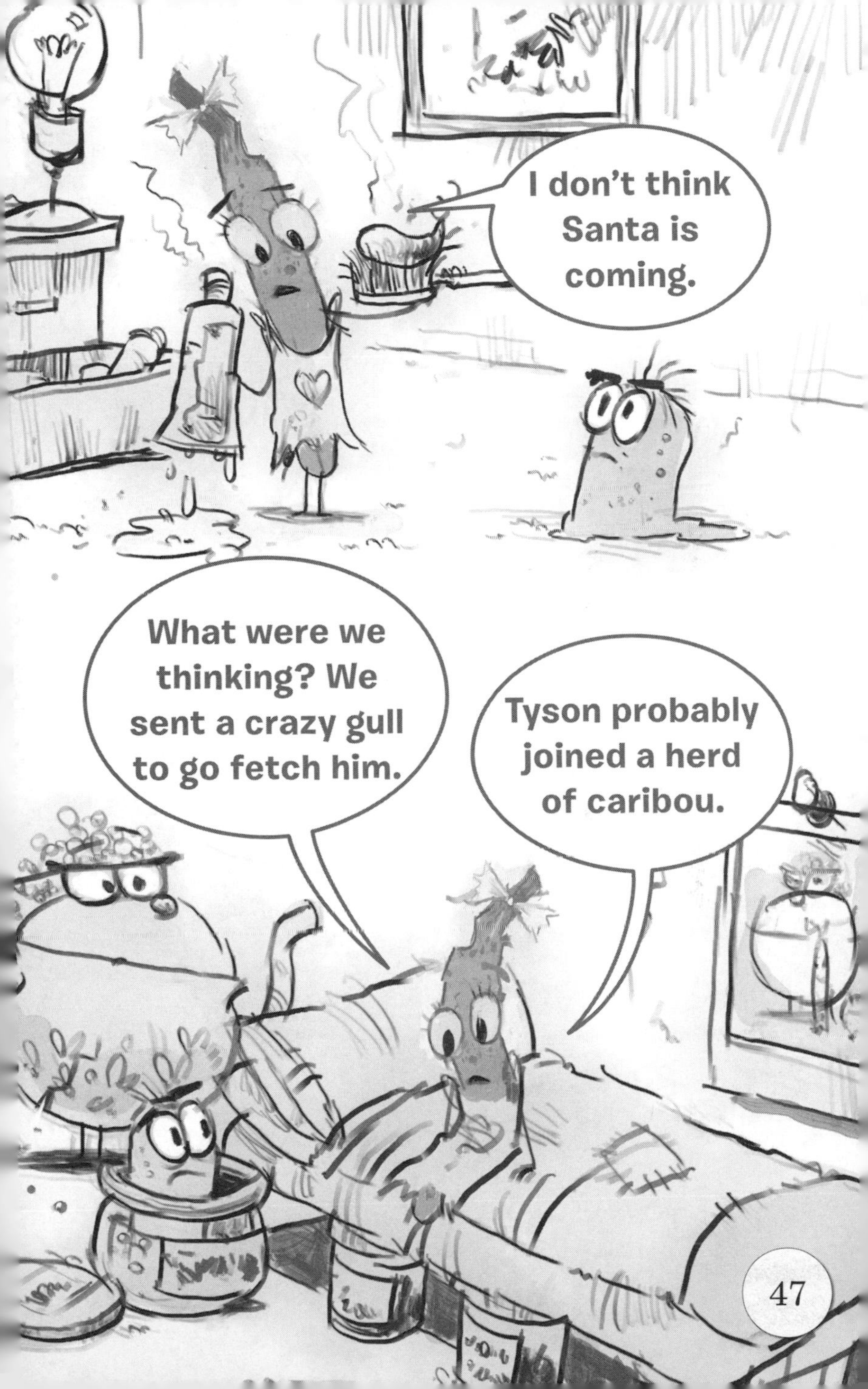
I don't think Santa is coming.
What were we thinking? We sent a crazy gull to go fetch him.
Tyson probably joined a herd of caribou.

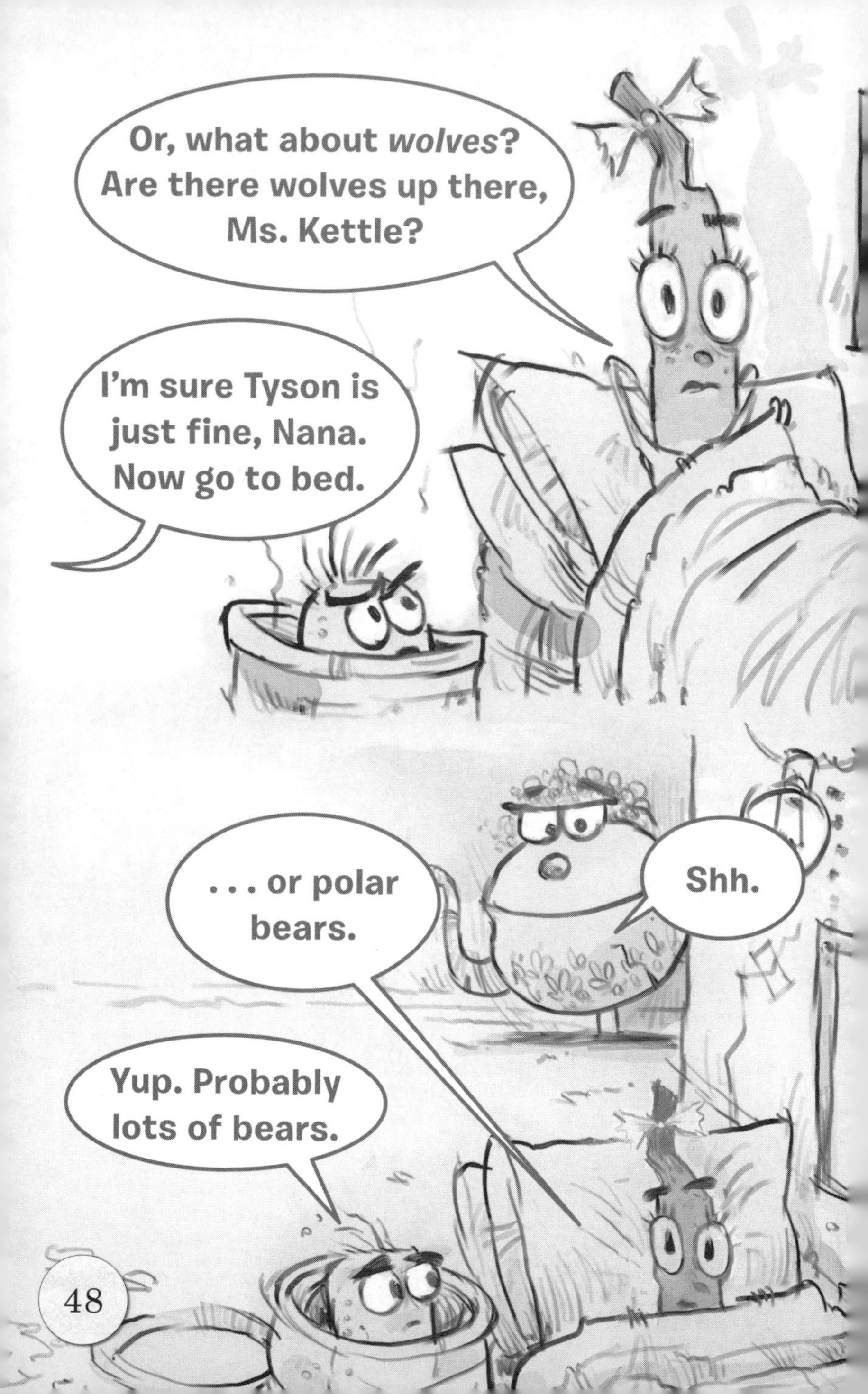
Or, what about *wolves*? Are there wolves up there, Ms. Kettle?
I'm sure Tyson is just fine, Nana. Now go to bed.
. . . or polar bears.
Shh.
Yup. Probably lots of bears.

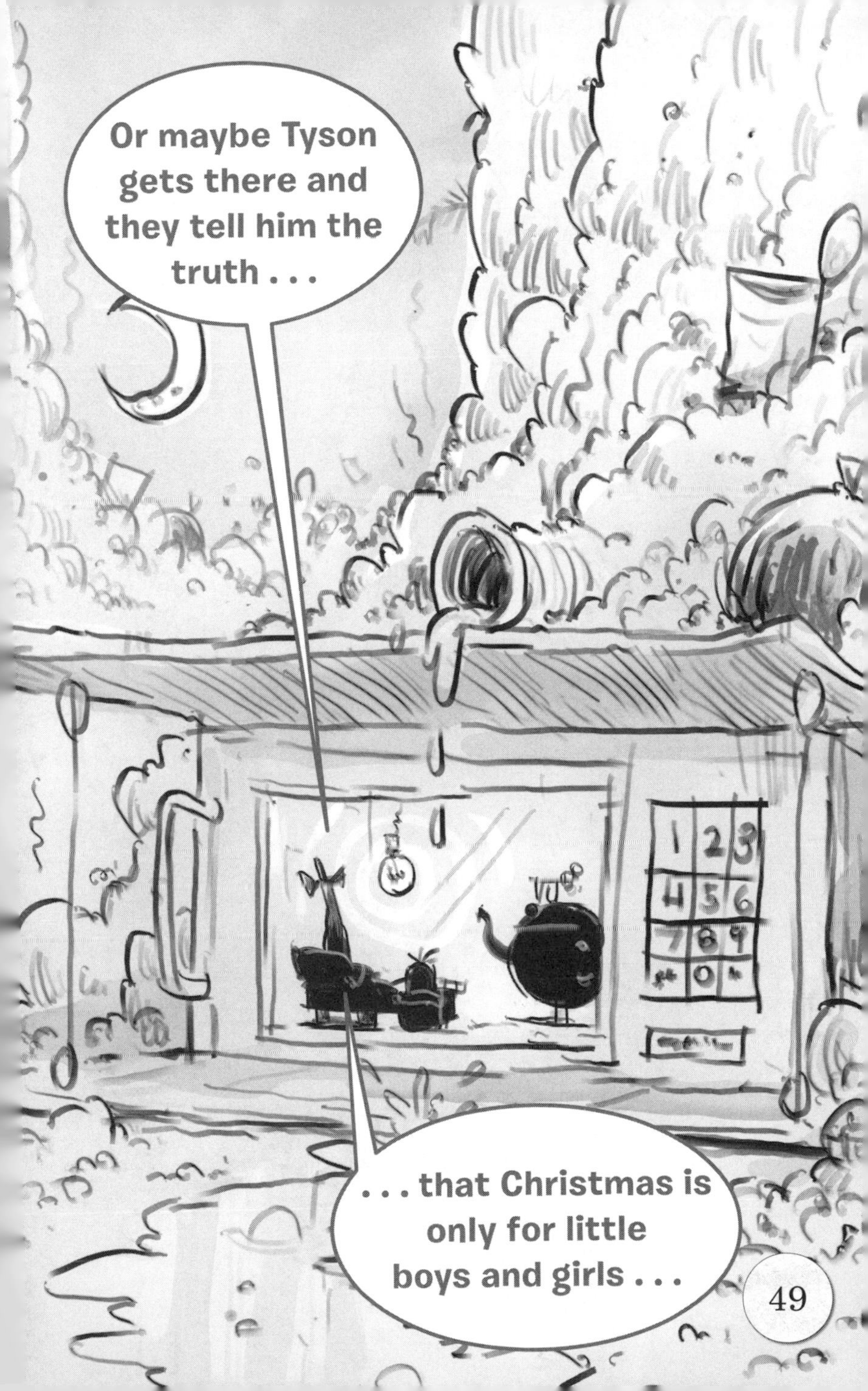
Or maybe Tyson gets there and they tell him the truth . . .
. . . that Christmas is only for little boys and girls . . .
1 2 3
4 5 6
7 8 9
0

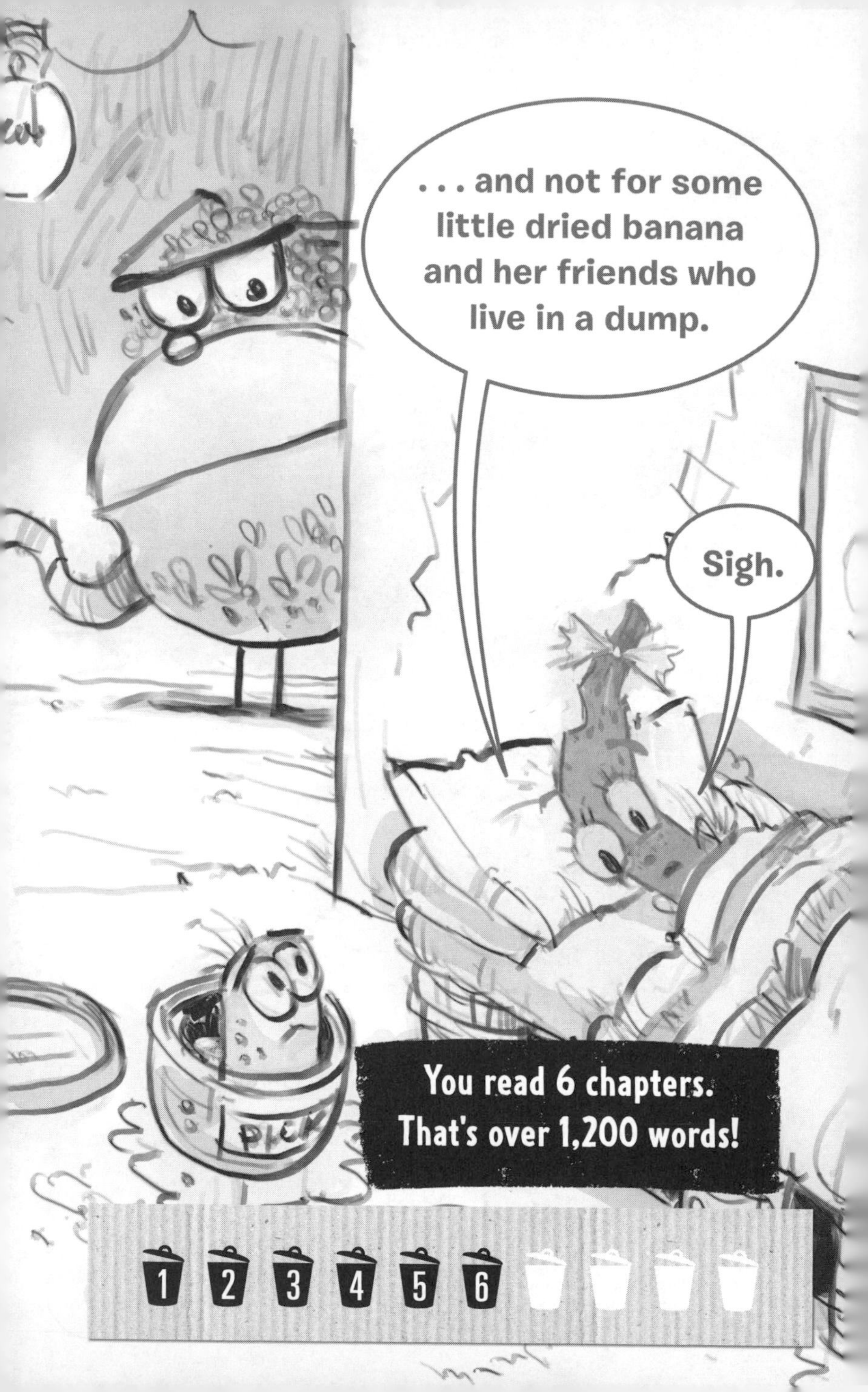
. . . and not for some little dried banana and her friends who live in a dump.
Sigh.
You read 6 chapters. That's over 1,200 words!
1 2 3 4 5 6

CHAPTER 7
SNOW!

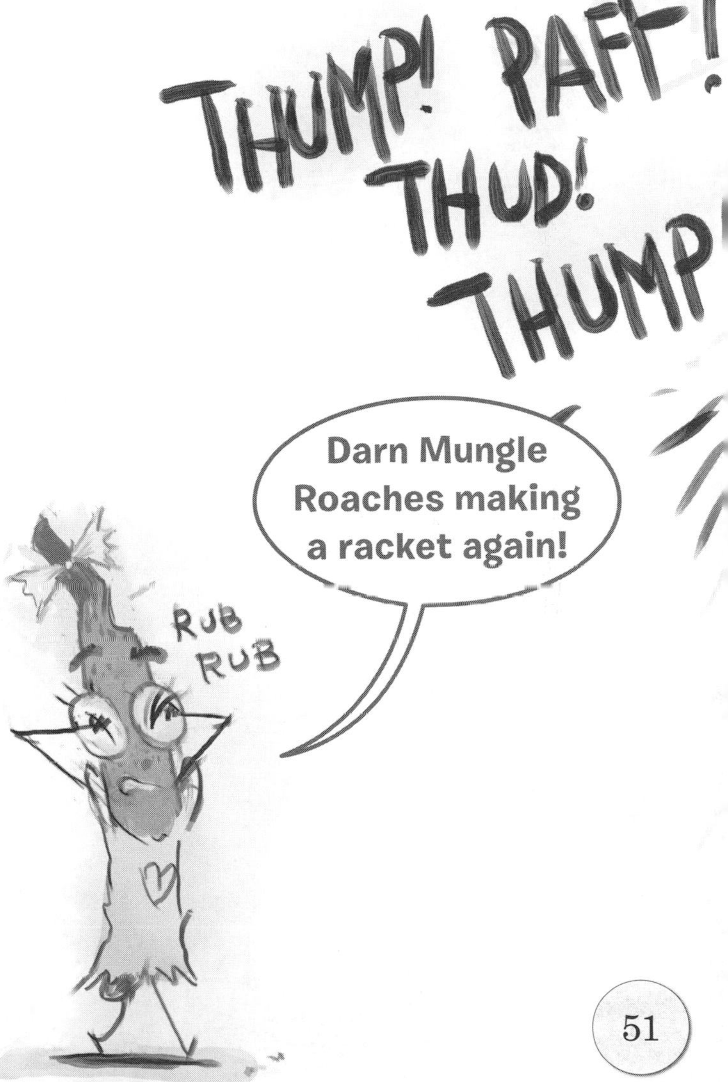
THUMP! PAFF!
THUD!
THUMP
Darn Mungle Roaches making a racket again!
RUB RUB

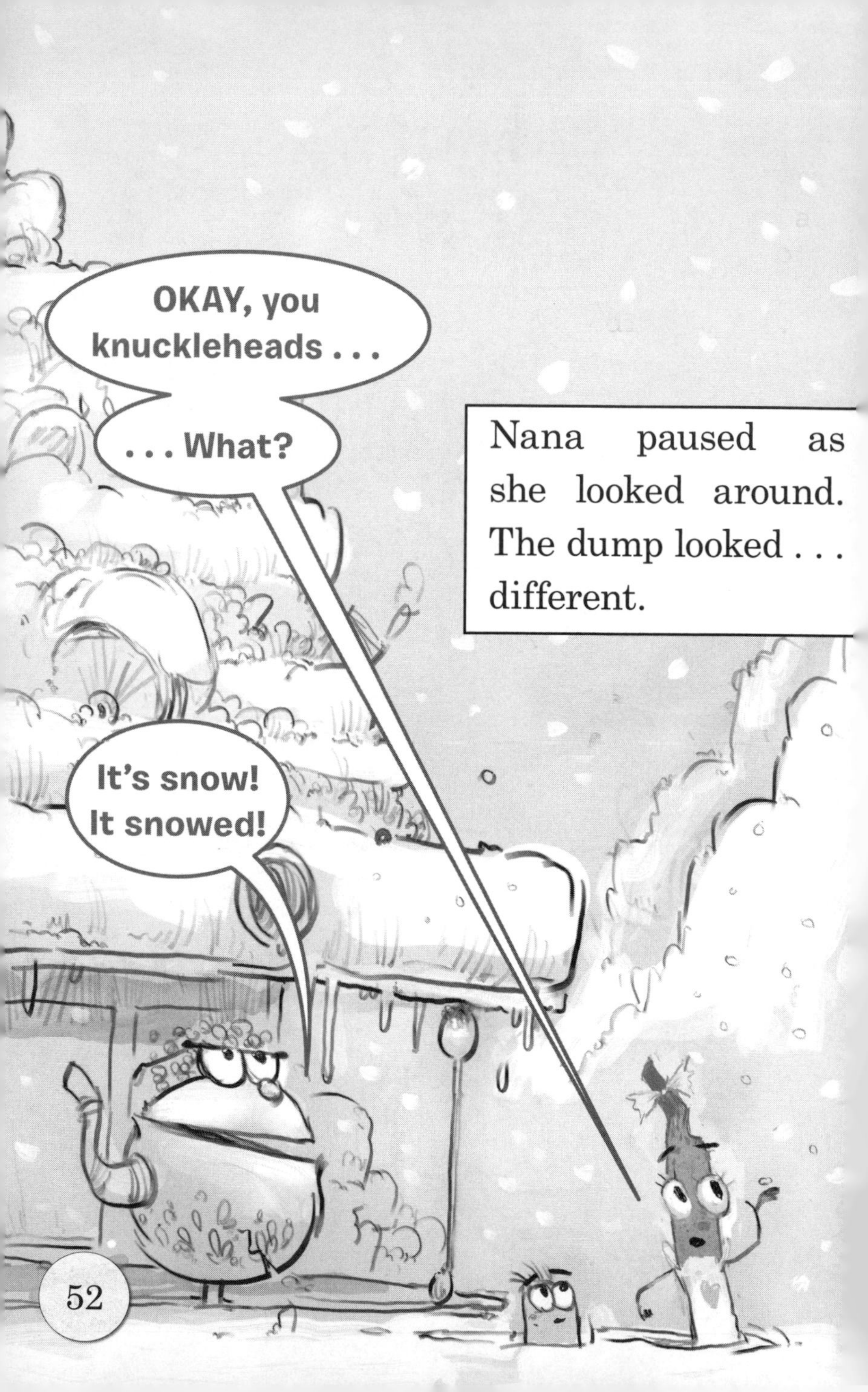
OKAY, you knuckleheads . . .
. . . What?
Nana paused as she looked around. The dump looked . . . different.
It's snow! It snowed!

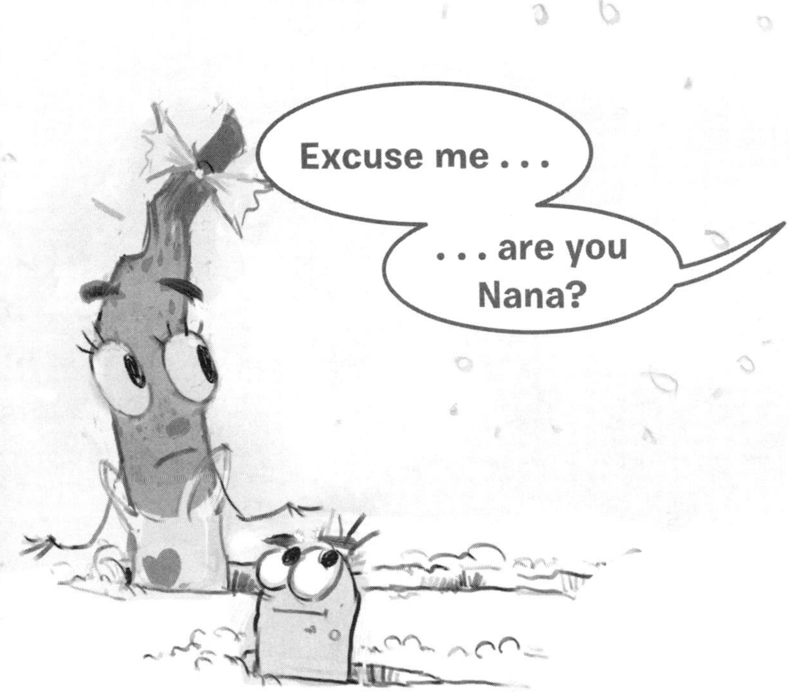
Excuse me . . .
. . . are you Nana?

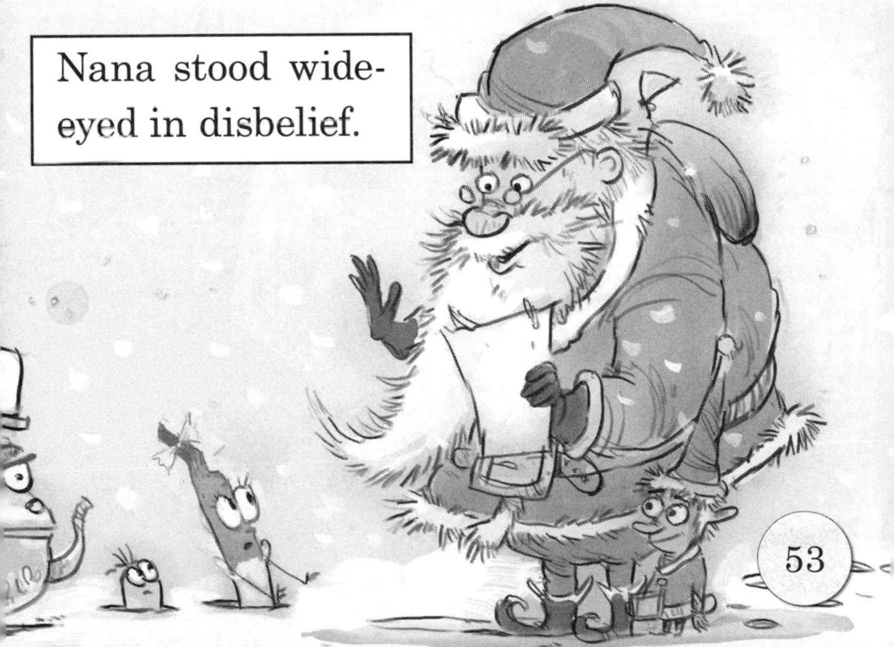
Nana stood wide-eyed in disbelief.

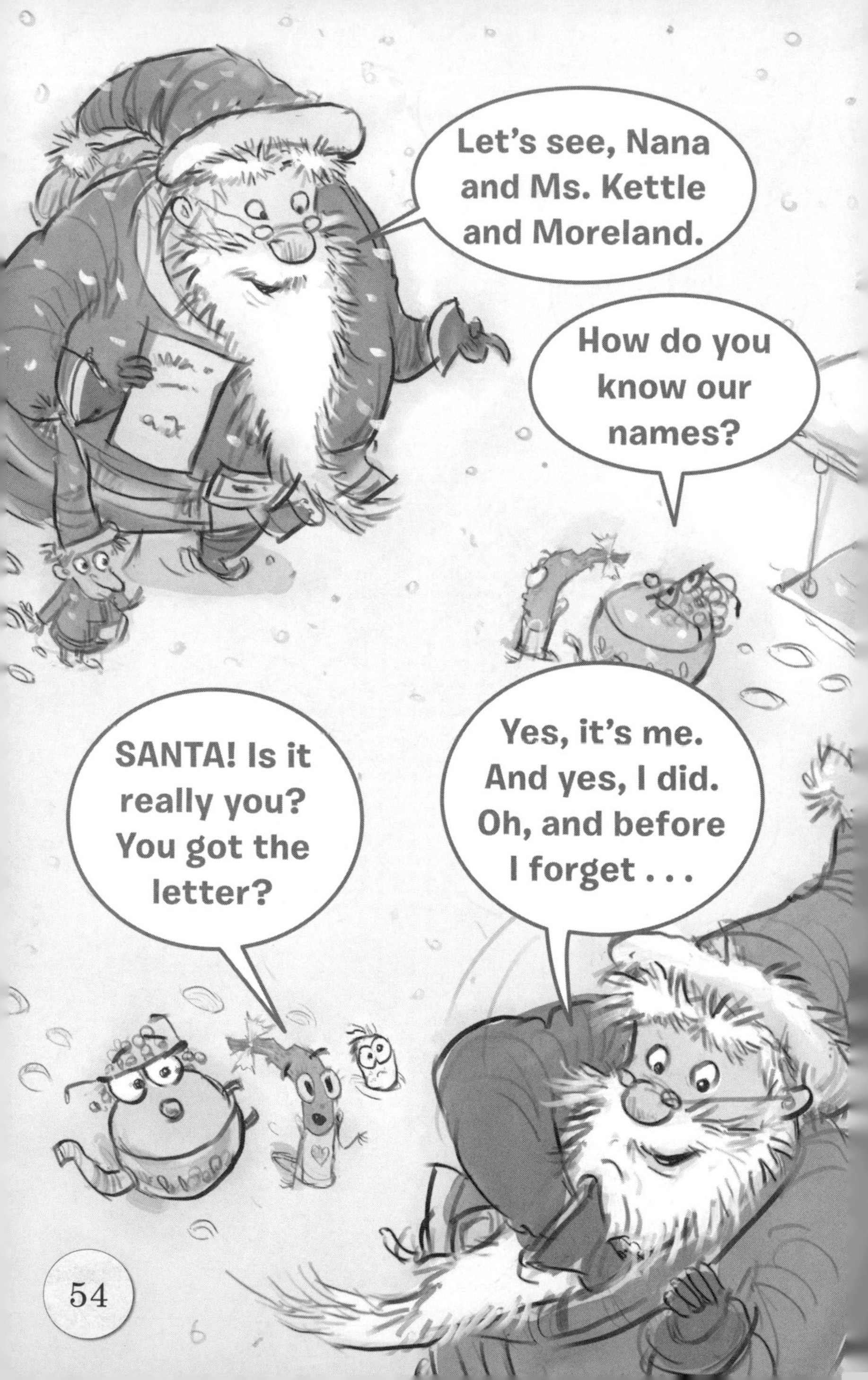
Let's see, Nana and Ms. Kettle and Moreland.
How do you know our names?
SANTA! Is it really you? You got the letter?
Yes, it's me. And yes, I did. Oh, and before I forget . . .

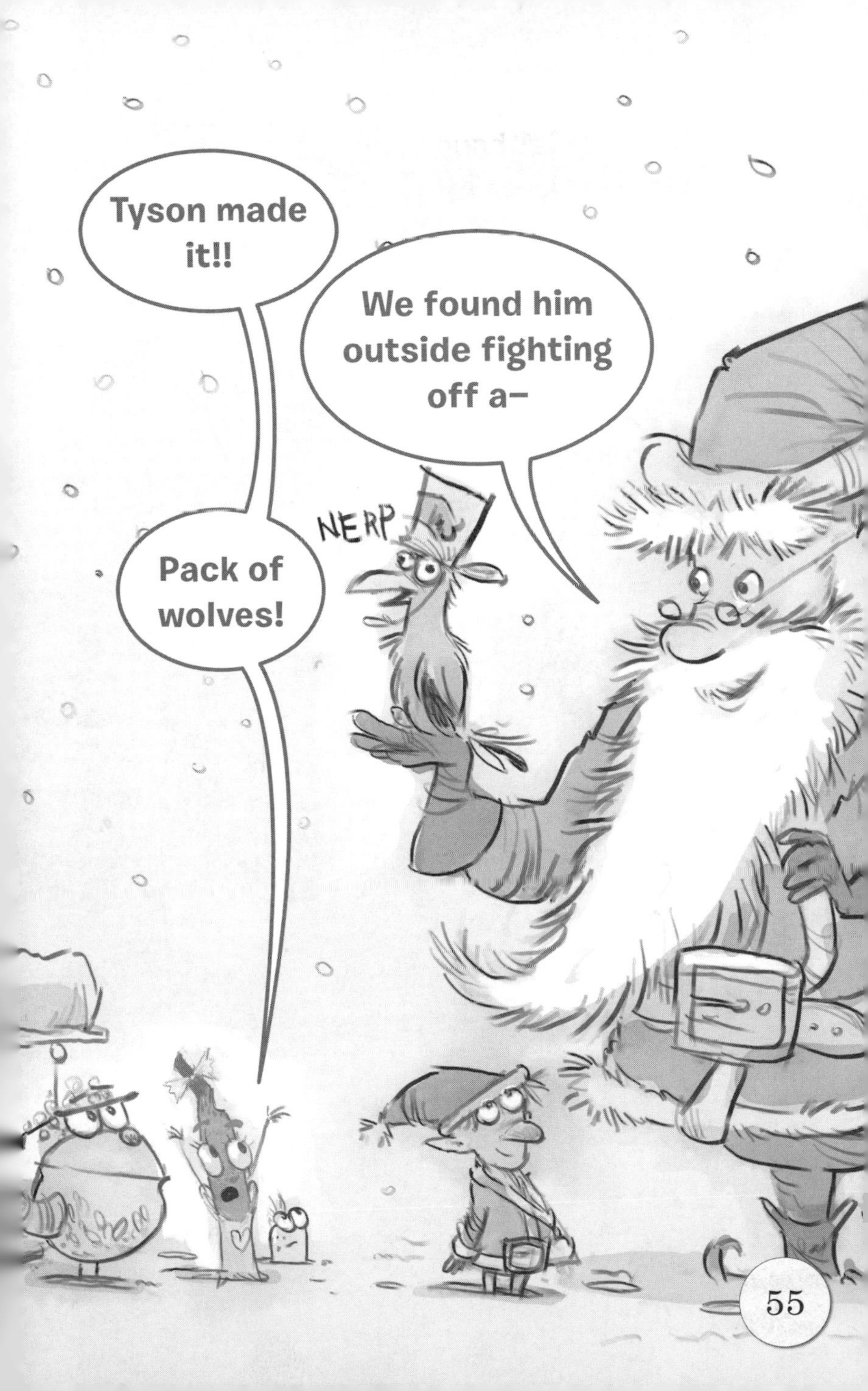
Tyson made it!!
We found him outside fighting off a–
NERP
Pack of wolves!

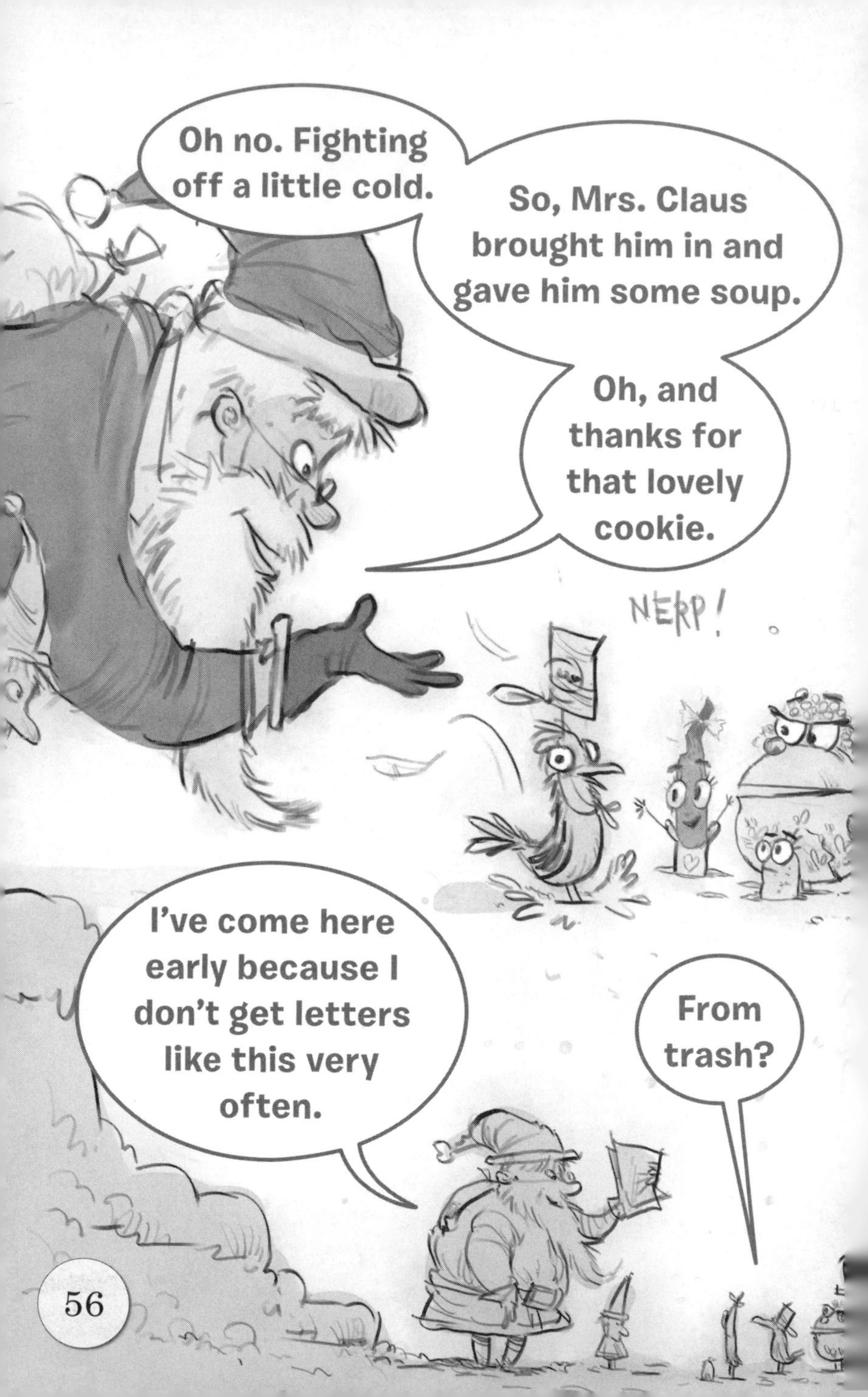
Oh no. Fighting off a little cold.
So, Mrs. Claus brought him in and gave him some soup.
Oh, and thanks for that lovely cookie.
NERP!
I've come here early because I don't get letters like this very often.
From trash?

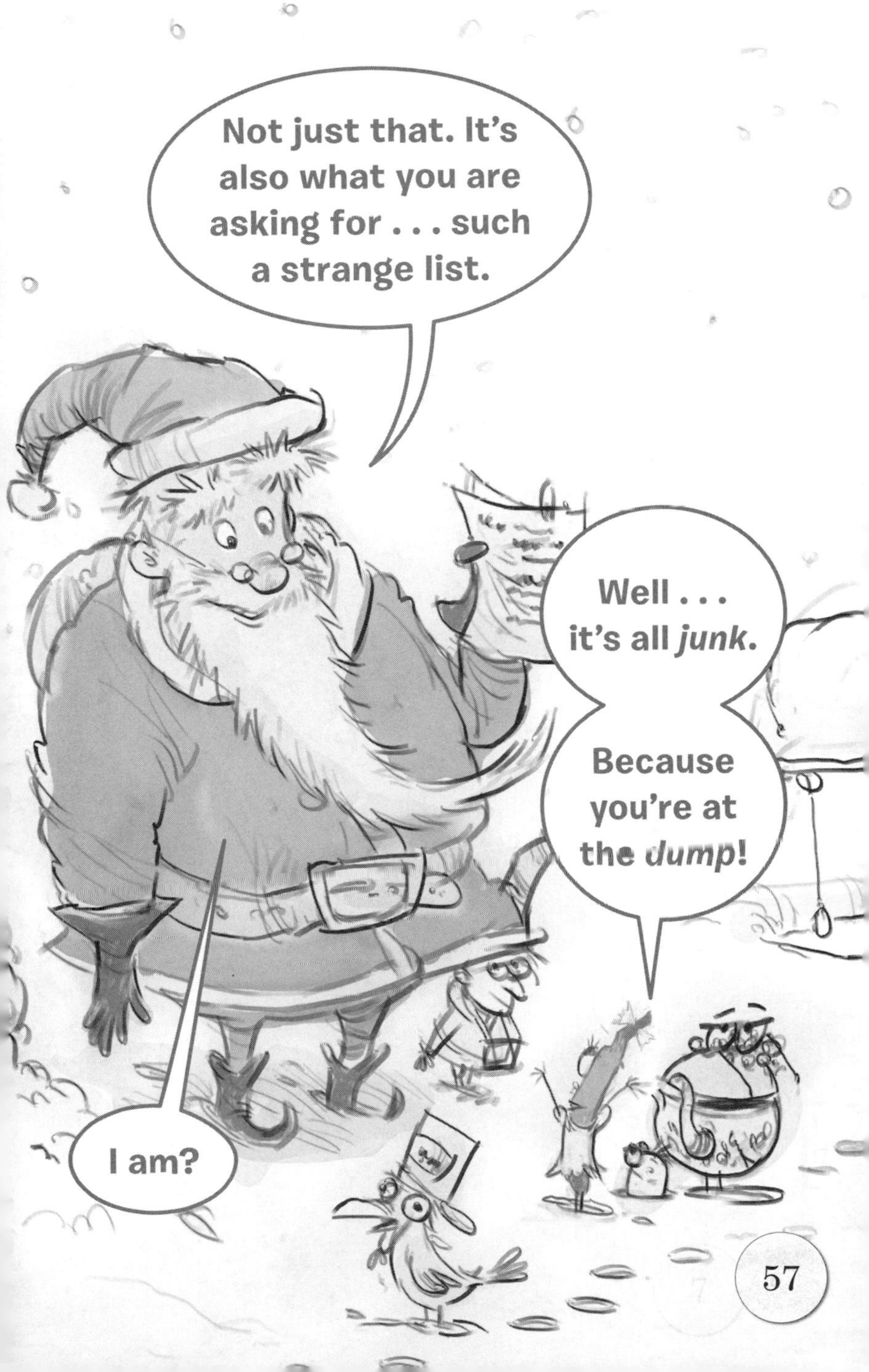
Not just that. It's also what you are asking for . . . such a strange list.
I am?
Well . . . it's all *junk*.
Because you're at the *dump*!

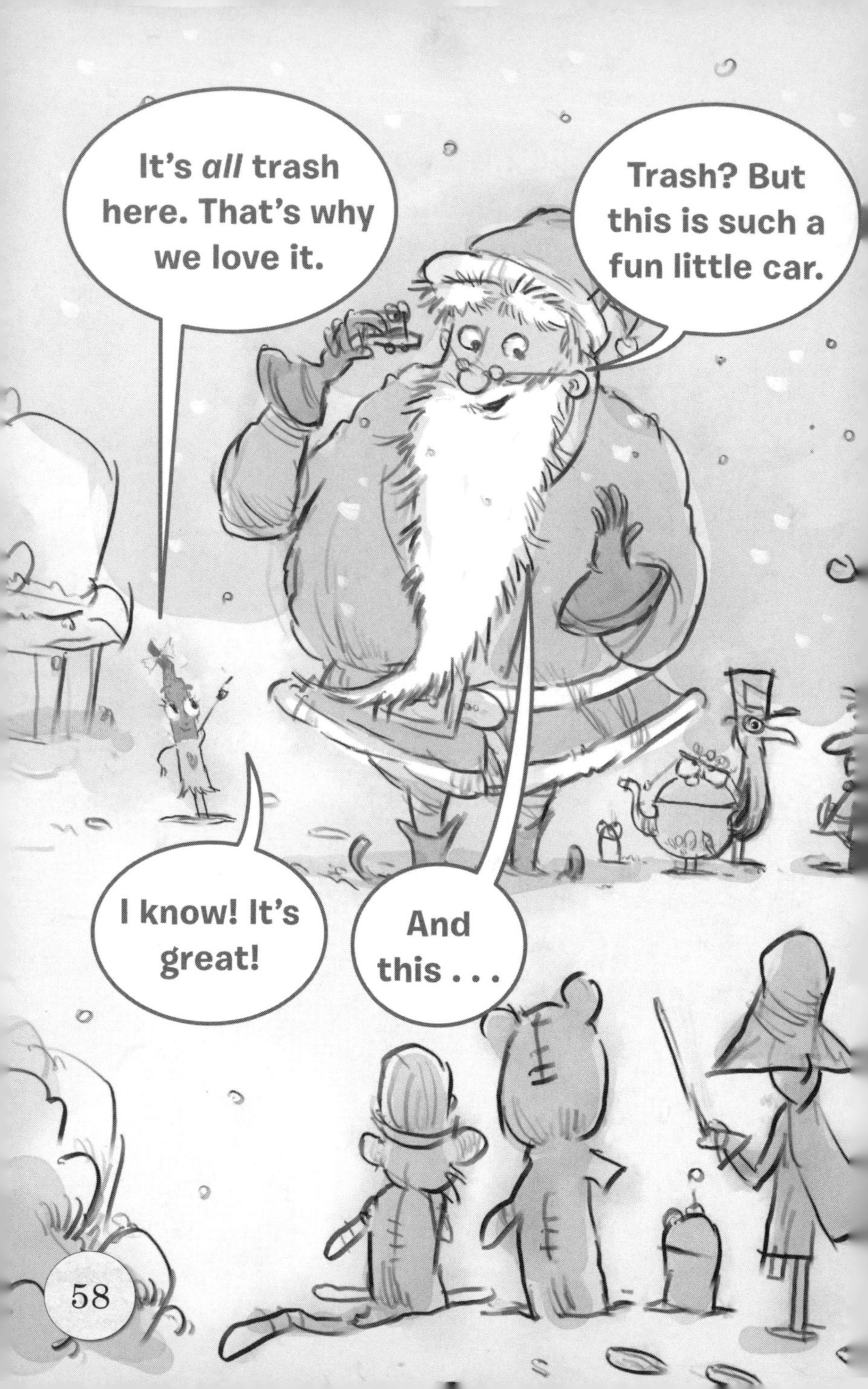
It's *all* trash here. That's why we love it.
Trash? But this is such a fun little car.
I know! It's great!
And this . . .

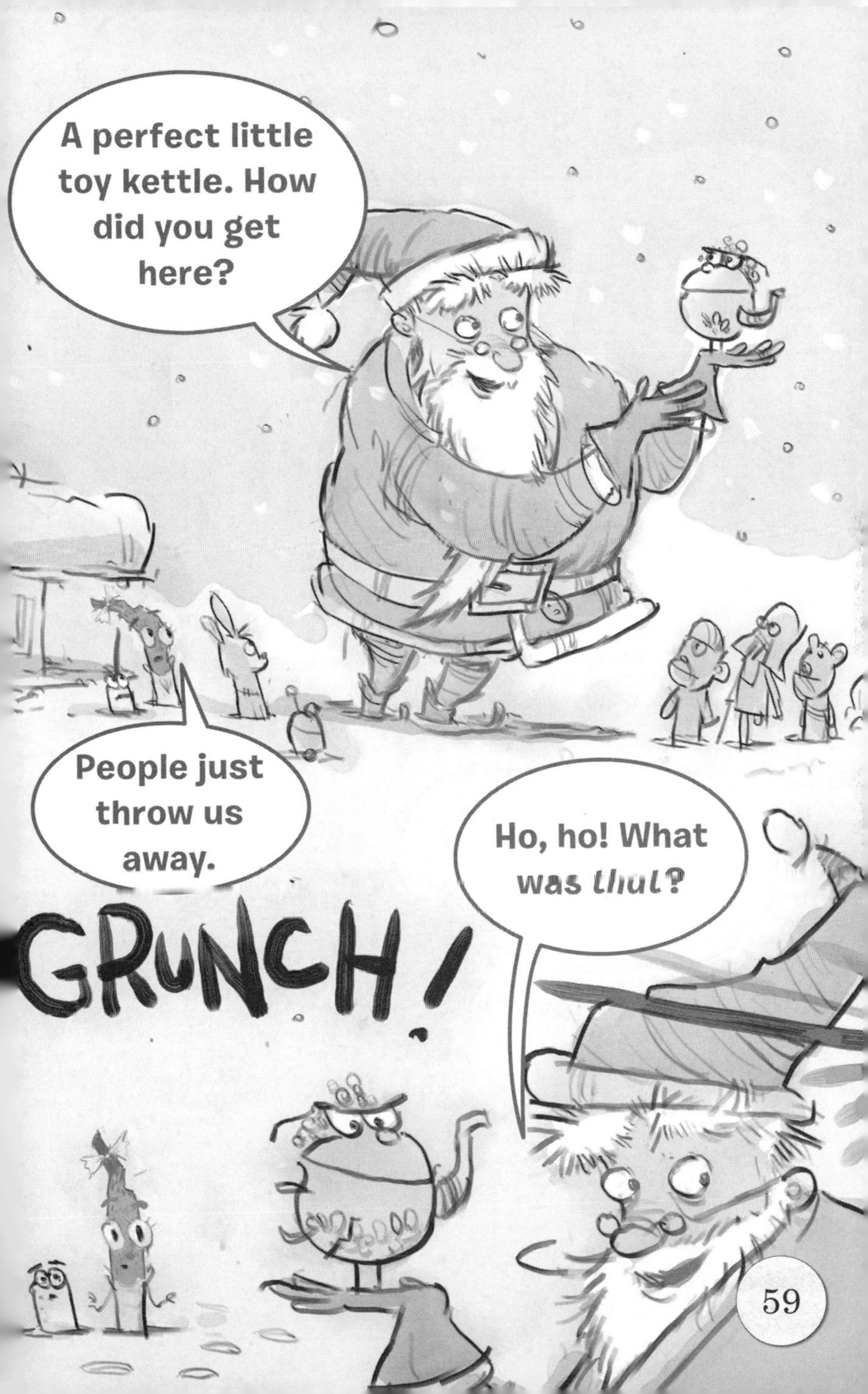
A perfect little toy kettle. How did you get here?
People just throw us away.
Ho, ho! What was that?
CRUNCH!

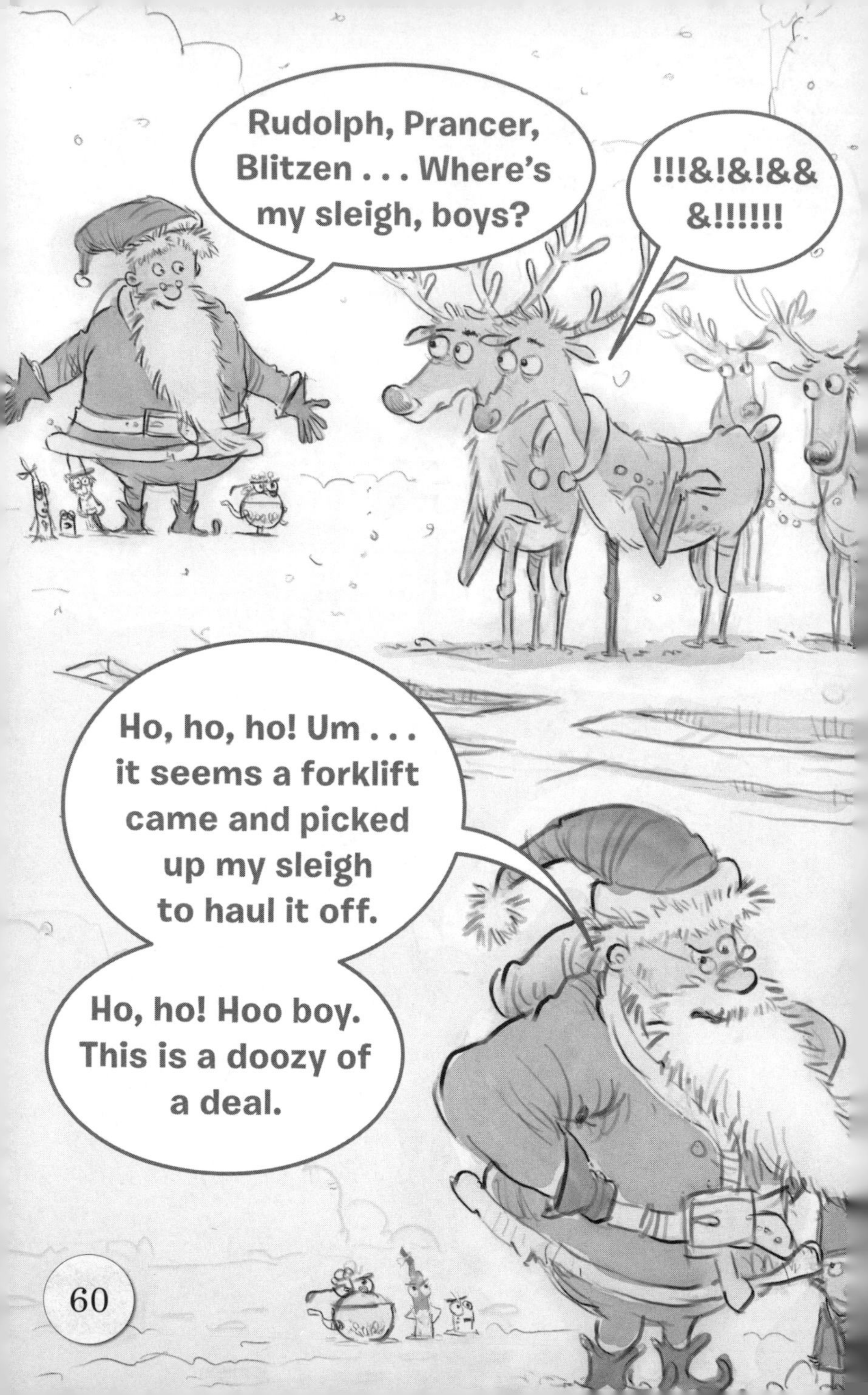
Rudolph, Prancer, Blitzen . . . Where's my sleigh, boys?
!!!&!&!&& &!!!!!!
Ho, ho, ho! Um . . . it seems a forklift came and picked up my sleigh to haul it off.
Ho, ho! Hoo boy. This is a doozy of a deal.

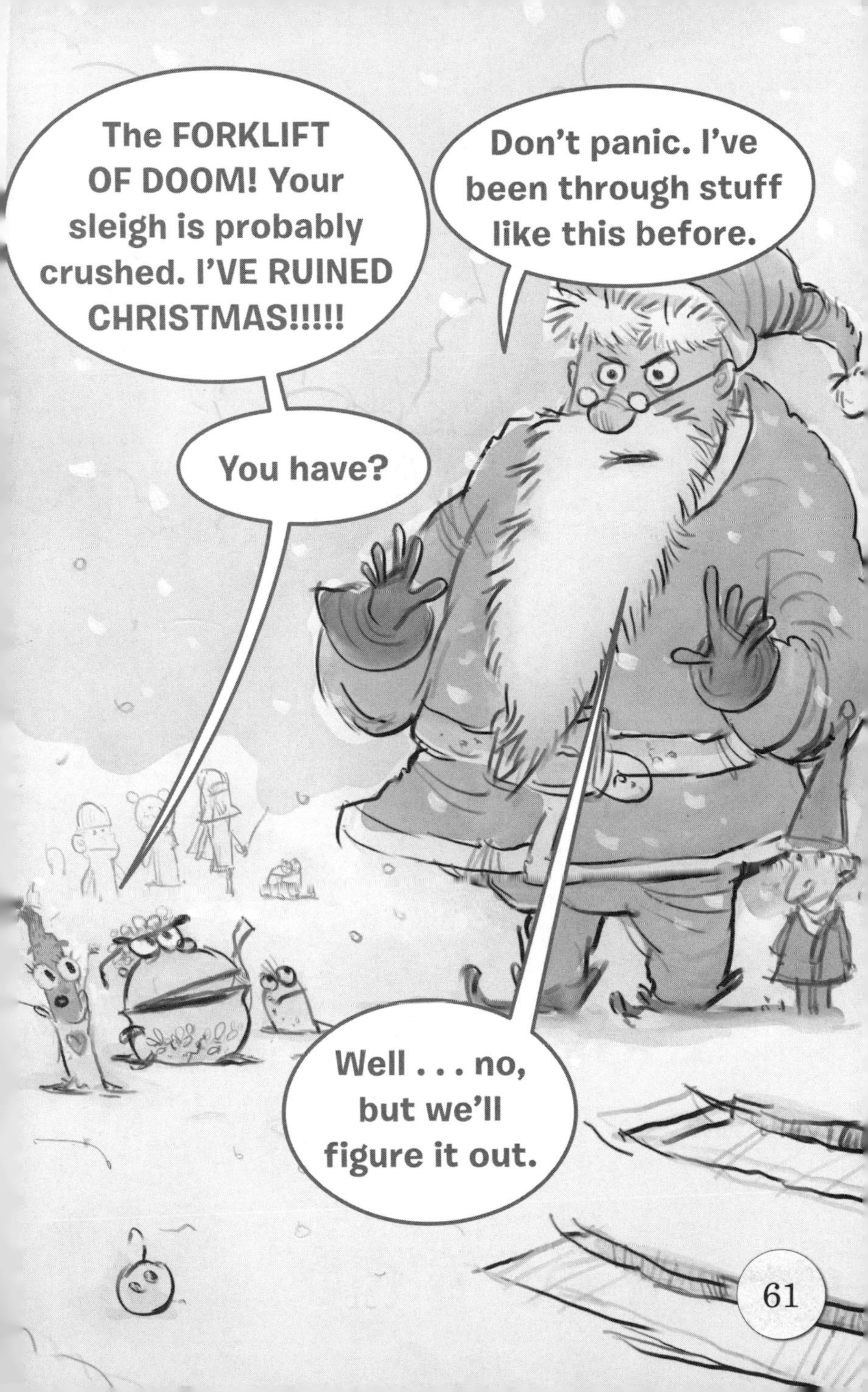
The FORKLIFT OF DOOM! Your sleigh is probably crushed. I'VE RUINED CHRISTMAS!!!!!
Don't panic. I've been through stuff like this before.
You have?
Well . . . no, but we'll figure it out.

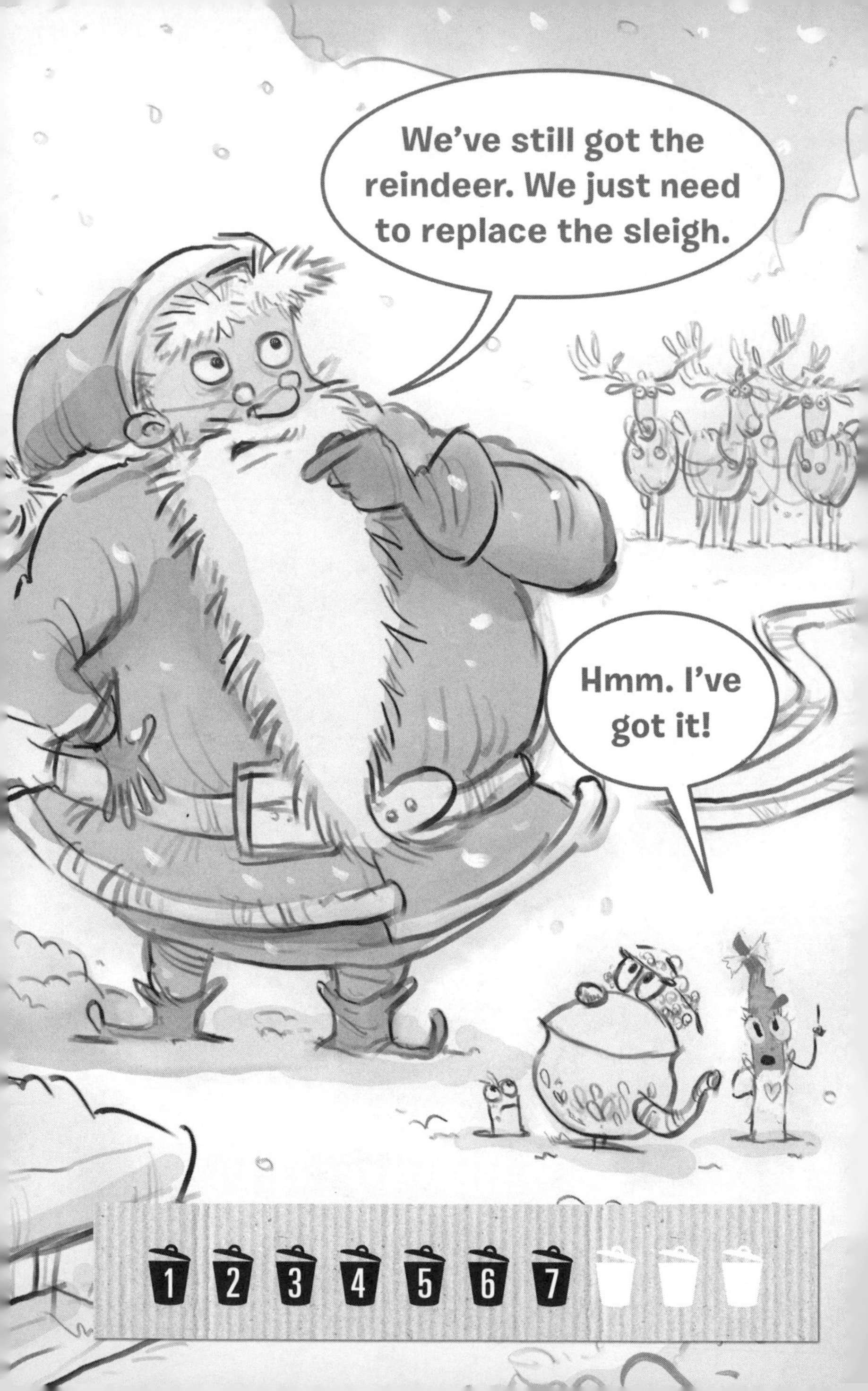
We've still got the reindeer. We just need to replace the sleigh.
Hmm. I've got it!
1 2 3 4 5 6 7

CHAPTER 8
JINGLE JANGLE

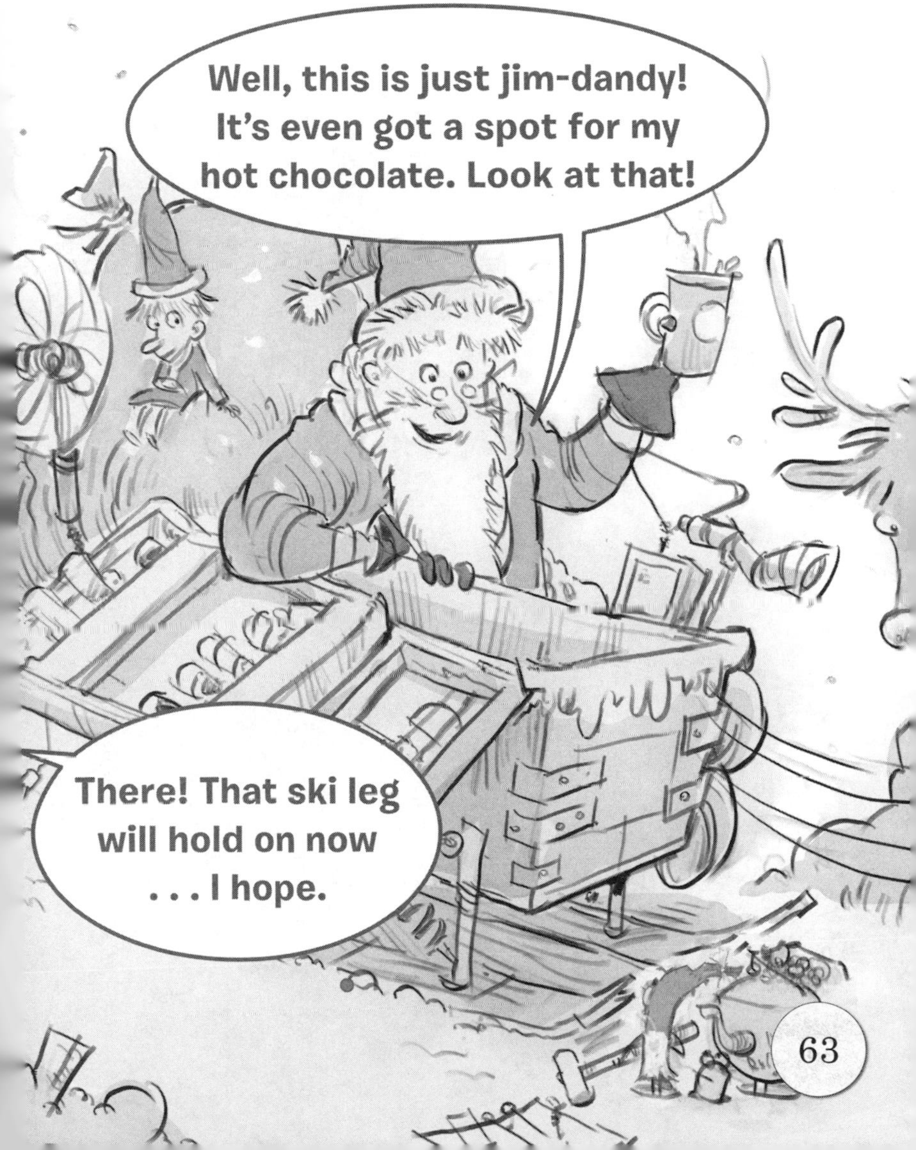
Well, this is just jim-dandy! It's even got a spot for my hot chocolate. Look at that!
There! That ski leg will hold on now . . . I hope.

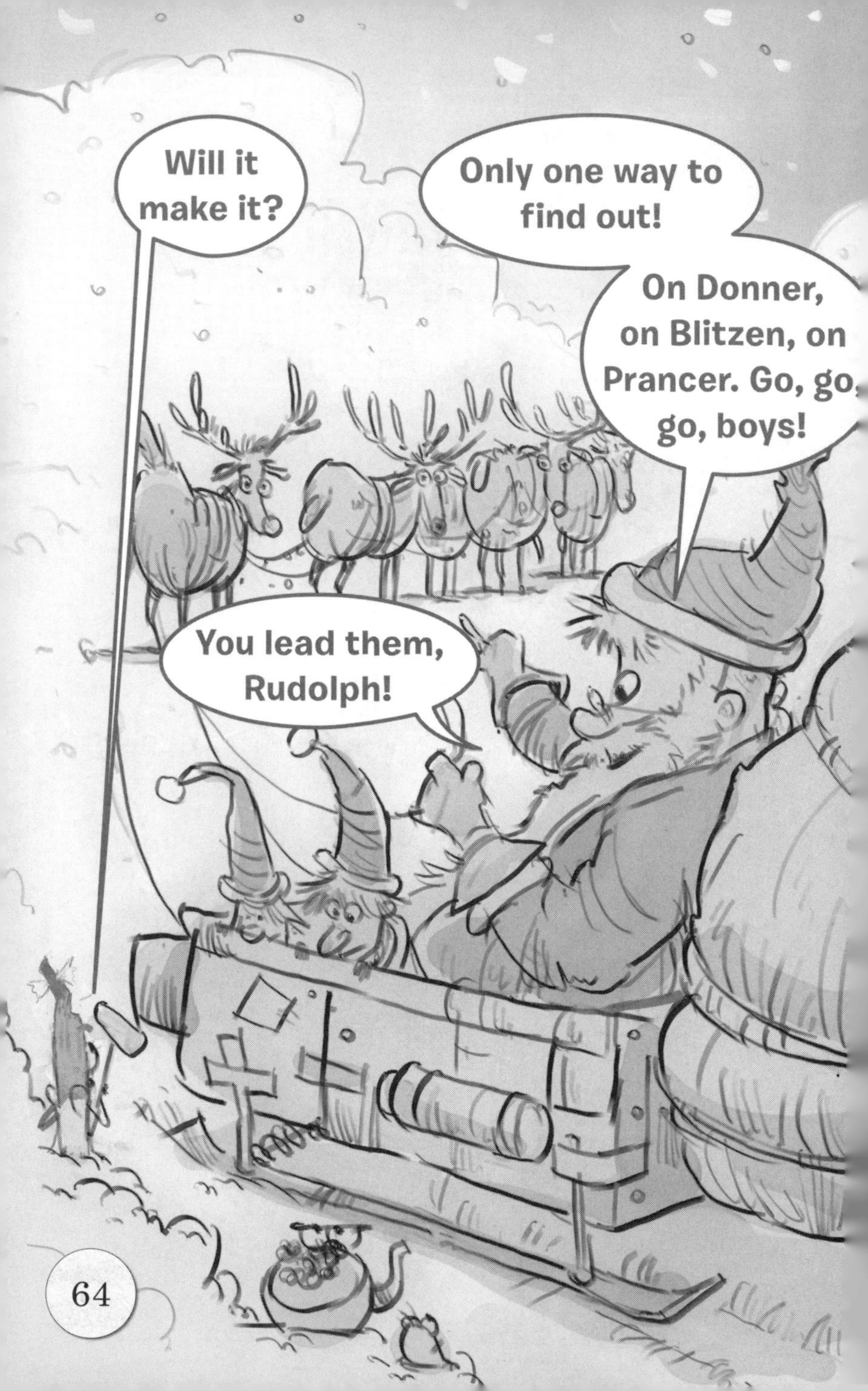
Will it make it?
Only one way to find out!
On Donner, on Blitzen, on Prancer. Go, go, go, boys!
You lead them, Rudolph!

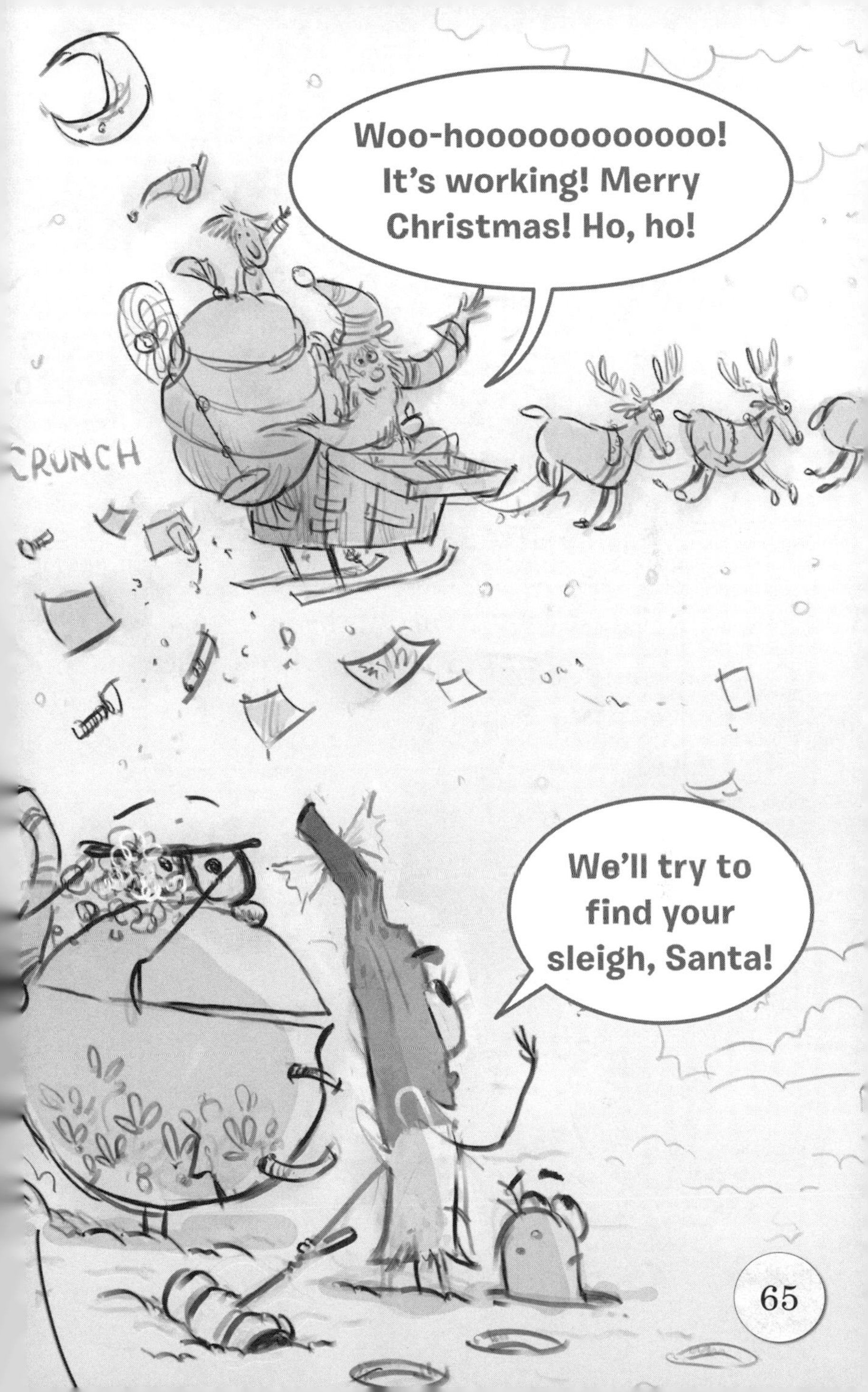
Woo-hoooooooooooo! It's working! Merry Christmas! Ho, ho!
CRUNCH
We'll try to find your sleigh, Santa!

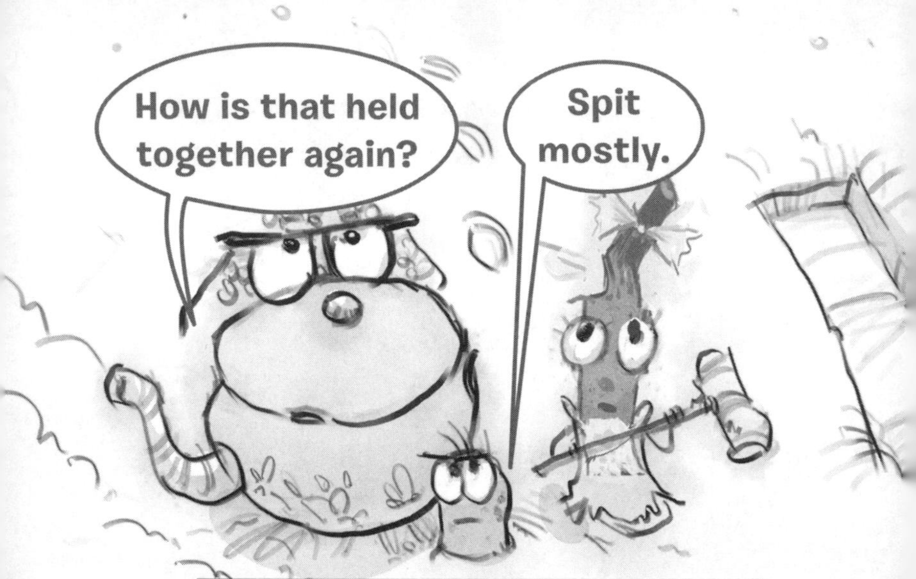
How is that held together again?
Spit mostly.

As they watched Santa's sleigh disappear, they heard a jingle, jingle.

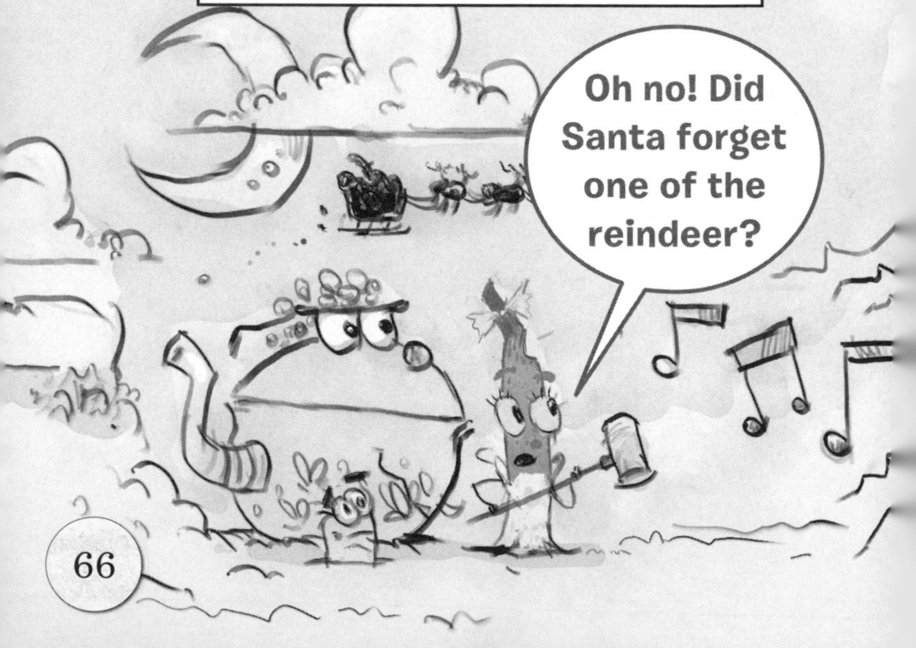
Oh no! Did Santa forget one of the reindeer?

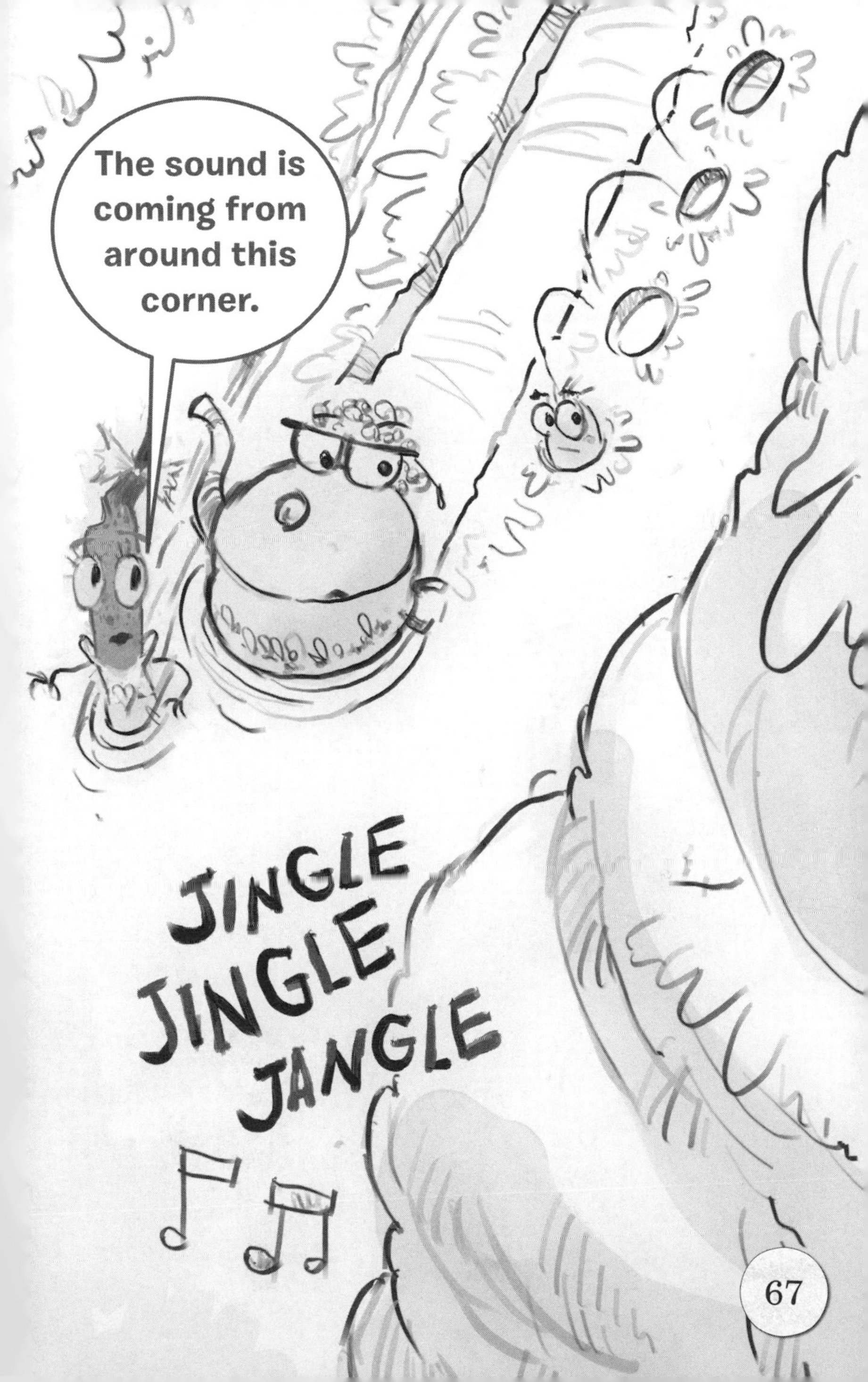
The sound is coming from around this corner.
JINGLE
JINGLE
JANGLE

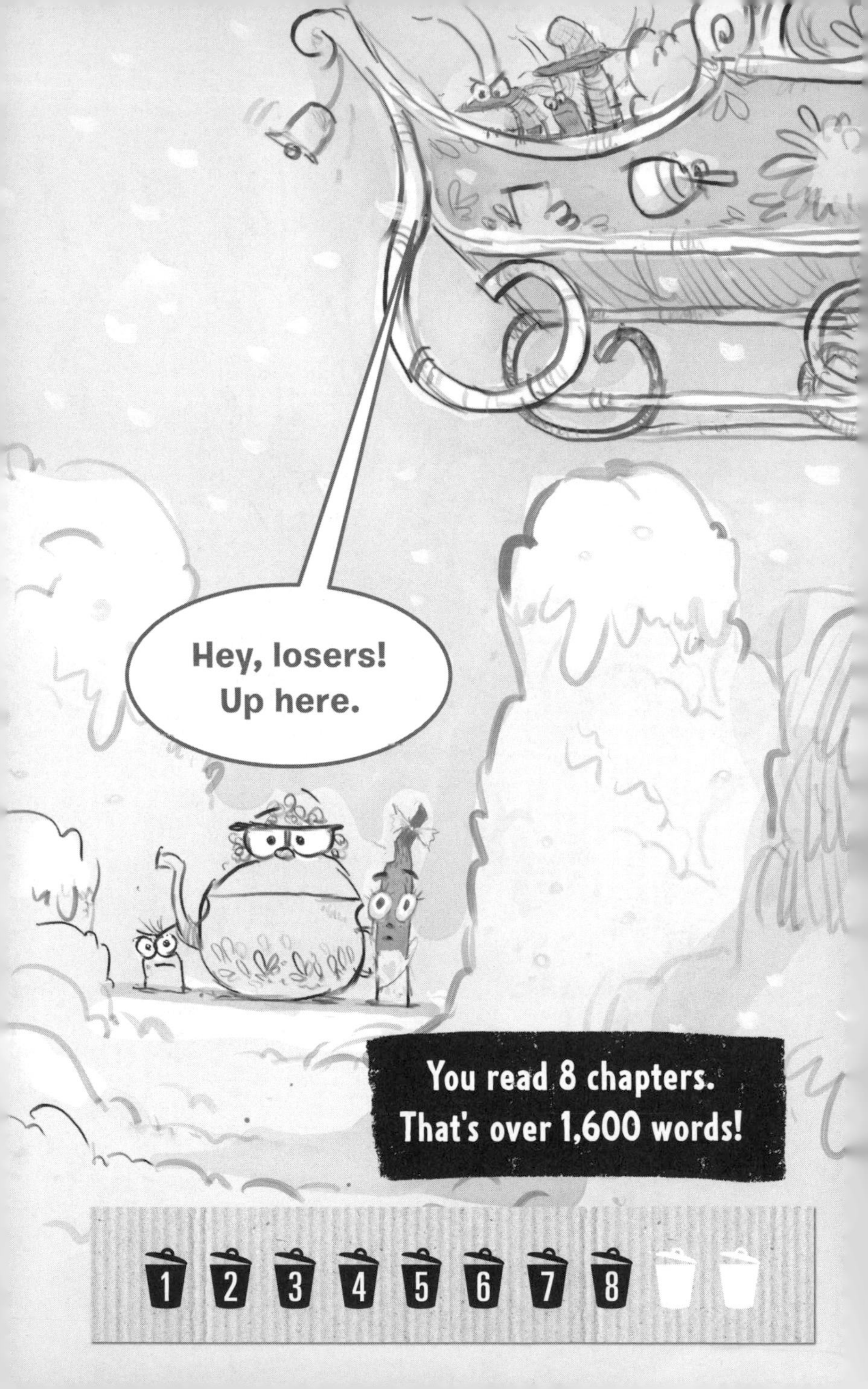
Hey, losers!
Up here.
You read 8 chapters.
That's over 1,600 words!
1 2 3 4 5 6 7 8

CHAPTER 9
A CHRISTMAS SNOT BUBBLE

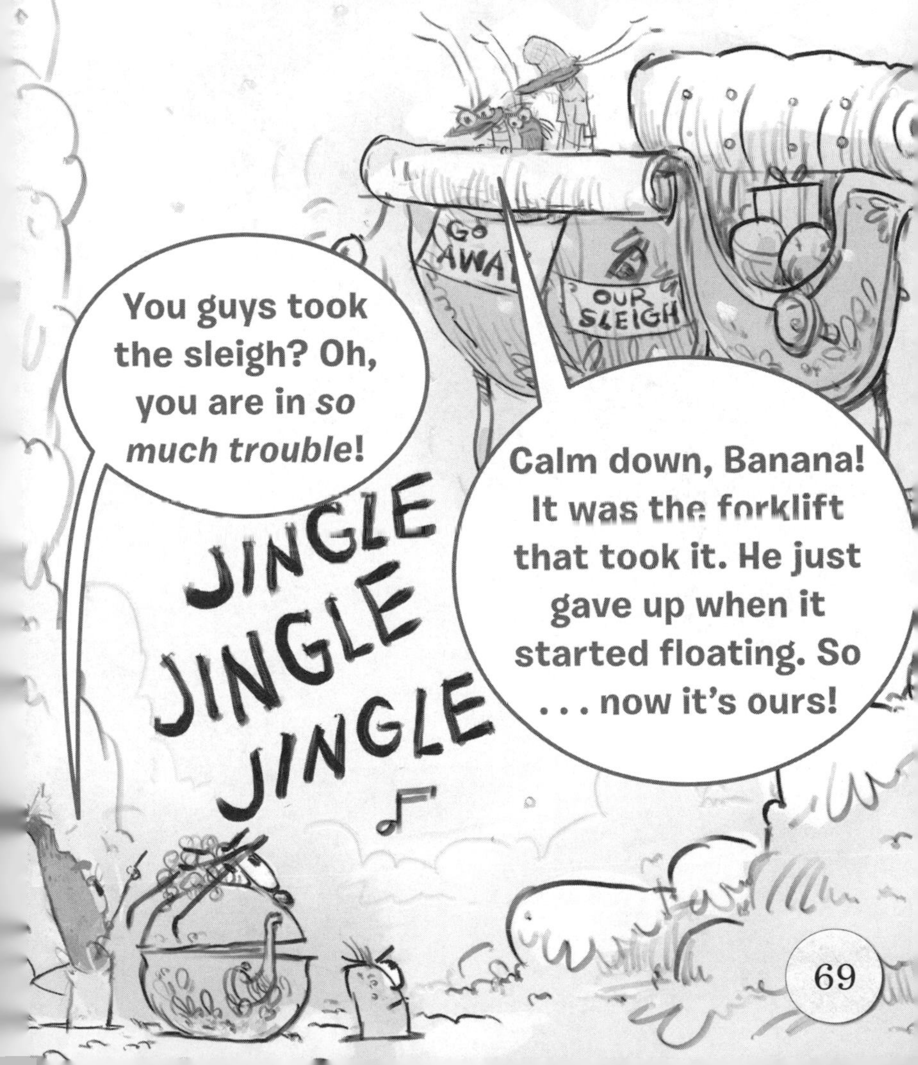
GO AWAY
OUR SLEIGH
You guys took the sleigh? Oh, you are in *so much trouble*!
Calm down, Banana! It was the forklift that took it. He just gave up when it started floating. So . . . now it's ours!
JINGLE JINGLE JINGLE

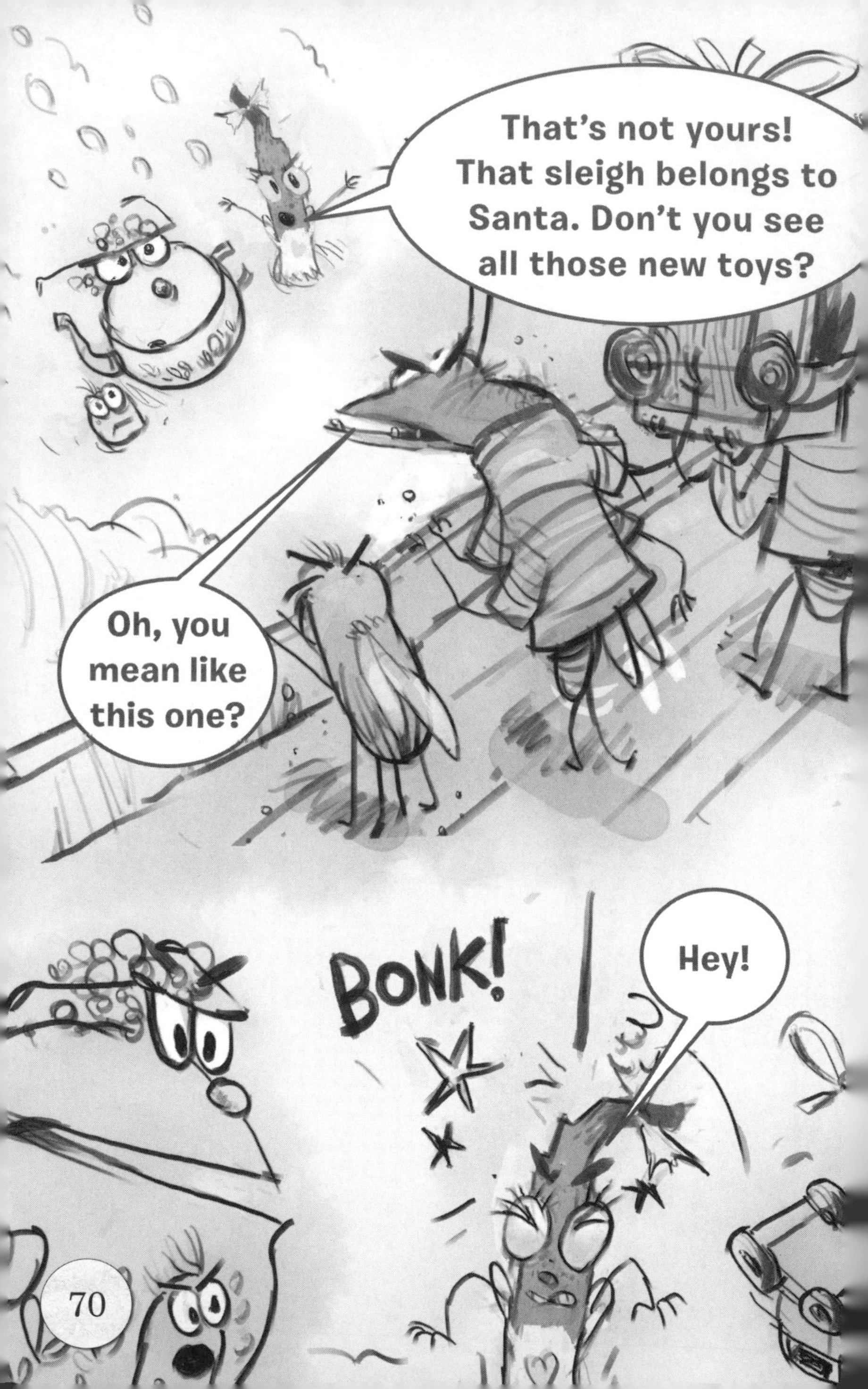
That's not yours! That sleigh belongs to Santa. Don't you see all those new toys?
Oh, you mean like this one?
BONK!
Hey!

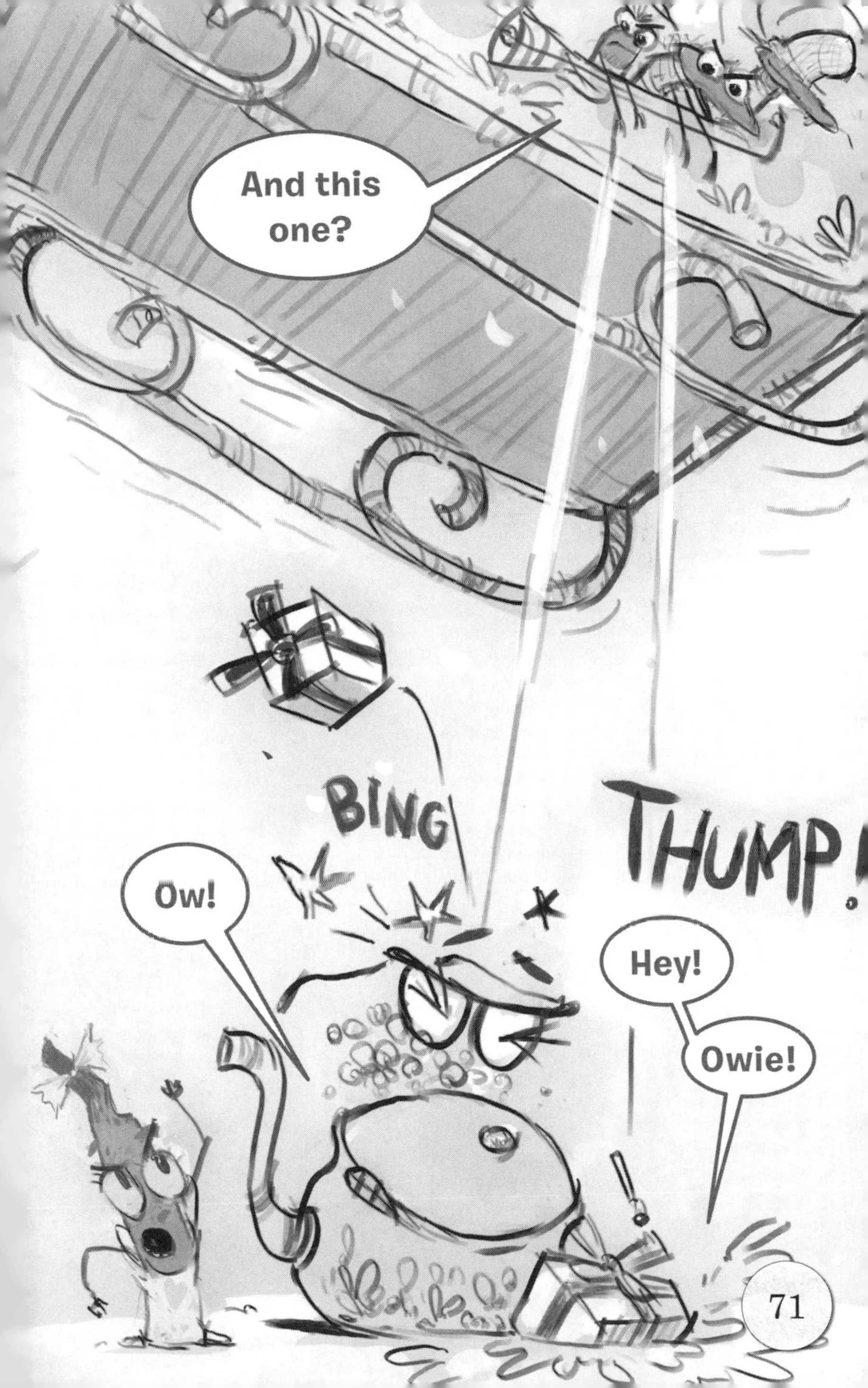

And this one?
BING
THUMP!
Ow!
Hey!
Owie!

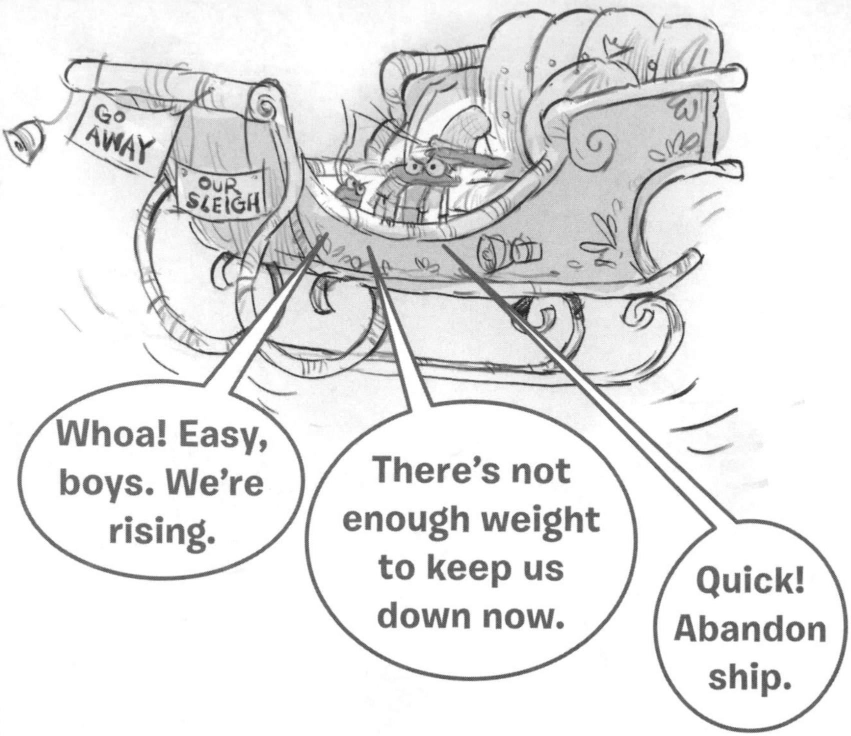
GO AWAY
OUR SLEIGH
Whoa! Easy, boys. We're rising.
There's not enough weight to keep us down now.
Quick! Abandon ship.

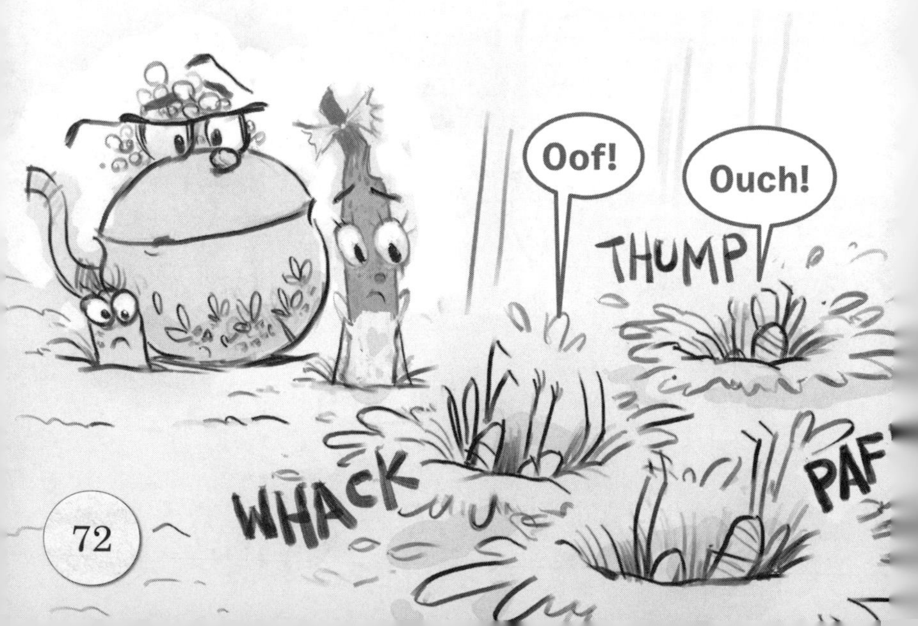
Oof!
Ouch!
THUMP
WHACK

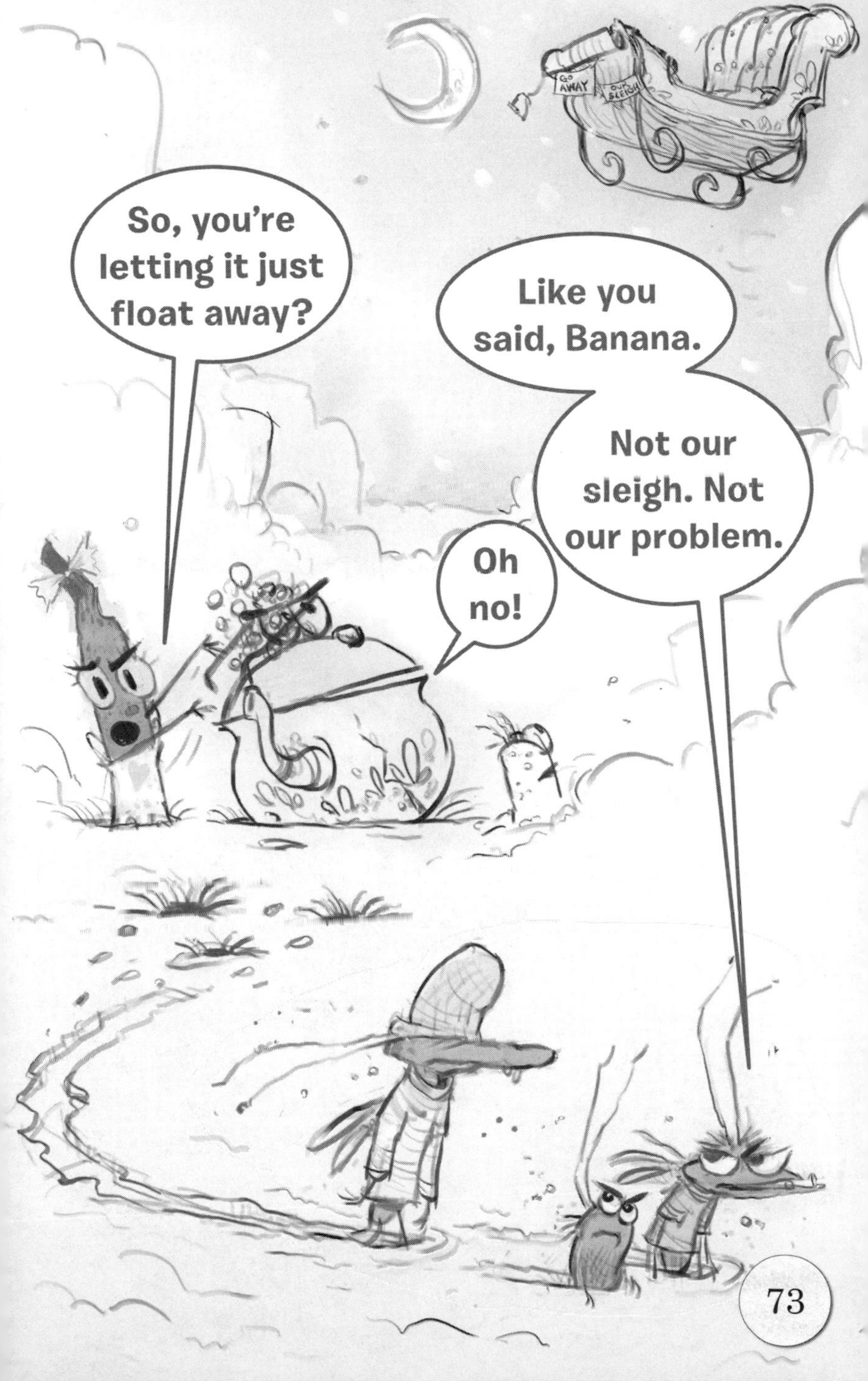
GO AWAY
OUR SLEIGH
So, you're letting it just float away?
Like you said, Banana.
Not our sleigh. Not our problem.
Oh no!

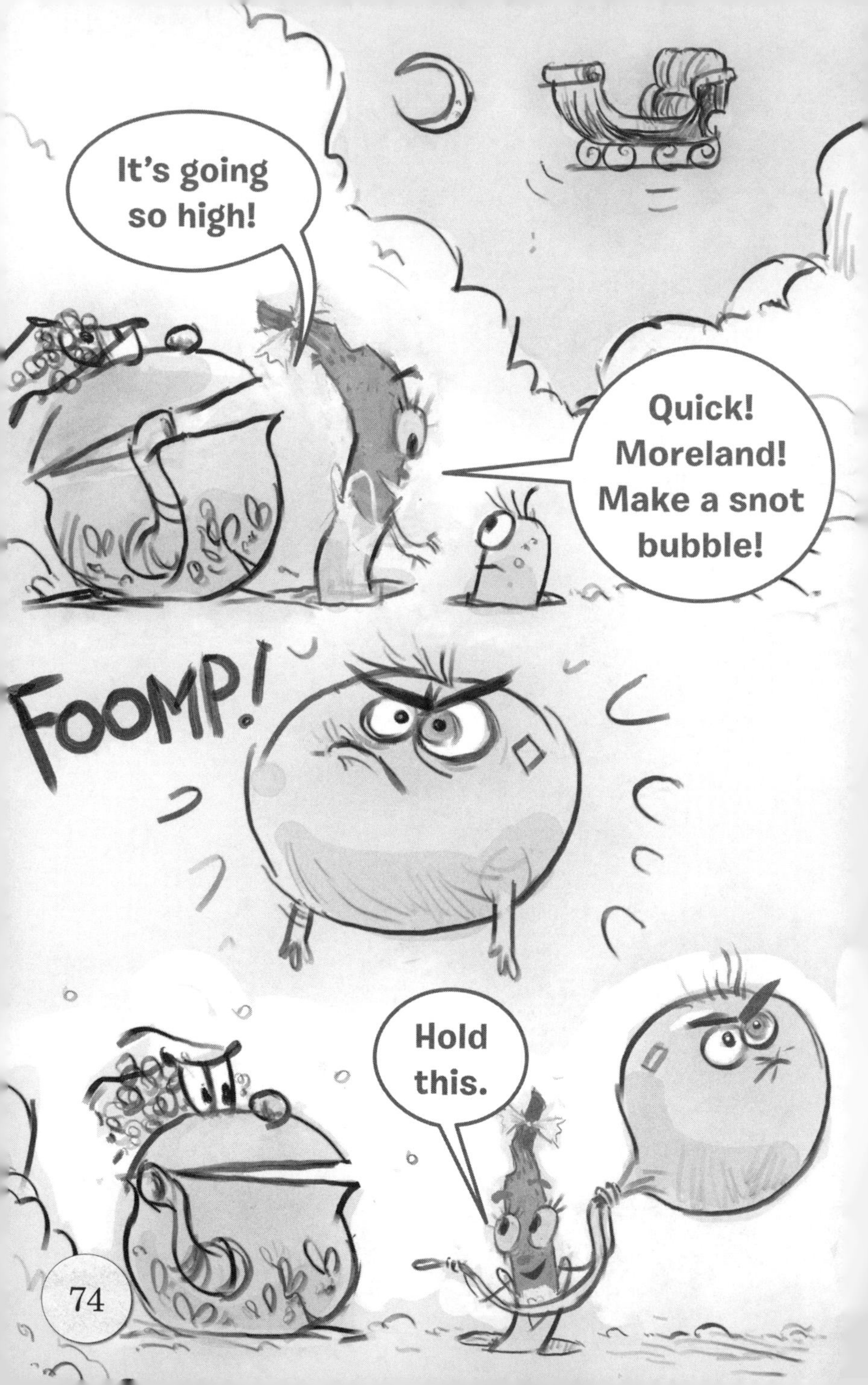

It's going so high!
Quick! Moreland! Make a snot bubble!
FOOMP!
Hold this.

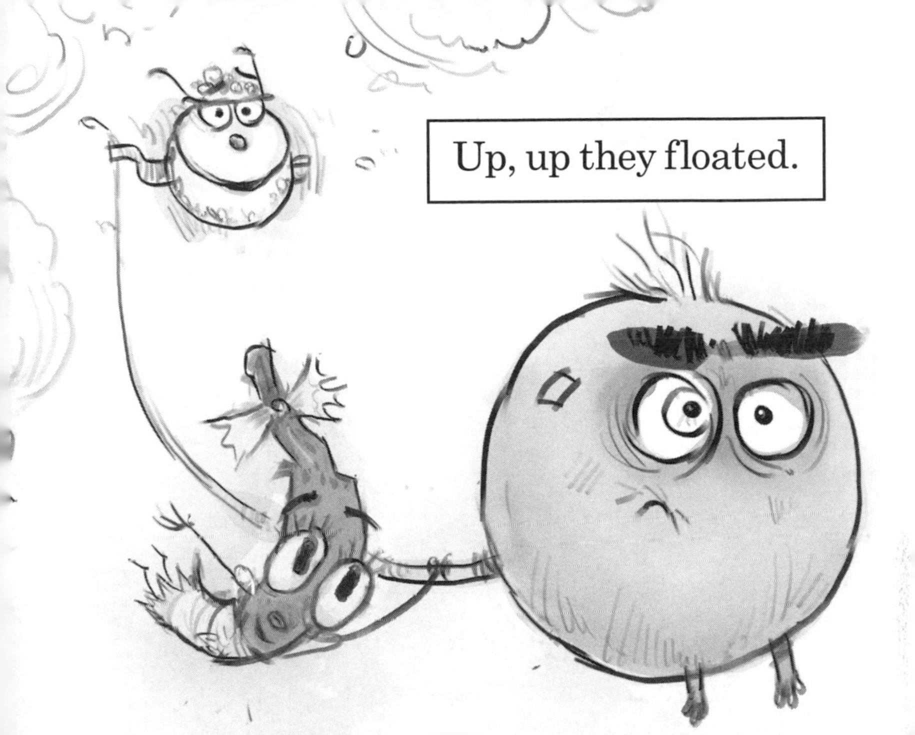
Up, up they floated.

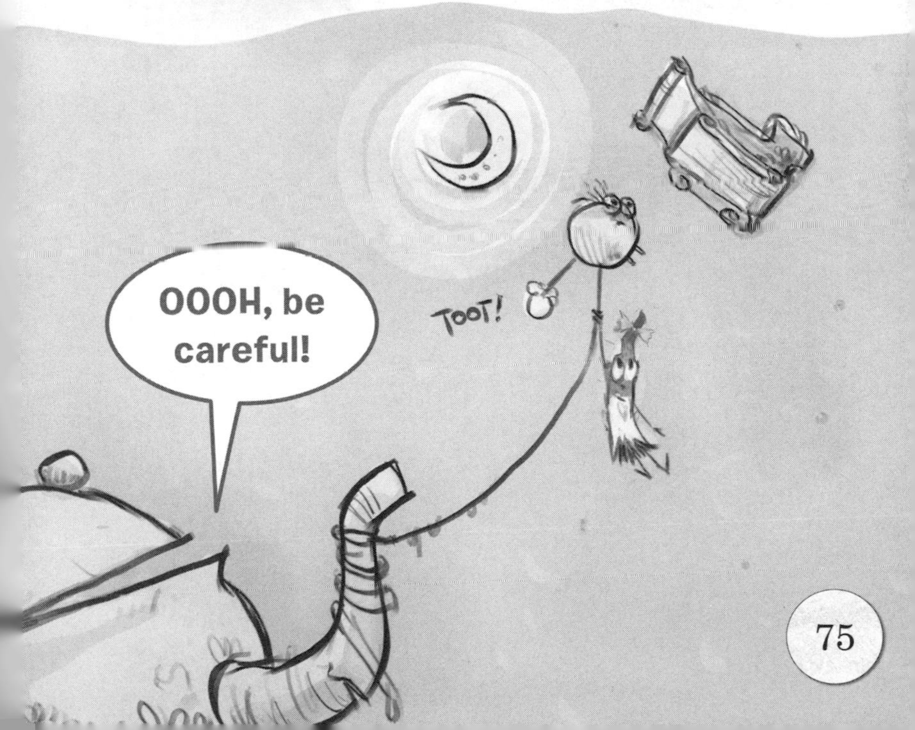
TOOT!
OOOH, be careful!

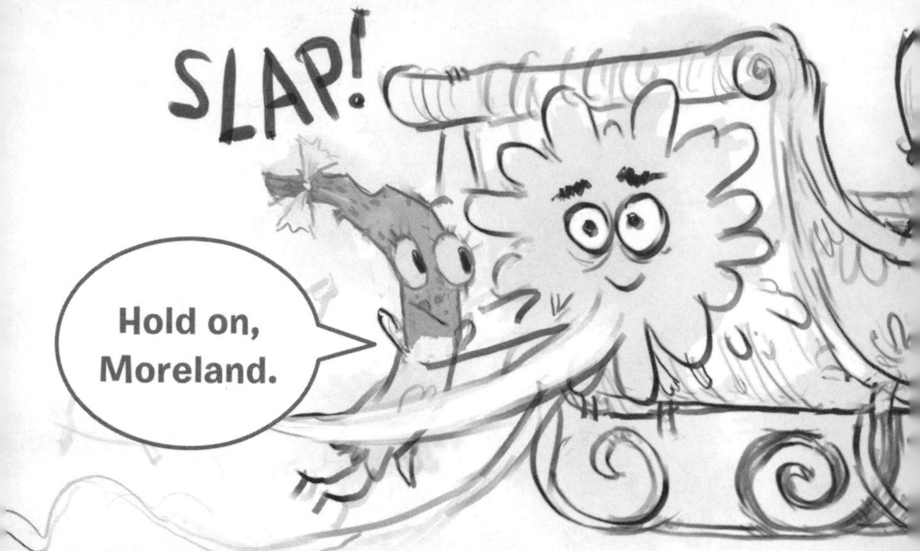
SLAP!
Hold on, Moreland.

Then Nana stuck Moreland to the front of the sleigh.

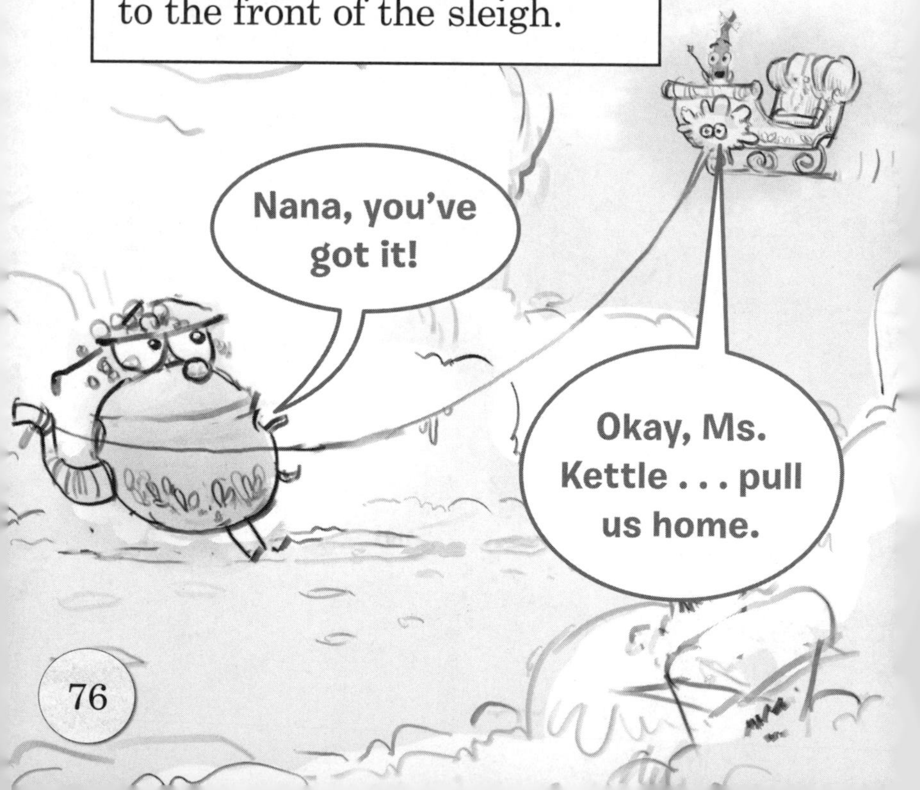
Nana, you've got it!
Okay, Ms. Kettle . . . pull us home.

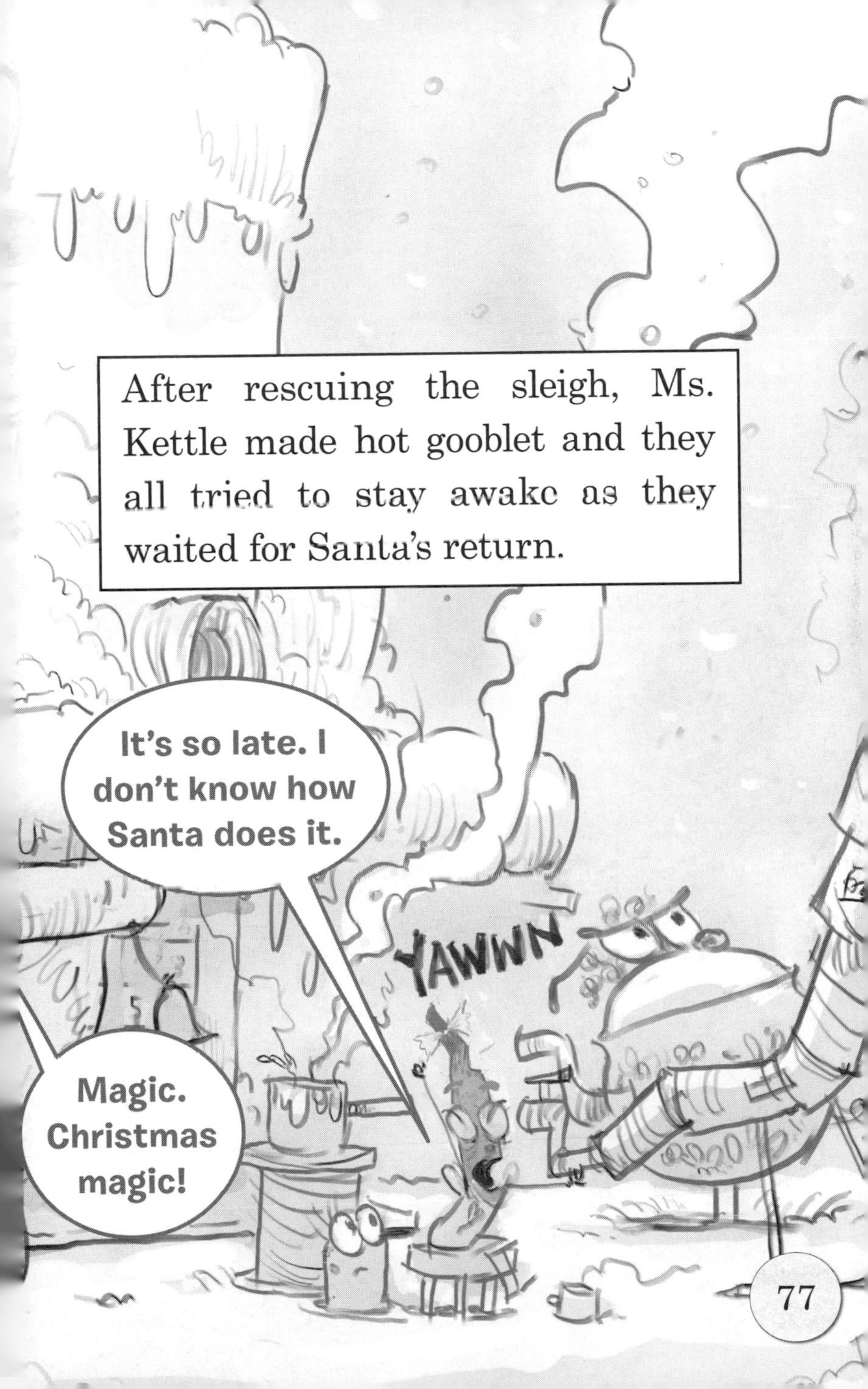
After rescuing the sleigh, Ms. Kettle made hot gooblet and they all tried to stay awake as they waited for Santa's return.
It's so late. I don't know how Santa does it.
YAWNN
Magic. Christmas magic!

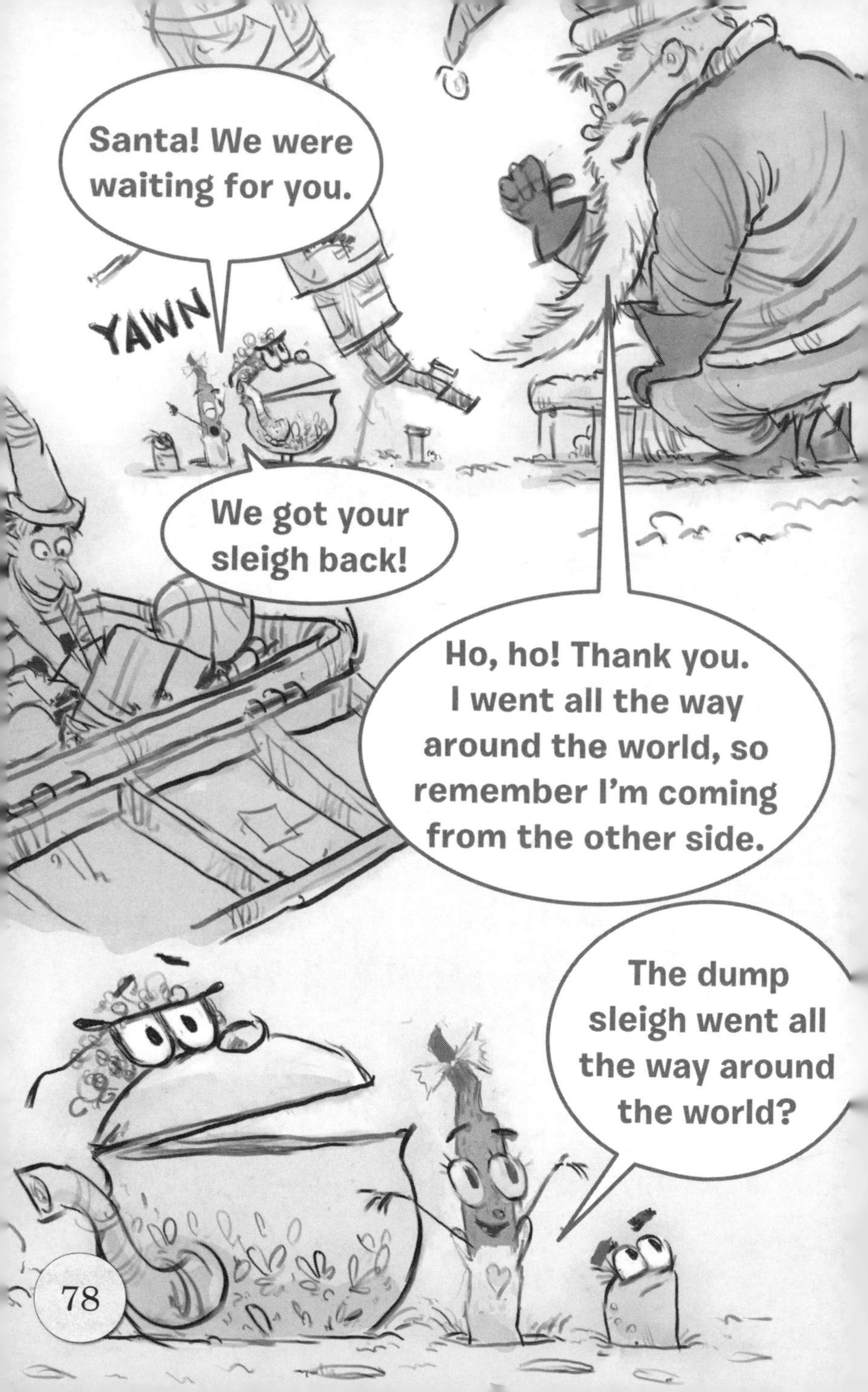
Santa! We were waiting for you.
YAWN
We got your sleigh back!
Ho, ho! Thank you. I went all the way around the world, so remember I'm coming from the other side.
The dump sleigh went all the way around the world?

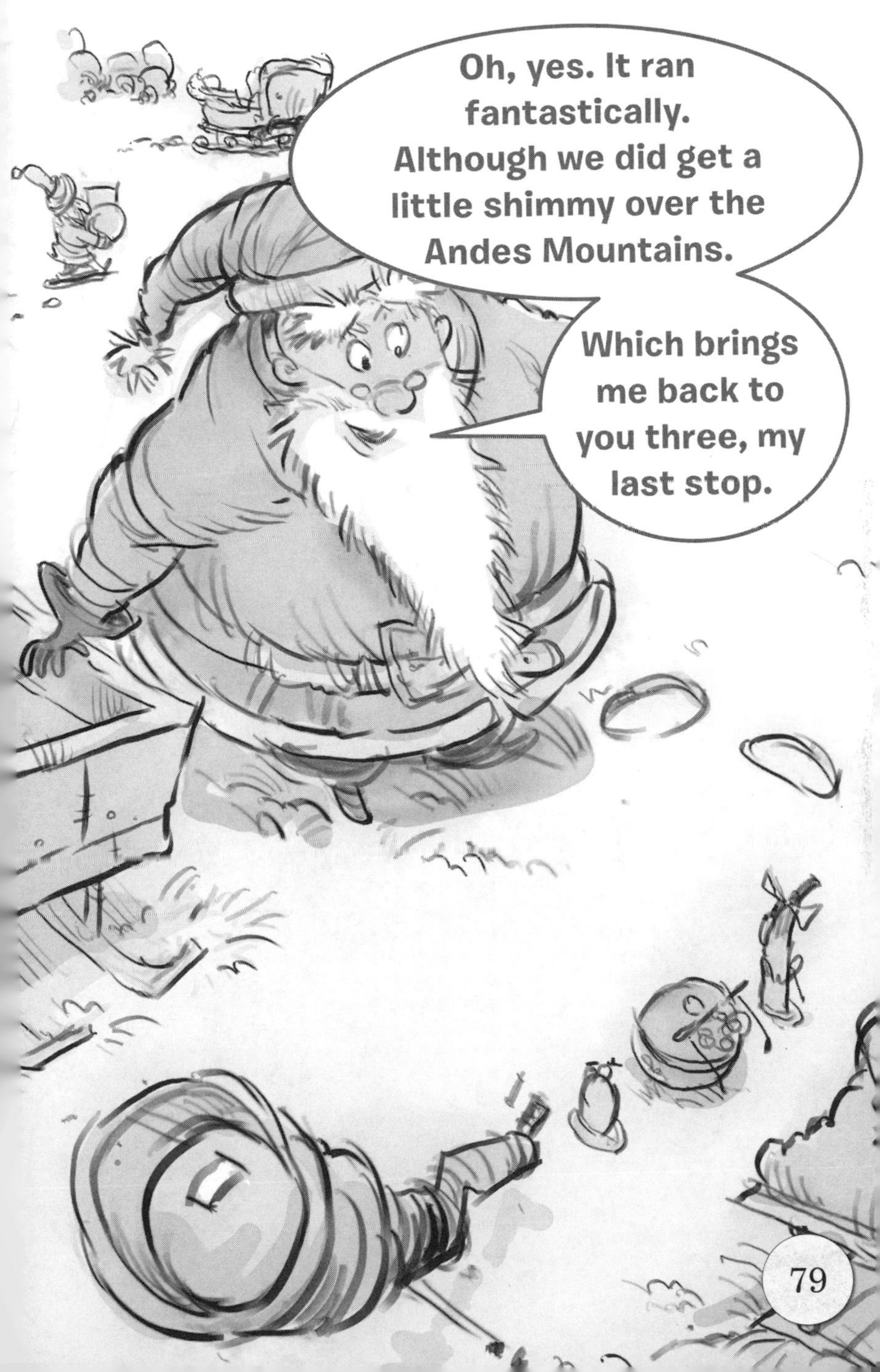
Oh, yes. It ran fantastically. Although we did get a little shimmy over the Andes Mountains.
Which brings me back to you three, my last stop.

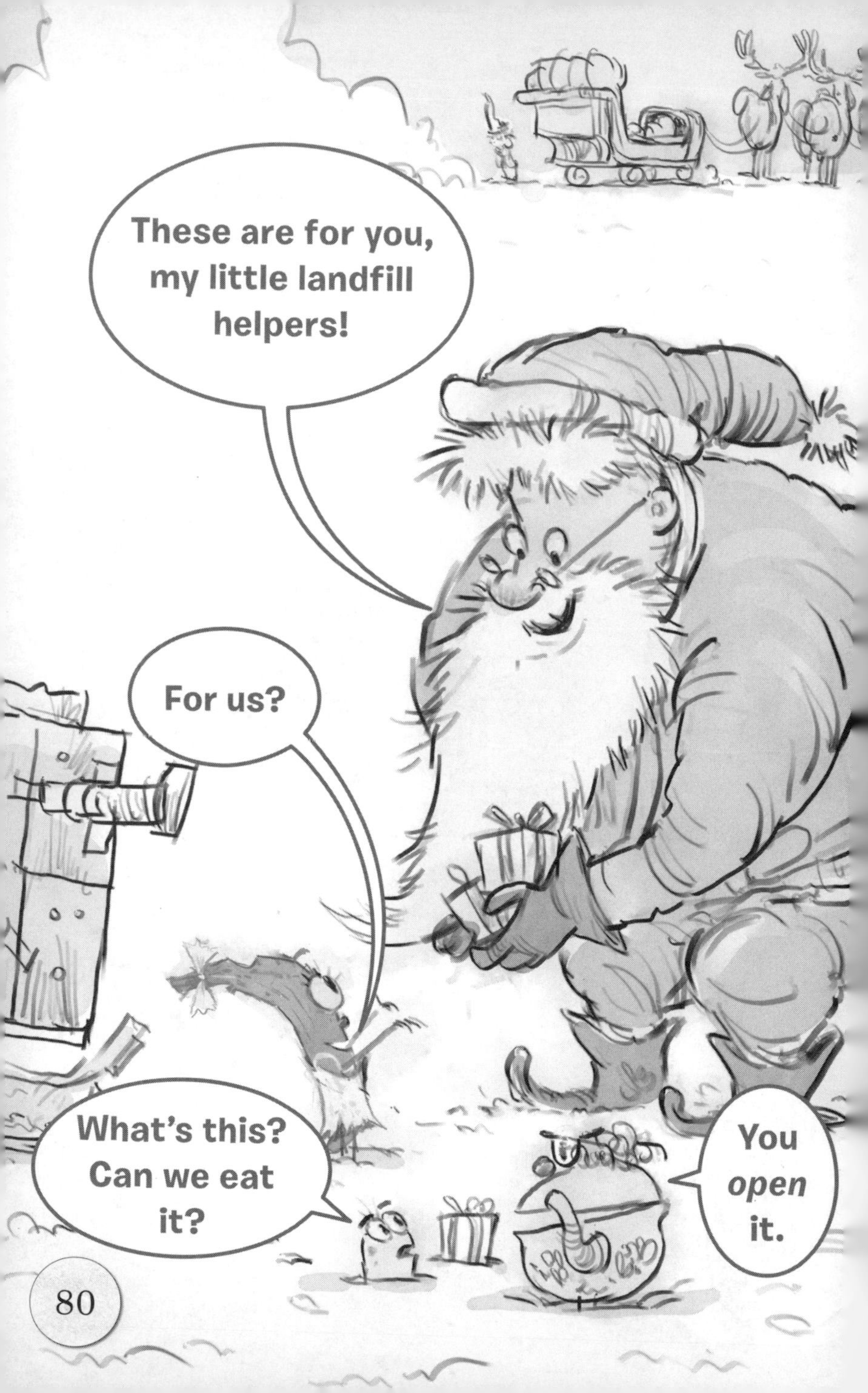
These are for you, my little landfill helpers!
For us?
What's this? Can we eat it?
You *open* it.

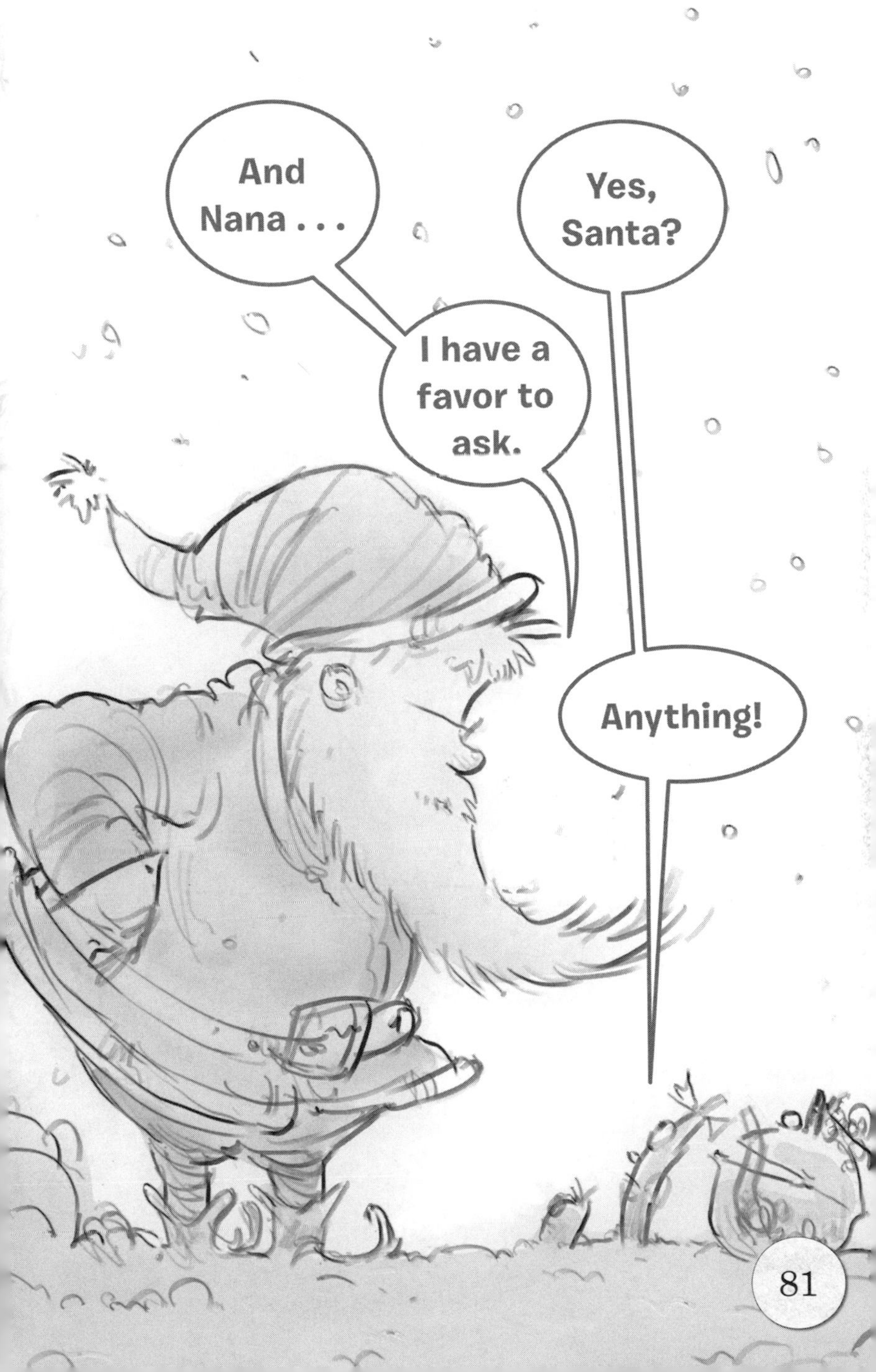
And Nana . . .
Yes, Santa?
I have a favor to ask.
Anything!

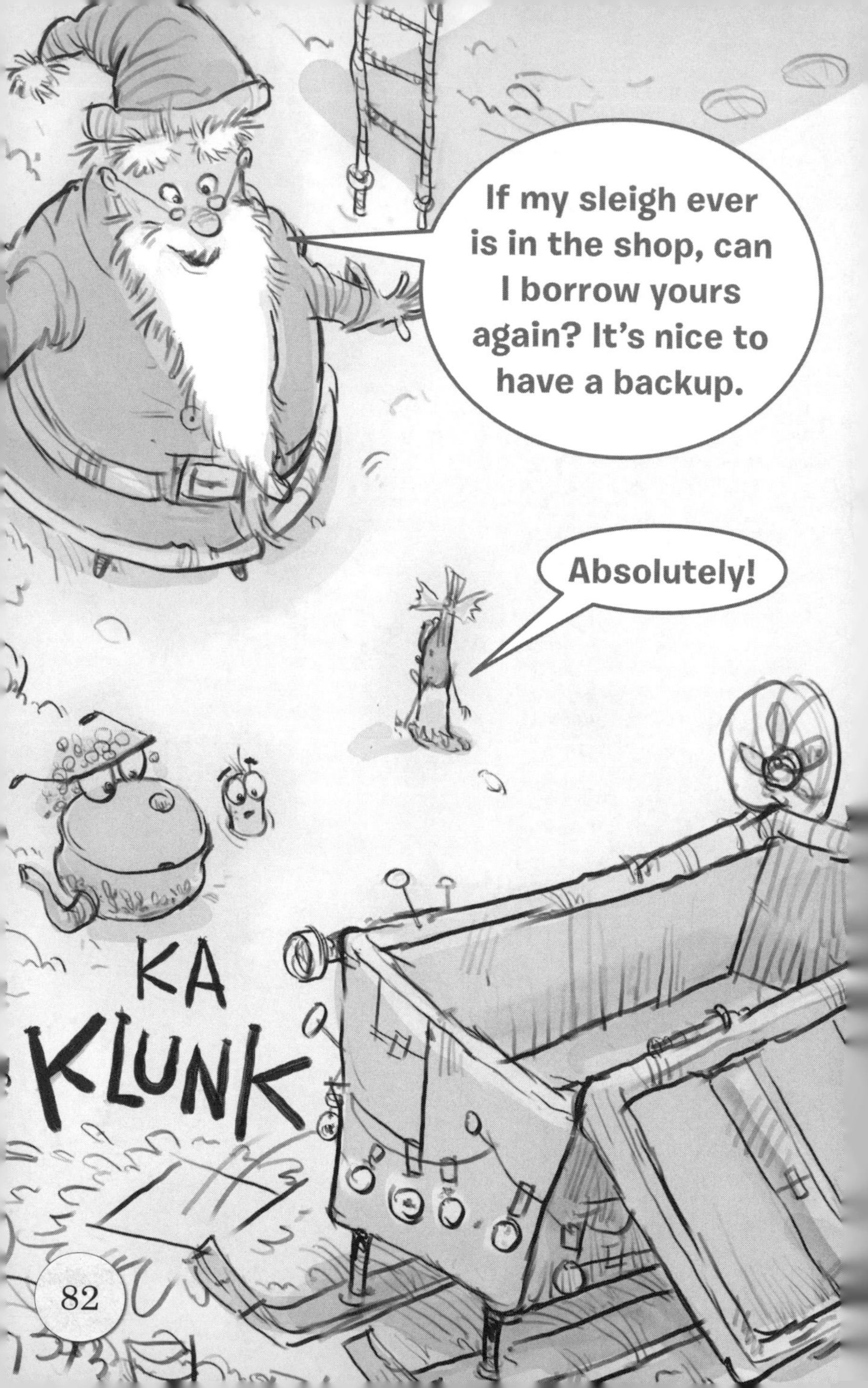
If my sleigh ever is in the shop, can I borrow yours again? It's nice to have a backup.
Absolutely!
KA KLUNK

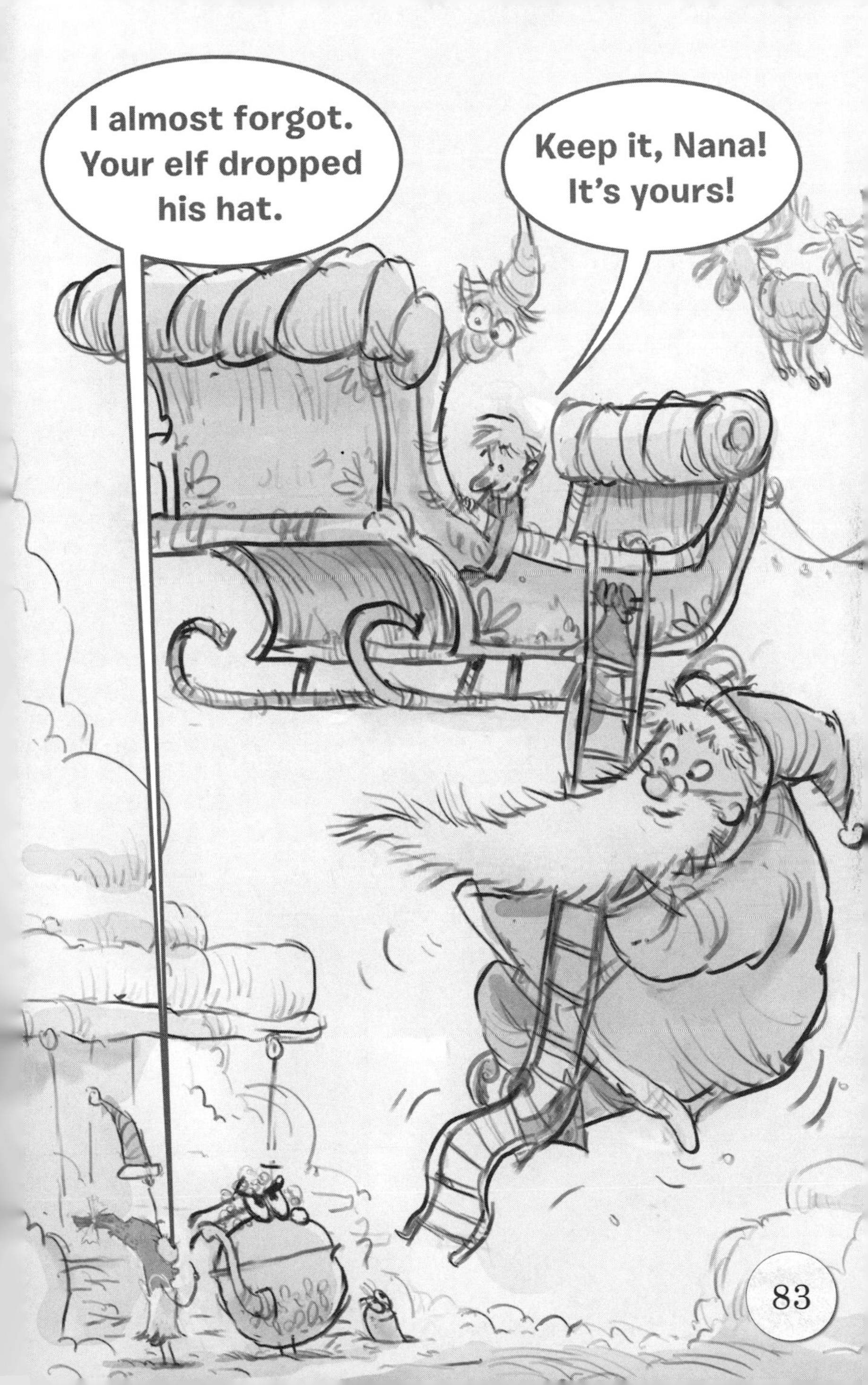
I almost forgot. Your elf dropped his hat.
Keep it, Nana! It's yours!

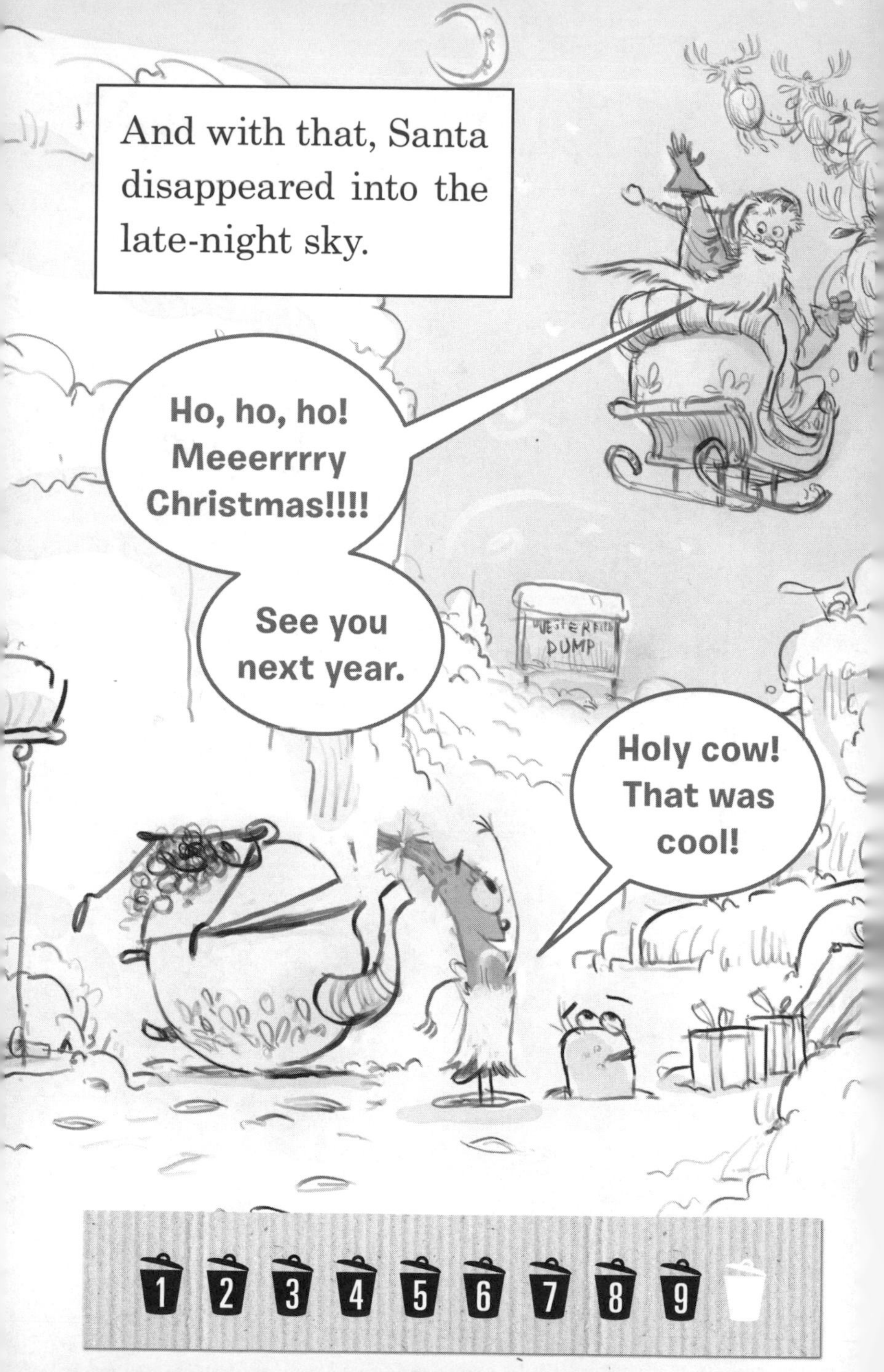
And with that, Santa disappeared into the late-night sky.
Ho, ho, ho! Meeerrrry Christmas!!!!
See you next year.
DUMP
Holy cow! That was cool!
1 2 3 4 5 6 7 8 9

CHAPTER 10
SURPRISE!

The next morning, when the three of them woke up, snow was still everywhere outside. It was Christmas Day!

Ms. Kettle opened her present and found a dingy old spoon.

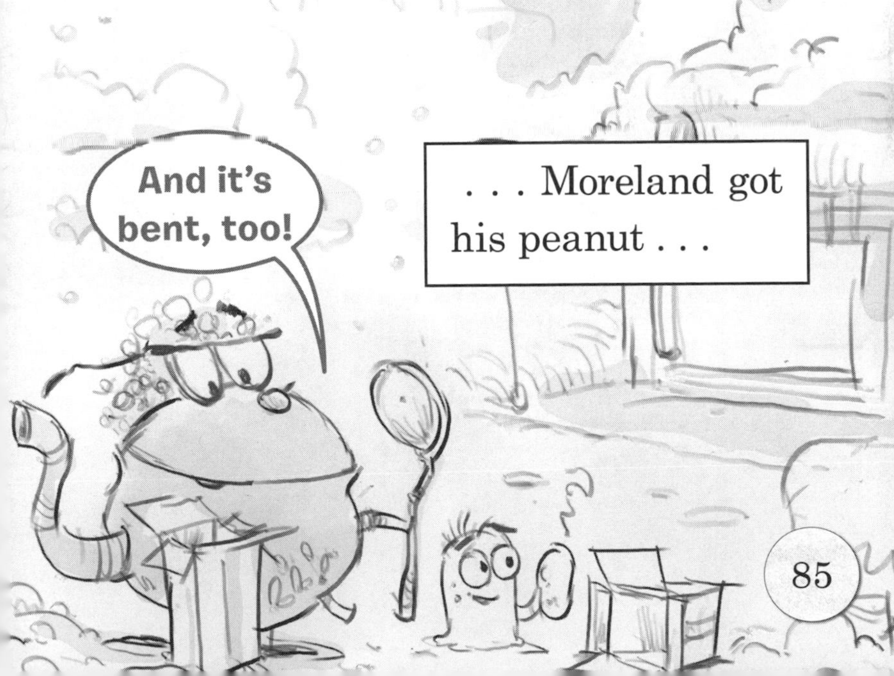
And it's bent, too!

. . . Moreland got his peanut . . .

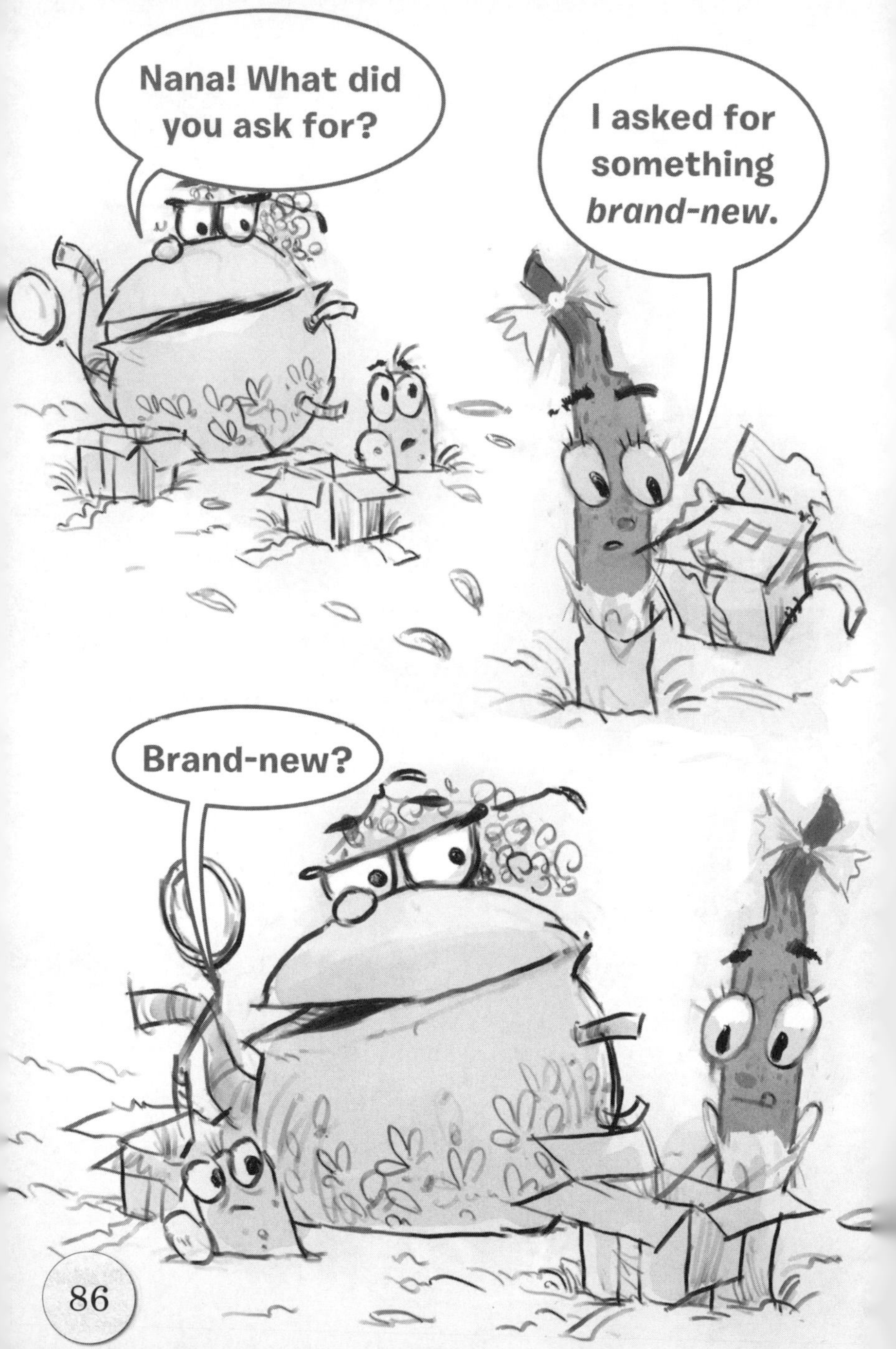
Nana! What did you ask for?
I asked for something *brand-new.*
Brand-new?

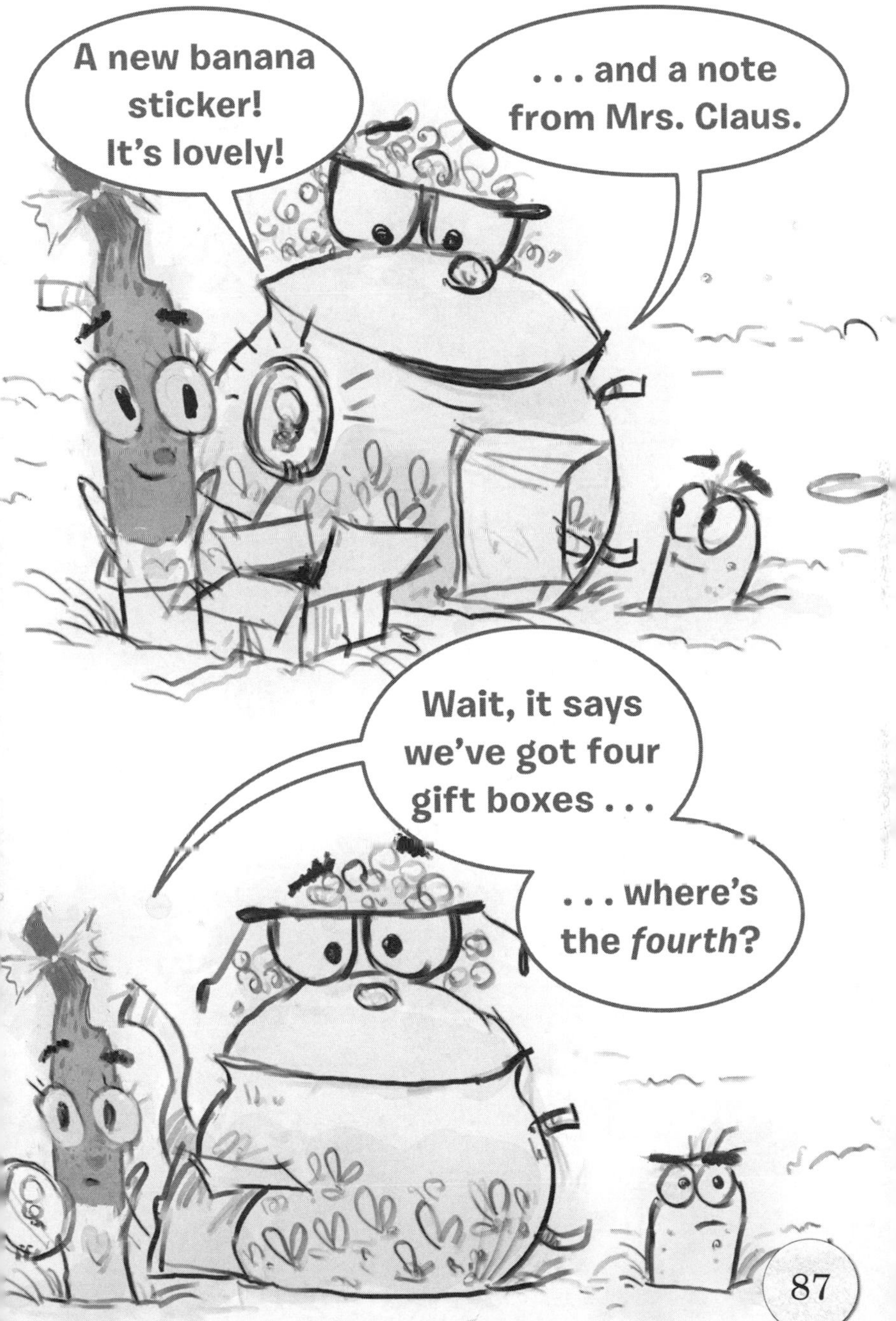
A new banana sticker! It's lovely!
. . . and a note from Mrs. Claus.
Wait, it says we've got four gift boxes . . .
. . . where's the *fourth*?

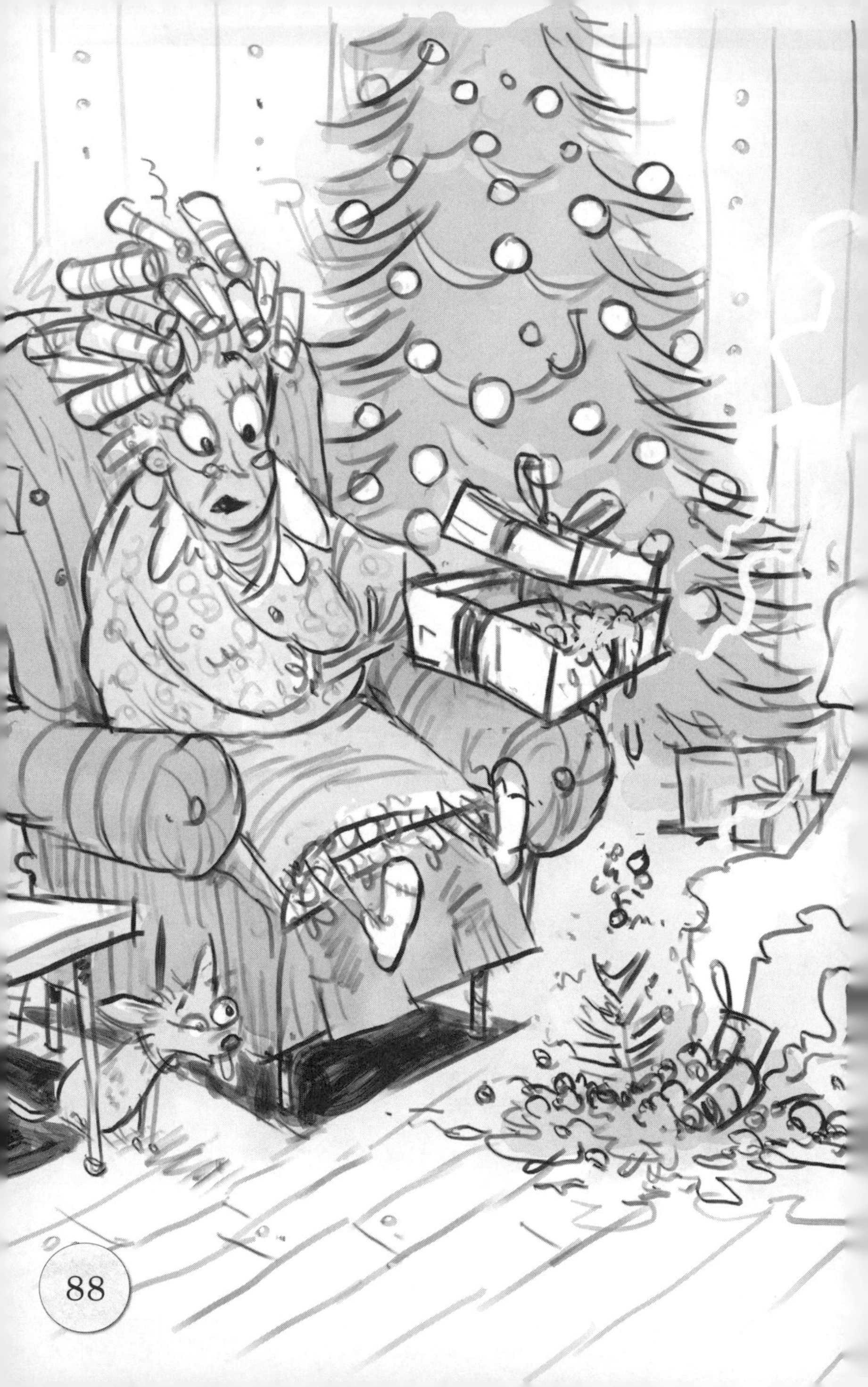

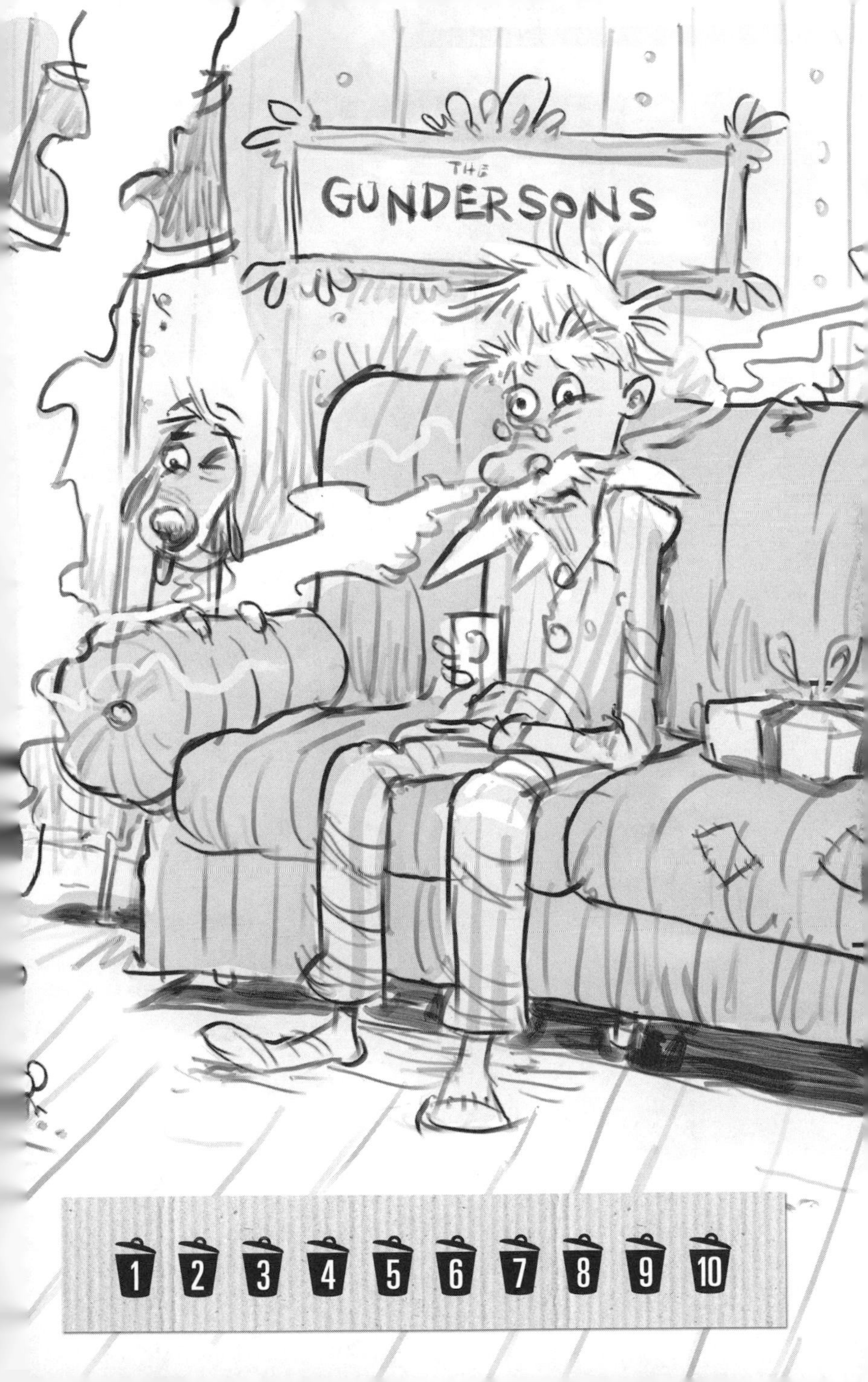
THE GUNDERSONS
1 2 3 4 5 6 7 8 9 10

CONGRATULATIONS!

You've read **10** chapters,

89 pages,

and **2,163** words!

All your help paid off!

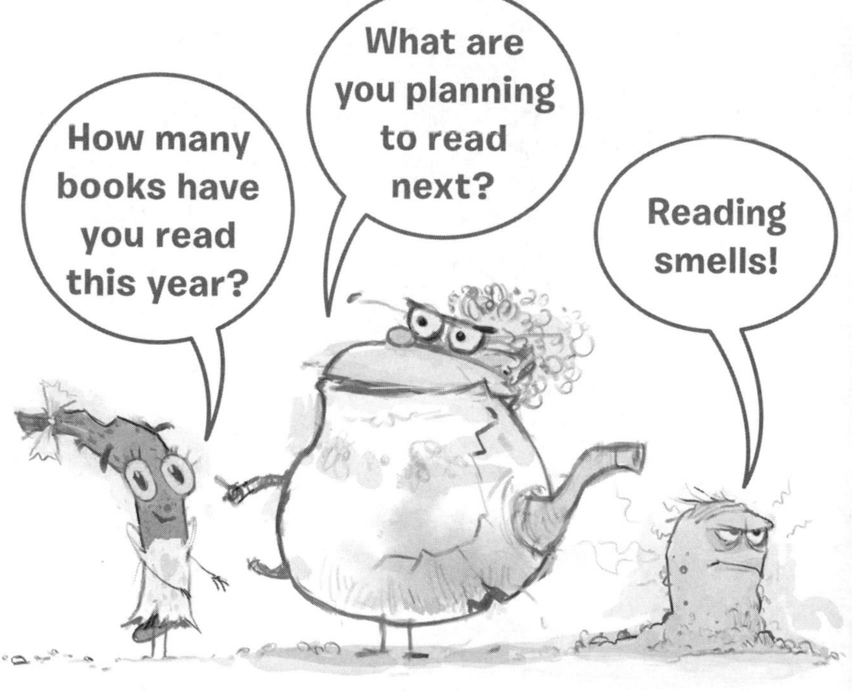
How many books have you read this year?
What are you planning to read next?
Reading smells!

SUPER STINKY GAMES

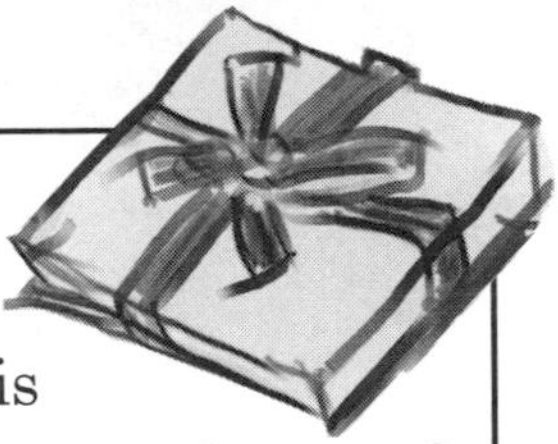

THINK

Nana loves Christmas and is excited to get her first present. Draw a picture of the Christmas gift you want most of all.

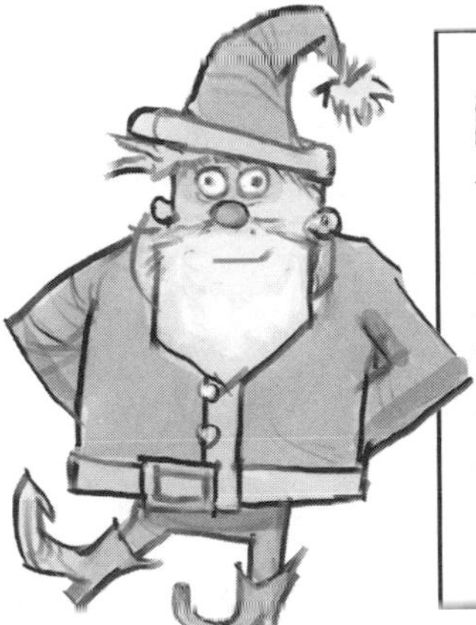

FEEL

When Nana learns about Christmas, she writes Santa a letter asking him to come visit her at the dump. Write a letter to Santa telling him what you love most about Christmas.

ACT

The whole gang is worried that Santa will get lost finding the dump on Christmas night. Draw a map of your house to help Santa know exactly where to go.

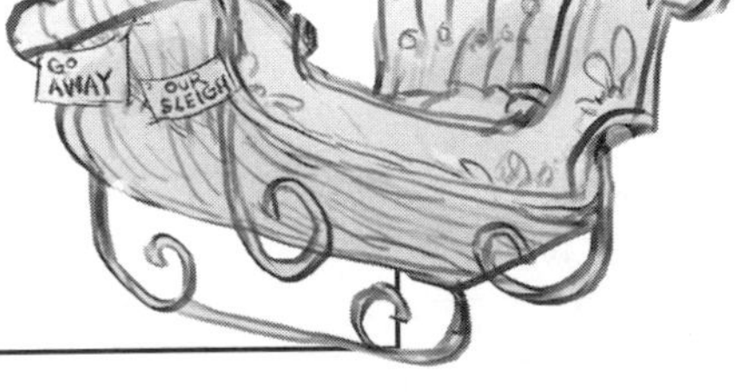
GO AWAY
OUR SLEIGH

WES HARGIS is an author-illustrator living in the desert of Arizona. He began his career in the Tucson newspaper industry and honed his craft late at night while landscaping in the hot sun during the day. The first children's book he ever illustrated was *Jackson and Bud's Bumpy Ride*. Since then, Wes has worked on lots of books, including *When I Grow Up* (a *New York Times* bestseller!) by "Weird Al" Yankovic and the Let's Investigate with Nate science series by Nate Ball.

Wes likes to draw on scratchy paper, but these days he mostly uses a big tablet. Wes loves hanging out with his kids and exploring the desert. He also loves making his own Mexican food and the color yellow-green (like Moreland).

He's married to his lovely wife, Debbie. They have three opinionated kids, two evil cats, and one happily clueless dog. And plants. Lots of plants.